COMBUSTIBLE MAGIC

MYRTLEWOOD MYSTERIES BOOK THREE

IRIS BEAGLEHOLE

Iris Beaglehole

PROLOGUE

As Rosemary and Athena slept peacefully in their beds, a woman stood on a hill under the light of the waning moon, overlooking the village of Myrtlewood.

Her eyes gleamed in joy at the news – such good news. Her contacts had come through, finally. A girl had entered the fae realm, and not just any girl, the one she'd been looking for all these years.

"Right here under my nose," she said to herself and cackled in glee.

There was finally a path in sight, a way to cut through to the realm, and this held the key to unlocking many years' worth of plotting.

"The power will be ours," she said to her companion, who hung back, overshadowed by trees.

The woman raised her arms, her dark hood sliding back slightly to reveal pale hair that gleamed pearlescent in the moonlight as she began chanting the ancient words, not heard for centuries.

She signalled for her companion to open the crate as the spell reached its apex. A burst of red and orange flew out. Circled in the air and then sped away.

The woman held her breath, unsure whether the spell had worked. It had been too fast, too much of a blurr to catch the details of what had been unleashed. She surveyed the countryside, looking for some kind of clue.

Down in the fields of Myrtlewood, all was quiet.

Then, as if from nowhere, a gust of wind swept through the back of the old Twigg farm.

The barn that had stood there for a hundred years suddenly burst into flames.

Agatha Twigg looked out her back window in horror as the bright orange fire engulfed the structure before turning an unearthly pink.

"Oh dear me, Marla!" Agatha called out to her niece. "Ring the authorities. Something big is coming!"

CHAPTER
ONE

It was a charming late spring day. Athena lay on the grass next to Elise on the lawn at the back of Thorn Manor. They both looked up at the sky.

The foundling children ran around on the other side of the lawn. Athena could see Harry's red hair as he ducked behind a magnolia tree, chasing dark haired Mei, light haired Elowen, and the tiny strawberry blonde twins who Athena had named Clio and Thea. It was peaceful to watch them play from a distance, although staring at the tufts of white clouds drifting through the clear blue sky was even more tranquil.

"You're lucky to live somewhere like this," said Elise. "It's beautiful here."

"It would be more beautiful if I was allowed to go out and do stuff on my own," said Athena. "Outside of school, I'm pretty much stuck here. Unless Mum feels like taking me out for a walk like a little dog."

"I hate to say it, but there might be good reason for that," Elise said. "Your mum was in quite a state when we saw her after you disappeared. We were worried about you, too."

"I know," said Athena. "I'm sorry. It was stupid. I never should have trusted him."

"You don't have to keep apologising," Elise said. "I mean, as long as you've learned your lesson." She twirled a daisy between her fingertips and then flipped it at Athena.

"Hey!" Athena jokingly slapped at her friend. They giggled for a few moments. "Thanks for coming over. It's gonna be a long time before Mum lets me actually go out and visit other people's houses."

"She'll loosen up soon enough," said Elise. "I mean, you're sixteen. It's not like you're a baby. You're almost an official adult."

"That's what I keep telling her," said Athena. "But does she listen? No. She's so stubborn."

"Just like someone else I know," said Elise, reaching for a little wad of grass. Which she ripped up and threw at her friend.

Athena blasted the grass away with a burst of air.

"You seem different ever since you went through," said Elise.

"I am different. For a start I couldn't really use my magic before. Not properly. There was something about that place that kind of sparked it all...kicked it off."

"It's not just that though," said Elise. "You felt it, didn't you? That feeling...when I went through. It was like...*going home*."

Athena turned towards her friend, giving her a knowing look. "It was the best thing I've ever felt," she admitted. "But I can't possibly tell my mother that. My father might understand, although I can never be sure with him. Plus, I can't really talk to him about that stuff. It's too personal."

"Fair enough," said Elise. "But he probably does understand, in his way. It's his home, his only true home. He's fae. For us, at least, we're part human. We should belong here just as much as we do there."

"Then why doesn't it feel like this?" Athena asked. "Why does this place feel so…"

"So heavy and lifeless?" Elise suggested.

"Exactly," said Athena. "I mean, I know that there's life all around me, but it all feels so dull compared to the other realm. It's like, it's like I was living in black and white, colour blind, and all of a sudden, everything's in Technicolor. You know, like in that old Wizard of Oz movie."

"That's exactly what it's like," said Elise. "My mum's never been through. But my grandmother grew up there and she knows. The doorways used to always be open. And people could just wander through. Sometimes they'd pop in for dinner and exit at the end of the evening."

"I wish it was still that way," said Athena. "But that was, I don't know, a hundred years ago or something."

"Yeah, my grandma's really old," Elise replied. "Naiads live for a long time."

"That's good to know," said Athena, smiling at her friend. "Hopefully you'll live for a long time, too. Sometimes it feels like you're the only one who understands me. I can't talk to Mum about any of this."

Athena held out her hand towards Elise.

Their fingers met, sending sparkles all around them. It reminded her a little bit about the moment she'd shared with Finnigan.

Despite the usual heaviness to her heart when she thought of him, the sparkles that shone out lightened everything again.

Athena didn't need to waste her energy on him. She wasn't going to make a stupid mistake like that ever again.

CHAPTER
TWO

The envelope sat on the kitchen table. It had been delivered with the morning post, but Rosemary hadn't opened it yet. She knew exactly who it was from. No one else would send such elaborate gold and purple brocade stationery.

"What do you think it says?" Athena asked.

They both stood over the table as Serpentine prowled around them as if she owned the house. Thorn Manor was unusually silent. Nesta and Dain had taken the foundling children to the park. The lack of background noise only made the envelope seem more ominous.

"I don't want to think about it," said Rosemary. "I know it's from our cousins."

"I'll open it," said Athena, picking up the envelope.

Rosemary's heart thudded in her chest. She was worried Athena would see something she shouldn't. "No. Give it here." She took the envelope and sat down at the table with her cup of tea. She'd asked for the favour from Elamina because she'd been desperate, and it wasn't the teen's fault. She didn't want Athena to feel like she was some kind of object to be bargained over. "Okay, here goes."

She opened the stiff expensive card of the envelope and pulled out an equally expensive looking piece of paper, complete with the Bracewell-Thorn's gold monograph in the corner.

"What does it say?" Athena asked.

"It's an invitation to dinner. Not exactly what I was expecting."

"You thought they were going to ask for your firstborn child?" Athena joked.

Rosemary gave her a serious look. "I'm indebted to them for the help they gave me to get into the fae realm. I told you..."

"So what? That was just a little favour. They gave you some spell ingredients. What's the big deal?"

"I'm afraid they're going to make it into a very big deal. And don't joke about firstborn children. You know, Elamina seems to quite like you. I wouldn't be surprised if she tried to steal you."

"I'm not a thing to be stolen, Mum."

Rosemary eyed her daughter warily. Elamina could be deceptive and charming when she wanted something. She hoped Athena wasn't naïve to that fact.

"Exactly, but my cousins might see you as some kind of pet," said Rosemary. "You know, they assume most other people are beneath them. Especially me."

"So we're not going to go and see them," said Athena.

"I guess we have to," Rosemary replied.

"Maybe going to dinner will be returning the favour," Athena suggested somewhat optimistically.

"I very much doubt that. But I do need to find out what it is they really want. And this is the best way to do that. I can ask them directly."

"When's the dinner?" Athena asked. "And do we have to dress up really fancy?"

"Tonight. And wear whatever you like," said Rosemary. "A brown paper bag would be fine. Least it would give them something else to be mocking and scornful about rather than just my very existence."

"What if we turn up butt naked?" said Athena.

"Sounds a little bit gross."

"Yeah. I don't know. Just making conversation. Doesn't it seem impolite that they summoned us for dinner at such short notice?" Athena looked at the invitation, which Rosemary had finally let go of. "What if we had plans tonight?"

"Exactly," said Rosemary. "They don't think much of us. Any plans we have are inconsequential to them."

"Some kind of weird flex," said Athena. "It's kind of rude, though, isn't it?"

Rosemary sighed. "They just wouldn't really think of us as real people."

"Though it is a little bit strange, isn't it?" said Athena. "Aren't they supposed to deeply value decorum?"

Rosemary shrugged. "Maybe they think they're honouring us with the invitation."

"All right. We'll go see them. I've always wanted to check out their house. You said it was a massive mansion."

"I've never been invited before," said Rosemary. "But that's how Granny always described it. Actually, I wonder what the old bat would have to say about this." She went upstairs, followed by Athena, half expecting not to see the little door to the tower. She was a little surprised that the door was visible from the upstairs landing, and even more shocked when she got there to see that there was a note pinned to it.

"More mail," said Athena. "We're popular today."

"I didn't know ghosts could write," said Rosemary. "It's definitely Granny's handwriting." She opened it up to read aloud.

8

My dearest descendants. I'm so relieved that Athena is back and that you are both well. I take this as my cue to leave you.

"Aw," said Athena. "She was growing on me."

"Like a delightful fungus," said Rosemary, although she did feel a pain in her heart at the thought of Granny not being around anymore. She continued reading.

This is not a final goodbye. It's merely a fare-thee-well-for-now. There are matters in the spirit realm that are calling me, requiring my utmost focus and urgent attention.

I apologise for not saying goodbye in person. I did not want to wake you or to disturb you.

Besides, I get the feeling having a batty old ghost hanging over your shoulders is starting to cramp your style.

Take care, my loves. I'm afraid you won't be able to summon me from where I'm going, but I will be back one day.

Until then, farewell and blessed be.

Rosemary felt sadness well up. "It's like I'm having to say goodbye to her all over again."

Without any warning, Athena put her arm around her mother's shoulder and gave her a little pat. "It's okay, Mum. She'll come back. And when she does, you can give her a right telling off."

Rosemary smiled.

"I suppose we'd better figure out what to wear tonight," said Athena.

"That's right." Rosemary sighed, remembering the dinner that she'd temporarily been able to forget. "Family," she said. "Even when they don't live with you, they have the amazing ability to drive you up the wall!"

THEY STOOD OUTSIDE AN ENORMOUS, looming black stone mansion belonging to the Bracewell-Thorns.

"Foreboding is the word to describe it," said Athena.

Rosemary rang the doorbell and some kind of fancy butler answered. He was tall with a black and silver waistcoat and a stony expression. They were shown in to an elaborately adorned cloak room, and the butler took their coats and then lead them through to an even more elaborate waiting area.

"Looks like we're inside a palace," said Athena. "And to think, these family members knew we were in poverty and never once offered to help."

"It's a bit gauche for my tastes," said Rosemary bitterly.

The butler disappeared into another room and then returned a moment later. "The Bracewell-Thorns are ready for you now." He bowed slightly and gestured for them to enter into a long stone hallway, lit with flaming lanterns.

"You've got to admit this part is cool, though," said Athena.

The hallway opened up into a large room with a high ceiling. Rosemary eyed the lengthy dining table with seating for over a dozen, complete with lit candles in crystal stands that glimmered, casting reflections back and forth between the chandeliers that loomed large on the ceiling. The whole room smelled like lily of the valley, Elamina's favourite perfume, but fortunately it wasn't too overpowering.

Rosemary's two cousins stood at the far side of the room. Elamina stepped forward. Her long white-blonde hair was done up as if she was prepared for a ball and she wore a grey and mauve evening gown, tailored perfectly to outline her petite figure.

Derse was dressed in a suit as usual, and glanced across at them, just as aloof as ever.

"Rosemary...Athena, how wonderful of you to join us."

Rosemary shot Athena a confused look. In all the years that she'd known her cousin, Elamina had never once before been so gracious or willing to acknowledge Rosemary's presence. She almost seemed warm in her demeanour.

It certainly must be an act, Rosemary thought, wishing that Athena would read her mind so they could have a conversation. Ever since she'd come back from the fae realm, Athena, having learned how to control the voices in her head, had very deliberately turned them all off, saying she didn't need the extra headache.

This was occasionally frustrating, but also a welcome relief. Overall, Rosemary preferred not to have to worry about her own mind being pried into by a nosy teen. It meant that Rosemary had slightly less to be teased about, at any rate.

Elamina, with a genuine smile on her face, or at least a genuine gleam in her eyes, came forward, taking both Rosemary's and then Athena's hands in a kind of half handshake. She then air-kissed them on both cheeks in turn.

"How wonderful of you to join us," said Derse, though his voice sounded wooden, almost robotic. Rosemary was surprised to hear him speak more than a word at a time. Whatever this charade was, he'd clearly been let in on it but couldn't act to save himself.

Elamina turned to him with a slightly wild look in her eyes, her smile faltering a little. She turned back to Rosemary, eyeing her rather casual outfit. "You look...well. It's so refreshing when middle-aged women give up the need to dress to impress."

That's more like it. Her cousin's passive-aggressive tendencies were strangely more comforting than the horrendously fake smile plastered to her face. Athena just looked surprised and vaguely amused. Rosemary didn't even bother trying to return the backhanded compliment.

"Please take a seat." Elamina gestured to the table.

Rosemary noticed little place cards with their names on them. Athena's place was right next to the head of the table, where Elamina sat down.

Preferring to ignore the assigned roles, Rosemary took Athena's seat and swapped the place cards over.

Athena gave her a mischievous look.

All was silent for a moment and then Elamina shook her head with a little giggle that was so out of character it shocked Rosemary.

"Thank you so much for joining us on such short notice." Elamina looked at her delicate silver watch. "And only half-an-hour late. I'm very pleased to hear that Athena returned happy and well." Her voice was almost musical.

"Erm," Rosemary started, unsure of what to say. Her cousin seemed to be locked in an internal battle between being her normal caustic self and taking on the faux-happy persona of a children's television presenter.

"Oh, now look," said Elamina crossly as two young servants approached with trays. "The entrees are arriving before I've even offered you a drink." She waved them away.

Rosemary felt her stomach rumble. She hadn't eaten before the rather long drive to the fancy neighbourhood. Her terrible sense of direction had sent them off on a round-about journey before Athena insisted on using her phone to navigate.

"Now, what would you have to drink?" Elamina asked. "Sherry? Wine? What do people like *you* drink?"

Athena stifled a giggle. Rosemary pressed her mouth into a thin line to avoid laughing. It was comical how much her snobby cousins were trying desperately to accommodate them, while also clearly having no idea how to be normal people.

"Red wine is fine," said Rosemary.

"Do you have any lemonade?" Athena asked.

"Certainly." Elamina smiled at Athena then clapped her hands. Servants stepped forward and she relayed the drink instructions. Moments later they returned with the beverages.

"Excuse me for asking," said Rosemary, feeling like she should at least attempt to be polite, given the comical situation. "But was there a particular reason for the invitation?"

"Oh, you don't beat around the bush do you?" Elamina batted her eyelids, as if trying to be charming. "I just wanted to see you – my poor dear cousins – after all you've been through. And we wanted to celebrate that Athena is back, safe and well. Isn't that a lot to celebrate, Derse?"

Derse just nodded.

"Thank you," said Athena. "It is nice to be back." She took a sip of her lemonade and squinted as if it was far too sour.

Rosemary followed suit and took a gulp of her own wine, which she admitted to herself was delicious and probably incredibly expensive.

"Now we can have the entrees." Elamina clapped her hands and the servants returned with silver domed trays.

"So, just a celebration?" said Rosemary. "Great. That's...That's lovely."

"Yes. And how was it?" said Elamina. As if asking about a holiday.

Rosemary gave her a deadpan look. "How was what?" she asked flatly.

"The fae realm, of course," said Elamina with a little laugh.

"It was..." Athena's voice trailed off and she stared blankly at the candles.

"I see, it's complicated," said Elamina. "I'm so sorry for asking. I've heard such wonderous things. I just...I don't mean to pry. But if you ever do feel like talking about it, let me know. I hear it can really cut to the heart of you...A place like that."

Rosemary raised her eyebrows as her cousin nattered on.

"I knew someone of fae heritage once," said Elamina. "Who'd been brought up in the fae realm but had somehow slipped through."

"Oh..." Athena started, but Rosemary shot her a warning look. This was not the time to talk about Dain's genetics. In fact, it was a time to withhold as much information as possible.

"That's interesting," said Athena. "I wonder how they got through. It's quite a hard thing to do, apparently."

"Indeed. I'm dying to know how you did it," said Elamina, looking between the two of them.

"It was a stroke of luck really." Rosemary tried to keep her expression neutral, though it was all she could do to stop herself glaring suspiciously at her cousin. *What is she up to?*

"Luck," Elamina repeated, sounding unimpressed.

"Yes, luck and a dash of cream," said Athena.

Rosemary shot her another warning glance. *Too much information,* she tried to think loudly, hoping that Athena had dropped her psychic barriers temporarily in honour of the occasion.

"Well, I don't know how we did it," said Athena. "Maybe...barriers like that tend to ebb and flow, don't they?"

"Indeed," said Elamina. "I hear it used to be quite an open thing. Quite easy to slip back and forth. If you were magically inclined anyway. Such a shame that the old ways have been forgotten. Things have changed and not always for the better. I hear there is much potent magic there."

Oh, so that's what it is, Rosemary thought loudly. *That's what this is all about. She's hoping you have some fae magical secrets that she can get her hands on.*

"I must admit I did manage to slip through the barrier when I was a wild young child, on an equinox or two," said Elamina. "It's a pity I had no idea of the true potential of the magic it held."

"I can't see why you'd want to do that," said Rosemary. "It's really not all that hospitable over there, despite their obsession with manners."

"Oh?" said Elamina. "Do tell me more."

Rosemary bit her tongue to stop from rambling. She'd already shared far too much information.

"Is that what this is all about?" Athena asked, rather more forward than Rosemary was comfortable with. "Are you trying to get back there? Are you trying to get through the veil?"

Elamina gave a little laugh. "Oh, darling girl. I'm afraid that was merely a passing fancy...a childhood phase. I've moved on to much, much bigger things with my ambitions. That's all I'm going to tell you about that."

So that's what it is, Athena's voice projected into Rosemary's head. *She's trying to get to the fae realm and she's trying to get information out of us.*

I knew it was something like that, Rosemary replied. *And we are not going to help her. It's far too dangerous.*

Rosemary thought the appetisers were overly complex in terms of flavour profile, and not terribly enjoyable, while the main was bland.

Athena seem to be enjoying it well enough. They ate mostly in silence aside from the odd question about the fae realm or the family magic posed by Elamina. Derse, in his typical style, hardly said a word.

"Now, Athena, you're growing very powerful, aren't you?" said Elamina. She gave a flourish of her hand as she gestured for the staff to clear away the meals. "Now tell me about your magic, my dear cousin. How does it work for you?"

"I'm just figuring it out, really," Athena demurred.

Rosemary wanted to ask why Elamina was so curious about Athena, rather than about her. She didn't want to bring up the subject of her daughter's father's heritage in case it was revealing her hand too much in a game she didn't know how to play.

"Wouldn't you love to train with some *real* magical experts?" she asked Athena.

"Oh," Athena started. "I don't know." She paused for a moment.

"Actually, Athena has come a long way recently," said Rosemary. "We're both quickly learning to master our magic without any help from *you*."

She didn't mean it to come out sounding so bitter.

Elamina's smile never faltered. "I know!" she said, with a little clap. "How about you come and stay with us regularly, my darling little cousin."

The term of endearment made Athena wince. Clearly Elamina was not used to spending time with the teen folk.

"Uhh...That's okay," said Athena.

"As I said, we're perfectly fine with our magical training," said Rosemary.

"Come now, I have no children of my own," said Elamina.

Probably because you didn't want to risk losing your figure, Rosemary thought inside her head, wondering if Athena was still listening, and sure enough, the teen reached for her mouth as if to stifle a giggle.

She wants to keep you as a pet, Rosemary continued as a fluffy pink dessert course was placed in front of them.

"I can understand your hesitation," said Elamina. "After all, we've never been a very close family now, have we? I must admit, I was always jealous that you and Granny got on so well." She gave Rosemary a meaningful look.

Rosemary was startled by that revelation. It wasn't like Elamina to let her guard down.

"I know, I'm not the most friendly and well-liked person around," said Elamina.

You can say that again, said Athena's voice in Rosemary's head.

"I can't help the way I am," said Elamina. "But I'd like to make amends."

"I thought you brought us here because I owed you something," said Rosemary. "After you helped with that spell."

"Oh, nonsense," said Elamina. "What's a favour among family? Besides, it helped you get your daughter back...my dear cousin."

"I don't know what you're trying to bargain for here," said Rosemary. "Athena's not some kind of pawn. She's a human being, not a play thing. You helped me when I needed it and as you made clear in your letter, I do owe you one, but I don't owe you her." She gestured to Athena.

Elamina's smile dropped away from her face. "Very well," she said coolly, putting down her tiny dessert fork. "You've made your hostility perfectly clear, Rosemary." There was an edge to her voice that made Rosemary feel tense.

"I won't bother you," said Elamina. "Just know that I'm acting with goodwill. I'm trying to make amends for not being the best cousin or the best...person. And I may well have a lot more work to do on that score. But I'm trying and that's all I can do."

Rosemary nodded, feeling slightly ashamed of herself. "Okay. Thank you. I guess." She took the last bite of her overly sweet dessert.

"It's getting late. I think we'd better leave," said Athena. "It's a school night."

Elamina sniffed a little. "I'll have Charles fetch your coats." She clicked her fingers, summoning another servant.

On the way back to the car Athena gave Rosemary a very concerned look. "What was all that about?" she asked.

"Beats me," said Rosemary. "Perhaps our dearest darling cousin is finally losing the plot."

CHAPTER
THREE

Athena sat in class, feeling unfocused as she often had recently. She'd been unable to sleep the night before and was sure she'd heard strange sounds coming from the forest, though it could have just been her mind playing tricks on her in a half-dreaming state.

Mr Spruce waffled on about automancy, which was apparently the art of magically getting something to work for itself.

Instead of focusing on the topic at hand, Athena was miles away. Her eyes closed, just slightly, and she could almost picture it.

The fae realm...

Those purple trees and pearlescent cobblestone paths.

...that feeling like a fish being dropped back into water, at home again.

She'd wanted to come back home to escape the countess. And, of course, because after Finnigan's betrayal everyone she knew and cared about was in the Earth realm. But coming back seemed to take a toll on her body.

Everything felt so heavy.

"At least attempt to pay attention," Elise whispered, next to her.

Athena opened her eyes again and looked around the classroom. Mr Spruce hadn't noticed that she'd been daydreaming and almost napping in class, but Beryl certainly had and shot Athena a smug smile.

Beryl had been bragging about how it was only because of her that Athena had come back from the fae realm. The nasty girl had been lapping it up...How disengaged Athena had been...How poorly she'd performed at school recently. But it was hard to focus around things that seemed so grey and lifeless compared to the other world she'd briefly inhabited.

For most of the others in her small circle of new friends who'd gone over to rescue her, the fae realm had the opposite effect. It had felt unnerving and confusing and unpleasant. They were relieved to get back to the solid reality they were used to.

But Elise understood.

Athena reasoned it was because she was naiad on her mother's side, and they were beings from the fae realm. Elise felt the connection and the glorious joy of being there, that sense of finally fitting in and being comfortable.

Mr Spruce cleared his throat. "Now for something practical!"

He rummaged in the pile of odd implements behind his desk and brought out a box containing some old brass instruments. He handed them around to the class.

"Are they some sort of magical contraptions?" Felix asked.

Beryl laughed. "These are obviously just torches of a regular kind."

"Torches?" asked Deron. "This don't look like no torch to me. We've got a lot of plastic torches at home."

Beryl shot him a disgusted look.

"These are indeed dynamo torches," said Mr Spruce. "And we've been using them to teach this class for many decades. So while they might be dated I can assure you they work perfectly well. The point is that for automancy you must use your mind, not to influence the kinetic energy around the device in order to move it, but to connect with the device itself. The idea is to get the device to turn on, in its natural essence, and therefore move itself. Let me demonstrate."

He sat down at his desk, placing one of the brass windup torches in front of him. Then he put his hands on his temples and kind of zoned out, going cross-eyed as he looked at the device.

Felix laughed at the face Mr Spruce was making, and Elise elbowed him. It was clearly still her job to keep everyone in line. Athena gave her a supportive smile.

Mr Spruce hummed a little, and the handle of the dynamo began to turn, just slightly at first, and then a little faster. And faster still, until a light began to shine out of the front of the torch.

"There you have it!" said Mr Spruce proudly, lowering his hands as the handle stopped moving. "Now, you will practice. And don't even think about using kinetic energy to move the handles. They've been especially charmed so they'll only work with automancy."

The class began practicing. Athena didn't feel interested enough to engage in the task. She looked around to see Beryl, focusing in frustration as she stared cross-eyed at the device. Athena would have laughed, only none of the torches in the classroom were moving at all.

Felix looked like he'd given up and was shooting magic shaped like tiny paper planes back and forth with Deron who had abandoned his dynamo too.

"Ugh, it's no use," said Beryl, screwing up her face. "Why bother with automancy when kinetic energy is perfectly sufficient?"

Mr Spruce bellowed a laugh. "Miss Flarguan, surely you know that automancy is far more than just getting a torch to light up. It's a whole magical speciality. We are starting small because it's challenging to master."

Athena tried to stop herself from smirking at the obvious discomfort of her nemesis, but Beryl was right, there was hardly any point in trying. She folded her arms and leaned back in her chair. If none of the other students could get the thing to work she had a fat chance of succeeding.

"Not even going to try?" Mr Spruce asked.

"Err," said Athena. "I'm having trouble concentrating today."

"Go ahead," said Mr Spruce. "I have it on good authority that the Thorn family are experts in automancy."

"That might have been the case a long time ago," said Athena, thinking of the way their magical manor house liked to do things automatically as if it was a sentient being. "Unfortunately, my mother and I don't quite yet know what we're doing with magic."

"Now, now, this speciality is complex. It takes most people many years of studying, even just to get the basics. You hear that class?" Mr Spruce said, scratching his long, white, frizzy beard as he addressed the room. "You're not expected to move mountains today. I'd be delighted if any one of you got even an inch of movement from the contraption in front of you. I expect it will take you some weeks to get it to turn on at all."

Beryl had an expression of ardent determination on her face as she continued to stare at the dynamo, clearly hoping to prove herself.

Athena sighed and stared at the torch in front of her, but it wasn't long before her eyelids began to droop again, revealing some sort of imprint of the purple light shining through the fae realm at night and that feeling of connectedness.

Every time she thought back to that place, it came with the sting of betrayal.

Finnigan.

She'd trusted him. And yet, all he did was hand her over to his mistress, the Countess of West Eloria. The memory made her surge in anger, followed by sadness. But the worst part was that she still had feelings for him.

She couldn't escape from her own emotions. There was something that felt good about being with Finnigan, and about the fae realm in its entirety, which is why she'd stuck close to Elise when she was at school. Elise understood.

It was the same with the young foundling children who were temporarily housed at Thorn Manor. Being around them reminded her a little of that unearthly place. They, having lived there for so long, glowed with some of its essence. This was also perhaps why she didn't mind all the time she was spending with her fae father, despite not completely forgiving him for how he'd behaved when she was a child.

Dain was fae and she was fae. And as much as part of her wanted to cut herself off from all of that, along with the pain of betrayal, another part of her delighted in it so much that she simply couldn't. In the fae realm things worked for her. Her magic came easily. Her mind was clear. Even being there a short amount of time had helped her hone her powers in a lasting way, far more than months of practice in the Earth realm had before. It was like she was made for that place. She fitted there. It worked.

She glanced back down at the brass object in front of her, still half in a restless daydream. It was like she could see through the layers of metal. It had been created for a purpose. It belonged...Just like Athena felt she fitted when she was at home in the fae realm.

There was something about the dynamo contraption that oddly reminded Athena of the house that she lived in. Thorn Manor had this intense sense of purposefulness about it, like a being alive in its own right.

All of a sudden she could see it – sense it – as if it were an innate truth. Everything had such a spark within it. And when activated, it could do so much more than expected.

She focused closely on the device in front of her. In her mind she could see down, through the layers of brass, through the cogs and screws, into the heart of the object: its essence. Athena felt the inner spark light up like a fire igniting to life.

The handle of the dynamo twitched.

Yes!

There was a humming sound. All eyes turned towards Athena's desk, to the contraption that was now moving of its own accord. It began to turn, quicker and quicker, out of control, so much so that the torch spun around on the table, shining a light throughout the whole room.

Mr Spruce stood up, bursting into loud applause. "Oh brava! Brava!" he cried out. "I've never seen such a thing! That was simply stupendous for a first attempt!"

Athena felt a swell of pride. She noticed Beryl glaring at her from across the classroom, but she couldn't help smiling. Despite the fact that she hadn't even been trying very hard, at least she'd managed to do one thing right this term.

CHAPTER
FOUR

Rosemary watched from the kitchen window as Athena and Dain ran around on the lawn outside, entertaining the children. Little Clio and Thea had finally started talking, though they didn't remember anything about their past, not even the names they'd had before Athena had given them new ones. They giggled as they ran around, guided by the vivacious Harry and shy Elowen. Mei was there too, only she, unlike the other foundling children, had a known family. The others remained mysteries.

"They're such placid children, aren't they?" said Detective Neve, who sat at the nearby table, sipping a cup of freshly brewed tea.

"Maybe that's part of the magic of the fae realm," said Rosemary. "It's true. They hardly ever cry or bicker. They're nothing like the challenge Athena was as a little one."

"You're probably right," said Neve. "They're ethereal, like that place rubbed off on them. At least that makes them easy to look after."

Rosemary readily agreed. The children had been no trouble at all. All she needed to do was make sure they were fed and bathed, and Dain was doing a great job of entertaining them. Two weeks had passed since their return from the fae realm, but this wasn't a permanent home for them, and the uncertainty was starting to bother Rosemary.

"How's Athena going?" Neve asked.

Rosemary beamed. "Brilliantly, at least today. She came home raving about autofancy or something. Apparently school went well today!"

They watched as Athena swung Harry around in a circle, while the other children squealed with glee. The children were so sweet and full of wonder.

"What do you think will happen to them?" Rosemary asked.

"We've been trying to track down the families, as you know," said Neve. "But the magical authorities are busy with emergencies."

Rosemary raised her eyebrows questioningly.

"I probably shouldn't tell you," said Neve. "Police business, but as for finding the families these children belonged to, our best leads are old historic cases." She took out a manilla folder from her bag and opened it on the table. "I'm not technically supposed to show you this, as it's a police investigation. But in the circumstances..."

Rosemary excitedly skipped over to the table to look at the documents.

"We've got the groceries!" Marjie said, bustling into the kitchen in a multi-coloured floral dress. Nesta followed close behind wearing her usual bright-red cape over plain black clothing. Her dark hair was pulled up in its customary high bun.

Rosemary smiled. Nesta had become a good friend over the past few weeks as she and Neve had assisted with the foundling children. Rosemary was used to hearing her soft musical voice with its slight Welsh lilt.

The house had recently been full of friends, something Rosemary had been sure she would tire of quickly, but it was actually quite nice.

"Don't worry," said Nesta, approaching the table and seeming to read Rosemary's mind in the way she often intuitively did. "We won't stick around forever. We just want to help with the children until…oh, is this the file, love?"

Neve shot her girlfriend a smile. "Yes, just don't tell Perkins I showed it to you or he'll blow through the roof. You know what his temper is like."

"It's really no trouble having you all around," said Rosemary. "In this big old house I can still have my own space if I want to, I just have to wander into one of the many empty rooms. Besides, how else would we cope with all the kids?"

"They don't have to be your responsibility," said Neve.

"As I said before," Rosemary responded, "I don't want to risk them going into foster care in case they have a horrible time. Besides, it's giving Athena a good chance to learn to take more responsibility."

Rosemary watched through the window as her daughter threw tiny blonde Elowen high up into the air.

"Or at least that's the idea," said Rosemary with a sigh. She crossed to the back door and yelled out to Athena. "Be careful not to injure them!"

"Is that little Elowen?" Marjie asked, squinting. "She just loves to be thrown around. She thinks it's hilarious when Herb holds her upside down!"

"She's a sweet kid," said Rosemary. "Barely knew her own name. I think she's about four years old."

"From the old newspaper records, we think she's little Elowen Dawson who went missing forty years ago," said Neve.

"A lot can happen in forty years," said Nesta. "Where are her family now?"

"The last report we have says they left town. Moved to Burkenswood, probably to keep the other children safe."

"I don't blame them," said Rosemary. "Who would want to stick around somewhere that constantly reminds you of your missing baby?"

"Have you spoken to the family?" Marjie asked.

"Not yet. I tracked down a sister. The parents have passed away."

"It's strange, isn't it?" said Rosemary. "Tracking down family members and trying to find out whether they want to adopt their missing siblings or cousins who disappeared decades ago but are still little kids."

"It's certainly not normal police business," said Neve. "And we can't involve the mundane child welfare office because..."

"How do you explain something like this?" said Rosemary.

"Exactly," said Neve. "We've never needed a magical child services department before. Occasionally children have gone missing or returned, but it's quite rare, especially coming back from the fae realm. The problem is, so much time has elapsed over here, but the kids are still so young. And to make matters worse, the families don't tend to remember anything."

"Oh. That's right," said Rosemary. "So why did they move away?"

"The specific magical amnesia seems to take a while to kick in," said Neve.

"We'll have to watch that we don't all forget what happened to us as well," Rosemary muttered, feeling bitter about her memory and how it had been tampered with. "I wonder if there's some kind of spell that might stop the memory magic from happening." She looked out the window towards Dain, who was running around with Harry and the twins. She didn't want any more fae meddling with her mind.

"I can try to help you with that," said Marjie. "My Aunt Morwenna was an expert when it came to memory. She had some spiritual books..."

"Don't remind me," said Rosemary. "Dain wasn't the only one that messed with my memory, remember? My own grandmother cast a spell to bind the family magic, making me totally forget it ever existed."

"Now, now," said Marjie. "You know she had her reasons."

Nesta astutely assumed that this was a good time to change the subject. "So you're going to call on them?" she asked Neve, gesturing to the files. "Elowen's family, I mean. It looks like you've tracked them down. Surely you have to let them know."

"I was planning on going there tomorrow," said Neve. "To visit the sister." She turned to Rosemary. "Maybe you could come with me and help to explain about the fae realm and the memory loss, since you understand it better than most."

"Don't you think that would be crossing a line?" Rosemary asked. "I'm not a cop or anything. It might be weird."

"I could bring you in as a sort of external consultant," said Neve. "We'd pay you an hourly rate, just like other contractors."

"You know, I never expected I'd become a professional consultant in magical memory loss and faeries," said Rosemary. "But Perkins will hate it, so count me in."

Neve smiled at her. Just then, a little dark haired girl ran to the kitchen and wrapped her arms around Neve and then around Nesta.

"Mummies!" she said.

"Mei, we've had this conversation before," said Neve. "I'm your cousin, remember."

The little girl giggled. "I know, Connie," she said, using what was clearly a childhood nickname, shortening Neve's first name, which happened to be Constantine. "But it's like you're big enough to be a mum. How did you get so big, anyway?"

"A lot of time passed, remember," said Nesta. "You were in the fae realm, and time was different there."

"But where is Mummy? My real mummy?"

The two women shot each other an uncomfortable look. "Your mummy's a lot older now," said Neve gently. "She didn't go to the fae realm like you. You stayed very small, and the rest of us got bigger and older."

"She must be huge!" said Mei.

"Not so much, actually," said Neve.

"When can I see her?" Mei's smile faded.

"I've actually arranged for her to fly in this weekend," said Neve. "She's going to stay at our house. Remember, the one we visited yesterday?"

"Why not here?" Mei asked. "Can she stay here with me and my friends?"

"Mei, we thought you might want to come and stay with us, too," said Nesta.

Mei pouted. "But I want to stay with my friends."

"We don't want to trouble Rosemary for too long," said Neve.

Mei looked at Rosemary expectantly.

"All things change, darling," she said. "It's up to Neve and Nesta when they're ready to move on. You're no trouble, really." Rosemary looked at Neve. "Don't rush. We've got plenty of room. And I'm sure even if we run out, the house will whip us up some more." She patted the wood of the house affectionately. "Nice house."

"Well," said Neve, looking slightly troubled. She kneeled down and took Mei's hands. "We'll see where your Mum wants to stay. You must remember that a lot of things have changed since you disappeared."

"I know!" said Mei excitedly. "Athena showed me amazing things."

"Amazing things?" Rosemary asked.

"Yes! She has this little box like a rectangle, and it glows. And you can do *everything* on it. You can even talk to people who aren't there, but not like a telephone, but like...their faces. And it's got all the information in the world! It's magic."

"I see," said Rosemary, smiling.

"Athena calls it her phone," said Mei. "But phones have cords and they are much bigger. I told her!"

Nesta and Rosemary grinned at each other.

"This is going to be an interesting adjustment period," said Neve with slight concern in her voice.

CHAPTER
FIVE

Athena stared at the wood panels on the ceiling. She was having trouble sleeping again. As she lay in bed, all she could think about was the fae realm and how good it had felt to be there.

She looked around her room. Everything about this place felt too heavy and hard and dense. It was home in many ways, except the way that sang to her heart.

The wind rattled the windows and whispered through the trees outside as she lay there.

Sure, everyone she knew and loved was in the Earth realm, but being here just felt wrong. At her lowest points, she almost wished she could talk to Finnigan, despite his betrayal. At least he might understand. What she really missed was the Finnigan she'd thought she'd known, not the one who had turned her over to the fae countess, but that boy didn't exist.

She wasn't ready to talk about her emotions or anything personal with her mother. The last thing Athena needed was Rosemary getting over-protective and possessive again. Even still, she couldn't keep going around in circles. She needed to do something.

There was nothing for it.

Athena climbed out of bed and got into her slippers and warm dressing gown. She opened the door out to her balcony.

For a moment, she thought she heard whispering voices, but when the wind stilled all was silent. Athena felt so alone.

Of course, she couldn't call to Finnigan, and she wouldn't have wanted to see him even if he did come looking for her. Worse, she suspected he wouldn't bother, now that he'd got what he wanted out of her, using her as a bargaining chip with the countess.

She might still have lingering feelings for him, but she wasn't completely stupid. And most of those feelings right now were different forms of anger, anyway. She pushed him out of her mind.

There were more important things than boys, after all.

The wind picked up again as Athena stepped silently down to the lawn, grateful that the house hadn't decided to remove her own personal exit, despite Rosemary's yelling and complaining about it when she'd realised the balcony and staircase had appeared. Though her mother's histrionics *were* probably more to do with Athena running away to the fae realm than the magical renovations in particular.

She crossed towards the forest where Finnigan had led her. She couldn't help but look around for him in the trees, though she had half a mind to blast him with her magic if she did catch sight of him.

If only there was a way that she could figure out how to get back to the fae realm without him, even just temporarily. It was almost as if that place was calling out to her, beckoning her home, but she knew she had to stay.

Maybe I can try to cut through the veil, just a little bit. That would be enough to keep me sane and contented for a little while.

She attempted to remember what Finnigan had done, vaguely recalling there had been lights in the air. They formed a kind of archway. But she didn't know how to make that happen. It was all a bit hopeless.

A gust of wind whipped through the trees; it almost sounded like whispered chanting, but Athena knew better than to let her imagination run away on her.

I'm a powerful witch...and powerful fae. I can do this. I don't need him and his theatrics. I have all the power I need.

She raised her index finger with the intention of trying to cut a door through the veil from this realm into the next.

If Finnigan can use his fae and human magic to get through both sides of the veil, then surely so can I.

Athena focused on the fae realm, that beautiful sensation, the feeling she'd had of being free and relaxed, contented and truly alive. It was the feeling of being at home in her heart. Images of the purple light filtering through the trees swam through her mind.

A tiny light burst from the tip of her finger. She moved it up and over, sensing a thickness behind the usual night air. It was almost like moving her hand through jelly as she cut into the veil.

A blast of energy shot through, bowling her over onto the grass.

Athena picked herself up and tried to see what she'd created. The air shimmered in front of her. She held out her hands and felt a warm liquid sensation floating through her.

Gorgeous patterns of light wove though the air as bursts of red, blue, and purple flew through from the fae realm.

Athena sighed and basked in the energy.

It was that same beautiful feeling, though it was only fleeting.

This is it, she realised. *This is the feeling of home. If only I could bottle it and take it with me wherever I go.*

After a few moments, the feeling was gone and the veil had stitched itself back together. Despite the temptation, Athena didn't dare try to make another opening in order to get through, in case she couldn't return again.

She slipped back up the stairs and got into bed, hoping that the contented feeling would last for at least a little bit longer.

CHAPTER
SIX

Rosemary and Neve stepped out of the car in a modest neighbourhood of Burkenswood. The morning air was still thick with a stubborn fog. Rosemary felt a slight thrill of nervousness at the prospect of helping Neve with policework, which put her at risk of rambling.

"I forget how early children wake me up these days," said Rosemary. "I didn't even realise it was still morning."

Neve smiled at her. "Are you ready?" she asked. "This could get interesting."

Rosemary nodded. She had put her hair up into a band, a bit like the style of ponytail the detective wore. She had dressed in some quite conservative clothing, a plain navy shirt and black pants, so that she didn't give off her usual vibe, which Athena referred to as Grandma-toddler-yoga-attire.

Neve knocked on the door. After a moment, a woman answered, pale with greying hair and a tired expression on her face. She held a piece of toast in one hand.

"Tamsyn Dawson?" said Neve.

"What's this about?" the woman asked. "I'm running late for work."

"Sorry to bother you. Shall we come back at a better time?" Rosemary said.

"No. Just tell me." Tamsyn sounded impatient. "Are you selling something, because if so you can shove—"

Detective Neve held out her badge and introduced herself.

Tamsyn's expression became even more serious. "What happened?"

"It's a long story," said the detective.

"I guess you'd better come in," said Tamsyn. They followed her into the open-plan kitchen and living area of the house. It had a musty smell. Rosemary noticed the linoleum yellowing and the veneer on the kitchen cabinets was cracking from age.

"You may not remember this," said Neve as she sat down at the kitchen table. "But forty years ago, a little girl went missing, who was related to you."

The woman shook her head in disbelief. "Is this some kind of cold murder case?" she asked with a look of horror.

"Not exactly," said Rosemary. "She's still alive."

"You're telling me I have a long lost relative who was kidnapped?"

"Sort of," Rosemary said.

Neve shot her a glance and Rosemary decided to let the detective do most of the talking.

"Look," said Neve. "To be perfectly frank with you, there was magic involved."

Tamsyn shook her head in shock. "No, no. We moved away...to get away from all that."

"Why did you move away from Myrtlewood? Do you recall?" Detective Neve asked.

"Something happened," Tamsyn said with a cloudy look. "I

36

don't know what it was. Maybe my parents didn't tell me. But something bad happened and we had to move away. We weren't allowed to talk about magic anymore. Oh gods, I missed it. I missed it so much."

"Would you like to know about the thing that happened?" Rosemary asked tentatively, unable to stop herself from talking completely.

"It's been a long time," Tamsyn said. "My parents are gone now. I suppose...I don't have to follow their instructions anymore." She shook herself. "Okay, sure. Hit me. What happened?"

"The little girl who went missing was your sister," said Detective Neve.

The woman's jaw dropped. She shook her head slightly in disbelief.

"She was abducted by the fae into their realm," the detective continued. "This is why you don't remember. They have a powerful magic that makes people forget things that might compromise them."

Rosemary nodded, relieved that the detective had a way of communicating that was so clear.

"It's not possible," said Tamsyn, crossing her arms. "I didn't have a sister. I would remember something like that."

"We understand this is a shock," said Neve.

The woman's posture stiffened. "Look, I don't know who you are and what kind of game you're playing. But I would've remembered something like *that*."

"Please," said Rosemary.

"No. Get out of here!"

"Do you want to know more about her?" Detective Neve asked.

"This is *not* happening," Tamsyn said. "It can't possibly be true. Leave now before I report you to the *real* authorities."

Rosemary and Neve shared a troubled look. The detective

shrugged and gestured for them to get up from the table. Rosemary went along with it. The woman was clearly stressed and arguing with her wasn't going to help. They left the house and made their way back to the detective's car.

"Well, that was awful," said Rosemary.

"It could have gone a lot worse. Believe me," said Neve. "At least we got through the door. At least she knew about the magic, even if she is about to dob us in to the 'real' authorities."

"It's a lot," said Rosemary. "Isn't it? It's horrible having your memory mangled. Like your whole sense of reality is being challenged. I know that's like."

Neve sighed. "We should have started with that. You could have talked about your experience and gently led her into it. I was too abrupt."

"No," Rosemary reassured her. "You were great. So clear and calm. I suspect there's not a perfect way to deal with a situation like this. And even if she does eventually believe us, what then? We can't just dump a little girl on the doorstep of a woman who doesn't remember her."

"This job is a lot harder than I thought it was going to be," said Neve. "You know, usually when the police return abducted children, everyone is overjoyed and relieved about it. It's a huge win, but this…"

"I wonder if there is something I can do to help," said Rosemary. "Some kind of spell."

"Thank you. That's the other reason I wanted to bring you along. I thought it might motivate you to see what you can do."

"Fair enough," said Rosemary. "I'm a total novice with magic, you realise. And as for police business? Well, I probably shouldn't have said anything at all, but I can't help it. My mouth just operates of its own accord."

Neve laughed. "You actually weren't that bad back there. And magically, you're more powerful than you think. You've already done the impossible. Twice. You've taken down the Bloodstone Society, which I thought would never happen. And you've made it to the fae realm. I think you can crack something as simple as memory magic."

"I fear there's nothing simple about it," said Rosemary. "And you make me sound much more impressive than I am. But sure. I'll see what I can do."

CHAPTER
SEVEN

R osemary's limbs felt heavy and tired as she and Neve arrived
back at Thorn Manor. They found Athena, Nesta, Dain, and
the foundling children all sitting around the dining room table.
Clearly, it was morning tea time.

Athena poured tea out for the adults and milk for the children.
Thea and Clio immediately began slurping their drinks happily
while Harry blew bubbles in his before being told off and beaming.

Athena offered Nesta milk.

"I'm afraid we're only allowed a low fat milk in the house, still,"
said Athena, looking at Dain. "It's not safe for him to be around
cream."

Nesta smiled. "I know, love. Don't worry. I don't mind what
kind of milk it is."

Athena served Nesta and then turned to Rosemary. "Find out
anything interesting?"

"I'm afraid I'm not at liberty to discuss my serious police business," said Rosemary, slumping down in a chair under the weight of
disappointment. "As a trusted and professional consultant..."

"Give me a break," said Athena.

"Well, we can say that it wasn't a particularly successful endeavour," said Neve grimly.

"Surprising," said Athena ironically. "If somebody showed up on my doorstep trying to pawn off a child that nobody remembered and who hadn't been seen in decades, I would be over the moon!"

The children laughed and clapped, not understanding the sarcasm in Athena's voice. Rosemary shot her a warning.

"Look. They're delightful," said Athena. "But it's an odd situation, you've got to admit."

"Shouldn't you get to school already?" Rosemary asked.

"Teacher only day. Anyway, I'm sure I'm learning a lot more about the responsibility of life just by having to look after all these kids."

"I'm sure," said Dain. "You're doing plenty by playing and having tea parties all day."

"Speak for yourself." Athena crossed her arms. "Somebody around here has to be responsible."

Dain sipped his black tea, raising his eyebrows at his daughter and smiling. "You turned out pretty well considering, I have to say."

"Considering what?" said Rosemary sternly. "It's not like you helped very much."

Dain made a face and Athena laughed.

"Considering that I have both of you for parents," said Athena.

Rosemary sighed. "Being a mother is the most thankless job!"

There was a knock at the door.

"Come in!" Rosemary called. But Marjie had already let herself into the house. "I'm back, and I brought cakes!"

The children cheered. Marjie carried two boxes into the dining room and set them on the table. Athena opened the one closest to her to reveal half a dozen assorted little cakes topped with cream.

Cream!

"Ahh, Marjie," she said, a note of worry in her voice.

Rosemary stared at the cakes, the hairs rising on her forearms in warning.

"Yes, dear," said Marjie.

"There's...on the cakes...Crea—" Athena stuttered.

"Oh!"

All adult eyes in the room turned towards Dain.

His eyes, locked on the cakes, seemed to glow as if covered in gold dust.

"This is not good," said Athena, quickly covering the cakes. "Mum. You have to hold him back."

Rosemary quickly moved to Dain's side of the table and gripped him by his arms. He began to struggle away from her, towards the cakes.

"Dain. No! You have a problem. But you've got to calm down."

For a moment, Dain held preternaturally still.

"I'm so sorry," said Marjie. "I should have remembered to check. I told the new girl at the shop, Lamorna, not to give me any of the cream ones for you, but she's obviously forgotten."

"Get them out of here!" Rosemary cried.

Athena picked up the box and made a dash towards the kitchen.

Rosemary heard the door to the back garden slam, just as Dain wrestled free of her grip. He flung open the other cake box to find there was no cream in sight, then he took a great leap over the dining chairs towards the door.

"Stop at once!" Rosemary cried. She watched Dain disappear in hot pursuit of the cream cakes, suppressing her urge to use magic. She didn't want to risk debris flying towards the children.

"Oh blast it all!" Marjie cried.

Rosemary ran after him. "Dain, I'm warning you," she said.

His hand was on the doorknob that Athena must have magically locked as she'd fled.

42

Rosemary could see her daughter heading quickly towards the trees, still carrying the box, but Dain could be much quicker. With his fully unleashed fae speed that he sometimes used while chasing the children she knew it would only take a moment for Dain to catch up.

Dain's hand was still on the locked door, scrambling to get it opened.

"Remember what happened last time?" Rosemary said, but the logical part of his mind had obviously vacated the building. "One more chance." She held her hands in front of her, and a light shimmered behind her palms. "I'm serious."

A growl issued from Dain's mouth. It sounded more like purr. He snapped the handle off the door as if it were no stronger than a candy cane and flung it wide open.

"That's it," said Rosemary.

She called forth her magic.

A golden ball of light issued from her hands and flew across the room, hitting Dain in the back. He sprawled forward, clearly concussed.

"It took you long enough," Athena said as she crossed back towards the house.

"I had to give him a warning," said Rosemary.

"Why? You know he doesn't think properly when he's in sight of a fix."

"We've got to do something about this," said Rosemary.

"Yeah, that's what you said last time," said Athena as they strolled back through the house. "And what have you done about it?"

"I've done some research," said Rosemary defensively. "I tried that spell from the old book Burk gave me, but it just made Dain sick, remember?"

"Oh well, at least we get to have whipped cream for morning

tea, now that Dad's unconscious." Athena's voice was tense when she called Dain "Dad." It was a new development for her to casually refer to him in this way and Rosemary hoped it was a good thing.

The children, who were now in earshot, cheered and clapped at the news. They were big fans of Marjie's cream cakes, despite the fact that they were hardly ever allowed them, except on rare excursions to town. On those occasions, Dain had to stay locked in the car for his own protection and everyone else's.

Rosemary understood that cream had an effect on the fae worse than most mind altering substances known to humans. They would lose all sense of integrity or propriety and become exceedingly generous. Fortunately, this didn't seem to apply to Athena, who must have skipped those parts of the genetic lottery and merely had an enthusiastic fondness for dairy.

Aside from its dangers, cream had proved to be exceedingly useful. Under its influence, the fae countess had sent them back to the human realm without so much as a second thought, even though she'd been pursuing them with violence moments earlier. Athena had cleverly laced her tea with cream that she'd smuggled into the fae realm.

Understanding the power of cream had helped to clear things up for Rosemary regarding Dain's history of irrational behavior, his gambling, and the way that her wallet had a habit of disappearing when he was around, back in the days when they were together.

The explanation hadn't meant she'd forgiven him. It was hard to come back from something like that. Despite often forgetting her anger towards Dain in the past, due to the amnesiac properties of fae magic, being betrayed over and over again by your first love took its toll.

It had almost made matters worse that she hadn't gone through the appropriate anger with him, or processed it.

Athena, who was immune to the fae memory magic, had been

dreadfully angry and resentful of her father, but recently, she'd seemed to warm to him slightly more than Rosemary was comfortable with.

While she hadn't been happy about Athena being previously so mad at Dain, Rosemary now had to contend with them both ganging up on her from time to time, even if it was just in a playful way.

Back inside the house, Rosemary helped herself to a chocolate tart and took a sip of tea, which Marjie had especially spiked with a generous helping of her special formula.

"Have you gotten any further with a cure for him, love?" Marjie asked.

"I keep asking her that," Athena said.

"I think I'm going to have to make up another spell entirely," said Rosemary. "I'll get to work on it after I visit Liam. Not that I know what I'm doing."

"Why are you visiting Liam all of a sudden?" Athena asked. "Don't tell me you two have a thing going on."

"Oh, really?" said Nesta. "Liam from the bookshop? He's quite handsome."

Rosemary felt her cheeks flush. "Nothing like that. I just promised I'd help him with something."

"But she won't say what," said Athena.

"It's not something I'm at liberty to share."

Marjie gave her a curious look.

"Oh, well," Athena continued. "At least if you're seeing Liam, you're less likely to get back with dad again. And we know that never was a good idea to begin with."

"I'm not getting involved with anybody, thank you very much!" said Rosemary. "We all know that only leads to disaster."

"Oh, it would be nice to see you with a nice man...or woman," said Marjie. She smiled at Nesta. "We don't discriminate."

Nesta gave her an awkward smile. "I know. You don't have to spell it out."

"Why don't you give us those spells that you tried last time on Dain?" said Marjie. "Athena and I can get started on some variations while you're out."

"Really, you don't have to go to any trouble," said Rosemary. "You've done so much already."

"Nonsense," said Marjie.

"What's the matter?" said Athena. "Are you worried that I'll figure the spell out before you do and show you that I'm better at magic?"

"That's the least of my worries," said Rosemary. "I wouldn't be surprised if anyone was better at magic than I am."

Athena sighed. "There's your imposter syndrome again, making everything worse." She gave her mother a sympathetic smile. "Don't worry, leave it to us. We'll have the spell cracked in no time. But at some point you're going to have to tell us what's going on with Liam."

CHAPTER

EIGHT

Rosemary drove down the quiet country lane towards the address Liam had given her. He'd asked to meet her at his home rather than at the bookshop, for the sake of his privacy.

Liam's cottage was a small white one with pale blue trim, a sweet little house to look at from a distance. But as Rosemary drew closer, the peeling paint and cracked whitewash became more evident. *It definitely could use a bit of care, and a fresh coat of paint.*

She stepped out of the car and headed for the front door, but just as she neared it, she heard the snap of a breaking twig from behind her.

She turned back to see a tall hooded figure wearing black robes and a grey mask, and carrying a giant metal spear.

"Not this again!" said Rosemary. The figure didn't say a word, but ran towards her at an alarming pace, raising the spear, poised to strike.

Rosemary was caught off-guard. She lunged out of the way, narrowly missing the attack.

It must be that cursed Bloodstone Society!

The figure turned back to face her.

Don't show fear, Rosemary instructed herself. *You're a powerful witch. Show them who's boss.* "Reveal yourself, you coward!" she said with mock bravado.

The attacker laughed a deep throaty chuckle. "Rosemary Thorn," a raspy voice said. "Prepare to meet your fate!"

"What a cliché. You can't really can't come up with anything more original than that?"

The figure laughed again. "You are a weak mortal. You will not stand in our way. We will return, victorious!"

"Yeah, yeah." Rosemary's patience was wearing thin and that helped her channel some of her pent up rage into a fireball the size of a small melon. She held it in both hands, staring down her foe.

The hooded figure hesitated. "You...I was told you knew nothing of your power. That taking you out would be easy."

"Then you were misled or someone got their wires crossed," said Rosemary with a frustrated sigh. "But either way, I've never been a fan of drawn-out fights, not even in movies, and definitely not in real life. Get out of here before I blast you to another dimension."

Rosemary had no idea how to do that, but she bit her tongue to save from rambling. This was hardly the time.

"Consider this a warning!" The figure raised the spear as if to throw it, but Rosemary was quicker. She shoved the fireball towards the weapon, blasting it out of the attacker's hand.

The figure shrieked and rushed towards her, but Rosemary was more prepared this time. She made use of the strength and flexibility that seemed to only work as a magically-induced survival mechanism and gave them a quick stiff kick to the head, hoping to reveal their identity.

The hood remained in place, however, as the attacker reared back, clutching their face.

Rosemary caught a glimpse of an emblem under the cloak. It was the familiar shield bearing the Bloodstone Society crest. She sighed. "Look, I'm sick of your crowd. Leave me alone. I've got places to be."

"There are hundreds of us and we are gathering power!" the figure shrieked. "We will return!"

A crackling sound burst from behind Rosemary.

She felt dread rising as she turned, preparing for more attackers. Instead, her eyes were met with a solid wall of fire.

"What the...?" Rosemary turned back to see that the mysterious attacker had disappeared.

The red and orange flames rose swiftly, in a mesmerising pattern.

Rosemary wanted to watch, but her instincts made her step back and check for other risks.

Her abdominal muscles clenched as the fire spread dangerously close to the side of Liam's house.

"This is not what I expected for my morning," Rosemary muttered to herself.

"Rosemary!" Liam called, coming out from his house. "What's going on? What did you do?"

"Nothing!" Rosemary replied. "I was just attacked...And now, well, I guess the attacker lit a fire somehow."

Liam looked at her, unimpressed.

"It wasn't me!" said Rosemary defensively.

"Fine. But can't you do something?"

"Not without a lot of water," Rosemary replied. "I don't know how to put out fires magically."

"There's water in the pond," said Liam. "Can't you..."

"Actually, I think I can help with that, now that you mentioned it."

Rosemary focused her attention on the water from the pond,

not far from the back of the house. Surely, it wasn't all that different from watering the plants she'd tended in her lounge only a few weeks before.

She closed her eyes and visualised the water spouting out, using the power of air to pick it up and pour it over the fire.

"It's working!" said Liam.

Rosemary looked to see that indeed, the water was spouting from the pond, sprinkling all over the flames, which had died back.

"Thank goodness for that," said Rosemary. "Sorry, Liam. Your house almost got singed."

"I thought you said it wasn't your fault."

"It wasn't. I'm just sorry it had to happen. And while I didn't make the fire, that attacker knows exactly who I am and knew where to find me. So you might want to reconsider whether you want to meet here."

"Who was it?" Liam asked.

"I'm not sure exactly." Rosemary described the mysterious figure. "I'm willing to bet it has something to do with that stupid secret society that seems to have it in for us. I'm sure I saw their emblem."

"The Bloodstones?" Liam asked.

Rosemary nodded. "I thought they'd given up, but apparently not."

Liam's lips pressed into a thin line. "Sherry told me she'd heard rumours of them making a comeback, or attempting to."

"Just what we need. Oh well, I suppose if we've vanquished them once it can happen again."

"The problem is, with their leader gone, there will be some kind of power struggle. They might get desperate." He rubbed his chin in contemplation. "Now that I think of it, some suspicious customers came into the book shop the other day. They weren't from around here, but they were seeking out texts on ancient vampire lore. One of them asked an oddly specific question on parallel dimensions."

Rosemary frowned. "Do you think they're trying to bring Geneviève back? I don't understand why they'd need the little brat."

Liam shrugged. "Their leader might have looked like an innocent child, but her reputation was infamous. She is believed to have caused chaos and destruction wherever she went for centuries, including instigating several wars and two near-apocalypses, and that was *before* she went undercover as the leader of a magical sect."

"Well, that's ruined my mood. I suppose I shouldn't visit your house if I'm only bringing you danger."

"Rosemary, if they knew to come to my house, then I'm no safer with you anywhere else, am I?"

Rosemary shrugged. "Fair enough."

"Come in."

She followed Liam inside. The cottage was simple with pale cream walls and plenty of bookshelves. Rosemary noticed many of Liam's books were old and leather bound, though she spotted a large collection of fantasy novels. She was surprised by the rather dainty watercolour paintings of flowers that adorned the walls. The furnishings were comfortable, not flashy. Old sofas and armchairs were draped with crochet blankets and there was a large fluffy rug on the floor. The lounge was cosy, especially when Liam lit the fire to take the chill out of the air.

Rosemary sighed and warmed her hands near the hearth. "I much prefer your fire to that one outside. It gave me the creeps."

"It was unusual. I wonder if it's anything to do with the fire at the Twigg farm a couple of weeks ago."

"I didn't hear about that," said Rosemary. "Which is strange in such a small town."

"Strange indeed. It was so warm this morning. And now all of a sudden it's freezing."

"Stranger things have happened," said Rosemary. "What is it you think I can help with?"

"We've talked about this," Liam said slightly defensively.

"Yeah...I know, in general, what you want me to do. I just don't know how to do it."

"Look, Rosemary, last time when I was in wolf form, you shocked me with your magic and it made the wolf go away, and it freed me temporarily. The next full moon is coming up in just over a week."

"Are you saying you want me to wait until you turn into a wolf, then shock you with magic every month?" Rosemary asked, unimpressed.

"If it comes down to it, then maybe," said Liam. "But I'm hoping there's a way you can bottle that sunshine stuff you produce out of your hands."

"Sunshine?" Rosemary wondered if what Liam had noticed might actually be some kind of combination of elemental fire and air – the two elements that came most naturally to her.

"That's what it felt like," said Liam. "I know it sounds strange, but maybe the sun kind of counteracts the moon."

"But you're still a werewolf during the day when it's full moon," Rosemary reminded him.

"Yeah, sure. It sounds silly and...I don't know. It's just my guess. The Moon is full when the Sun is opposite it, you know. The Sun and Moon have a kind of polarity."

"That sounds lovely and poetic," said Rosemary, though she wished Liam would get to the point.

"Look, I'm not sure about the actual scientific or magical truth. I'm grasping at straws," Liam admitted. "Do you have any other theories?"

"I'm afraid not," Rosemary said. "We can go with yours for now.

Surely there must be lots of books on werewolves? You work in a magical bookshop. Don't you know these things?"

"There are lots of books on how awful we are," said Liam. "The most useful things I've found are protection spells—the kind of thing I use a lot, to make sure I don't infect anyone else. But until the other day I'd never heard of anything like what you did. As far as I know, it's never happened before."

"Well, that's just ridiculous." Rosemary put her hands on her hips. "I don't know what I did. It was a fluke. We're totally in the dark."

"Could you try bottling it? Liam asked. "You know, like pouring your energy into some kind of vessel, and then when I need it I can just open it up."

"Why not smash it on the ground for dramatic effect?" said Rosemary. "Or, I know, in the bath. Maybe you want a magical bath bomb?"

"You're not taking this seriously."

"Forgive me if I'm a little wound up. I've just been attacked and had to deal with magical arson and now you tell me we have no clues as to how to deliberately work the magic you have such high expectations on me for."

"So you don't want to help me?"

"I certainly can try," said Rosemary. "Though, if I do manage to bottle some energy, we won't know if it works until it's already too late."

"That's true," said Liam.

"You'll have to chain yourself up in the basement, just in case."

"If I'm chained up, how am I going to have a magical bath?" Liam asked, amused.

"Liam, I'm afraid there are some things that I'm not going to be able to help you with." Rosemary laughed. "I draw the line at bathing you."

"I suppose I'll have to manage," said Liam with a wry smile, then his expression became more serious, his eyes stormy. "Thank you for trying to help. This *condition* has been plaguing me for years and I finally have hope that I'll be able to live a normal life without constant fears of hurting people or being ostracised by the magical community. I even wonder if there'll be some kind of cure."

"You mean if I can zap you with enough magic to stop you from ever changing again?" said Rosemary.

"I'm not sure if it's about enough magic," said Liam. "Or if it's about finding the precise kind, woven in the right way."

"Yeah, I get it," said Rosemary. "I wish I could ask other people for help because I have no idea what I'm doing and I don't want to hurt you. I only blasted you at the shop because I was being attacked by an enormous wolf creature. I don't really want to do that when you're standing here as a human, let alone as a friend."

"I've missed our friendship," said Liam in a soft voice, his eyes downcast.

"Me too," said Rosemary. "You were starting to act weird."

"I'm sorry. I just...I got a bit jealous after you shot me down. You've been hanging out with that vampire a lot. It gives me the creeps."

"Wow," said Rosemary. "Discrimination, much?"

"They're not natural, Rosemary."

"Any more than a werewolf is?"

"That's very different," said Liam.

"Is it, though? I mean you've both been infected with some kind of magical equivalent of a virus or something."

"That's one way to put it," said Liam. "But vampires are cunning, and they've been around for a long time. They're very strategic."

Rosemary thought of the very handsome vampire she'd taken a shine to. Burk had gone out of his way to help her when Athena went missing. He seemed trustworthy, but was that all a part of his vampire charm, luring her in?

"They amass a lot of resources," Liam continued. "And they have a different sense of morality. I mean, they feed on blood."

"And blood-enchanted food." Rosemary grimaced. "And apparently a lot of pig's blood."

"Still," said Liam, "I get the feeling they enjoy being what they are. Whereas, it's not like I can use my wolf to my advantage. It's only a curse, there's nothing good about it. I'd do anything to be properly human again."

Rosemary gave him a sad smile. "So you think this is something we can practice when you're not in your wolf form?" she asked. "You want me to shoot magic energy at you? I suppose you could give me feedback on whether it's had any effect on the wolfiness. If you're attuned to it enough to be able to tell."

"I think so," said Liam. "When infected with the virus, it's like a kind of wolf lives inside you. That's part of the reason I was so jealous. The wolf can make me aggressive sometimes, even when it's not the full moon. I do my best to quell it, but it's hard to control."

"So you can feel it there all the time?" Rosemary asked.

"Yes."

"Then I'll practice shooting you with magic and we can see how we go."

Liam gulped.

"Not too scared?" Rosemary asked him, her voice slightly teasing.

"Scared of what? Only the most powerful witch in town, shooting me with magic lasers?" Liam asked. "Why would I be scared of that?"

"They're not lasers," said Rosemary. "I'm a great ball of sunshine, remember?"

Liam laughed. "That you are, Rosemary. That you are."

NINE

Despite the pleasant hour she'd spent with Liam, Rosemary felt heavy and drained by the time she returned home. It didn't help her mood that the kitchen looked like a bomb site.

"What on earth is going on?" she asked.

Athena popped her head up from behind the counter, looking frazzled. "We've been trying to make a potion," she said. "But it keeps exploding. This magic stuff is way unstable."

"Tell me about it," said Rosemary. "Where's Marjie?"

"She's gone to the bathroom to clean herself up while I had a wee sit down on the floor."

"Oh dear," Rosemary said, approaching her daughter and giving her a fortifying hug. "This situation with Dain is not going to improve anytime soon, is it?"

Athena shook her head as Rosemary led her over to the window seats to rest properly.

"Magic is complicated where fae are concerned," Athena muttered.

"I was hoping we could get his little problem dealt with," said

Rosemary. "I suppose he's just going to have to work on his self-control, which is tricky when fae don't seem to have any around a particular high-fat dairy product. Come to think of it, isn't it odd that butter doesn't have the same effect?"

Athena shrugged. "Butter has the fat, but it has some of the other stuff taken out of it. Maybe it's the processing or maybe It's just that it needs all the components of cream to create that effect."

"How did you get to be so smart?" Rosemary asked. "Wait a minute, where are the kids?"

"Don't worry my dear," said Marjie. "Nesta took them out back. She's so good with children. She's always wanted some of her own, Neve told me."

"Well she's welcome to take some of ours," said Rosemary, flippantly. "We've got plenty here, and I'm a little bit worried that the next seasonal festival is all about fertility. Seeing as magic is real and all, we hardly need any more children at this time!"

She looked at Athena.

"Gross, Mum. Don't look at me. I'm not having any children, and you won't have to worry about accidents considering I'm never having relationships, ever!"

Marjie shook her head and tutted. "Why don't you go and get yourself cleaned up?" she said to Athena who grumbled as she shook herself and stalked off towards the bathroom.

"What's all that about?" Rosemary asked.

"The sting of betrayal," said Marjie. "It takes a long time to get over your first crush."

"Athena won't tell me the details of what went on," said Rosemary. "Just that Finnigan sold her out to some fae countess. I assume they wanted her and Dain to use as political bargaining chips. He was locked up in the same castle."

"And you can't see why she's bitter about relationships?" Marjie asked.

"Of course I can," said Rosemary. "It's just... She's cutting herself off from a whole world of human experience. It's bugging me how much she reminds me of myself right now."

Marjie gave Rosemary a knowing look. "And how will this insight affect you?"

"Oh Marjie, you know I have rotten luck when it comes to men."

"When it came to one man with a very specific dairy product addiction who isn't even human."

"That's a bit harsh."

"I don't mean offence by it. It's just the truth. Maybe if you were involved with anyone other than Dain it wouldn't be such a disaster."

Rosemary sighed. "I let Athena down so badly with my choices. I'm not going to do that again."

"And yet, here we are," said Marjie. "Listen, think about it this way. If you were giving advice to a good friend in your current situation, what would you say to her?" And with that, the older woman stood up, brushed off her apron and started cleaning up the kitchen, leaving Rosemary boggling at the astute question.

She got up to help Marjie as Athena returned and joined in the cleaning too. "Okay, so talk me through what you've tried so far, and I'll see if I can figure out what's going wrong," said Rosemary.

"Well," Athena said. "The first phase of the spell involves a fresh egg, quartz crystals, and plenty of sage, as well as salt."

"Sea salt to be precise," Marjie added.

"Yes, I know that," said Rosemary. "I tried it myself, remember. This one made Dain awfully sick. It didn't explode the kitchen, though."

"We've been trying to swap out ingredients," said Marjie. "Seems like any variation of the spell just creates total chaos... makes it unstable."

Rosemary read through the spell again, holding the piece of

paper she'd copied it onto by hand to save the book from getting messy. "It's such an old spell and it was originally supposed to deter fae from cream, but that was before the fae magic changed to protect them from vampires, and before the veil barriers were put up. If only I could understand how it's supposed to work... Then maybe I could make it better."

"I'm afraid I'm not really the expert here," said Marjie.

"I could try asking one of the teachers from school," Athena suggested.

"That's not a bad idea," said Rosemary. "They're bound to have a lot more experience in this sort of magic, even if they haven't focused on fae."

"It's almost like a healing spell," said Marjie, looking at the text again. "Actually, come to think of it..."

"What? said Rosemary.

"I feel daft for not mentioning it earlier," said Marjie. "It never crossed my mind that we should have been consulting Ashwyn at the local apothecary."

"What's that?" Athena asked.

"Oh, you know, the apothecary across the square from the bookshop," said Marjie. "They make all sorts of remedies. Well, perhaps not all sorts, otherwise we would have just got a pre-made one for our little fae spell. But they do specialize in treatments for all kinds of magical ailments and some mundane ones as well."

"This is more than just a regular magical ailment," said Rosemary. "Do you really think they can help?"

"It's worth a shot," said Marjie. "After all, they're experts at what they do. They're not going to be able to cure vampirism or stop someone from being a horrible werewolf, but for something like this, where the primary focus is actually an addiction, they might be able to do something or at least explain to you how this spell supposed to work."

Rosemary grimaced at Marjie's werewolf comment. It seemed like blatant discrimination and it made her fear for Liam, if his secret ever got out. *If the loveliest woman in town is awful about were-wolves, I hate to think how anyone else would react...*

"Do you think it's safe to tell your friend at the apothecary what Dad is?" Athena asked Marjie. "I don't even know if fae are supposed to be here in this world. Mum wants me to keep what I am a secret from vampires."

"Good point," said Rosemary. "We've got to play it safe. But the police know what Dain is. I'm pretty sure we could mention it to the local magical equivalent of doctors."

"They see all sorts of things around here," said Marjie. "And I'll vouch for Ashwyn and her lovely sister. They are good sorts."

"Alright, let's go then," said Athena.

"I can introduce you," said Marjie.

"We'll just have to check to make sure that Nesta is okay, minding the kids a little bit longer," said Rosemary.

"I'm sure she'll be fine," said Marjie. "I just checked a little while ago and she's got them down for their afternoon nap... most of them. Mei was reading quietly in the corner of the nursery."

Rosemary smiled. "It still surprises me how the house knew to make us nursery, even before we got home," she said.

"All right, Mum," said Athena. "Let's go. Before Dad wakes up."

CHAPTER
TEN

Rosemary and Athena followed Marjie into the apothecary and was surprised to see a familiar face.

The woman behind the counter had long blonde, wavy hair. It took a moment for Rosemary to recall that she was the one officiating at the Ostara ritual a few weeks before.

Rosemary looked around the shop to find dozens of shelves neatly stacked with assortments of bottles, all with neat white and green labels.

Athena had already become distracted by the different items on sale and had veered off to examine them. A large flower arrangement sat in the middle of the small shop, made up of freshly picked wild flowers and herbs.

The way everything was set out gave the shop a spaciousness and lightness. The whole feeling of the space was one of peace which no-doubt was partly attributed to the tranquil presence of the woman who ran it.

"How can I help you, today?" said the woman, smiling.

"Ashwyn! How nice to see you," said Marjie, introducing Rosemary and Athena. "We were just wondering if we could trouble you to help us out with a little problem we've been having, which is rather... complex."

"Of course, Marjie," said Ashwyn. "You know how much I adore little complex problems."

"Not so little, I'm afraid," said Rosemary. "Nothing is quite so simple when it comes to the fae."

"Let's see how we can help," said Ashwyn, with a knowing smile. "Please take a seat."

She waved her arms and four little stools appeared, surrounding the table.

"I see... Would you like some tea?"

"We just had tea," said Rosemary.

"Since when has that ever stopped you?" Athena asked.

"I just mean, don't go to any trouble," said Rosemary.

"It's no trouble at all," said Ashwyn. "I just happen to have herbal formula brewing. It's my new calming blend."

"That sounds wonderful," said Rosemary.

Ashwyn disappeared into a back room and Marjie smiled. "She always has some kind of tea brewing to offer people who enter the shop at any time. One of the nice things about coming here..."

"Well, if I'd known about that, I would have popped in more often," said Rosemary. "You know, my nerves can always do with some calming,"

"That's right, Mum. You should definitely be a regular client.

Ashwyn returned with tea. She was followed by another woman of similar height with long brown wavy hair. "This is my sister, Una," Ashwyn said.

There was something luminous about Una's skin. Rosemary thought she looked a little like Athena. The teen approached and sat down at the table. She smiled at the brown-haired woman and the woman smiled back, a glint of recognition in her eyes.

"What seems to be the problem?" she asked.

"It's my Dad," said Athena he's always had a problem... he can't help himself."

"Dairy addiction?" Una asked.

Athena gasped in surprise.

"How did you know?" said Rosemary, gobsmacked. She looked from one sister to the other, feeling her paranoia rising. Who were these women, really? They seemed so nice and genuine, but could that be a ruse?

"I might have some experience in that realm," Una replied. "I'm both human and fae, just like you." She looked at Athena, who put her hand to her mouth in surprise.

"You are? I thought there was something familiar about you," Athena said

"Yes," said Ashwyn. "Our mother was a gifted healer, but we have different fathers."

"I didn't know my father," Una added. "But Mother would talk about him, sometimes. She said it was a summer fling. But anyway, back to your problem... what's happening?"

" Dain has always been erratic," said Rosemary. "Flipping out and gambling and giving away everything we own."

"That happens when he has cream?" Una asked.

"Wait a minute," said Rosemary. "If you didn't really know your father. How do you know about this?"

"I might have suffered from something quite similar," said Una. "As I said before, Mother was a gifted healer and she was able to help me."

"But if you're like me," Athena said. "Then why don't I have that problem?

Una shrugged. "It could be genetics."

"I wouldn't be surprised," said Ashwyn. "If the power of your legendary magical genes had something to do with it, given that you come from the Thorn family."

"How do you know that?" Rosemary asked, raising her eyebrows.

Ashwyn laughed. "Marjie just introduced you. Besides, it's a small town. Everyone knew Galdie. I'd be surprised if there was a local here that doesn't recognise you already."

Una looked at Rosemary and Athena, curiously.

"But your mother managed to help you," said Rosemary, excitedly. "So... you have a remedy for us?"

"Not exactly," said Una. "The one that our mother managed to concoct for me was a potion and a spell. But it fortified my human side. If your father is a fully fledged fae, then that's not going to work."

Rosemary deflated in disappointment, her shoulders hunching.

"That's not to say we can't help," said Ashwyn. "We might be able to give you some pointers."

"Please, if you can help in any way," said Rosemary. "I had previously just thought that Dain was a totally irresponsible human being and I'm now having to adjust to the realization that he's actually a fae prince with an unfortunate predilection for flipping out over cream cakes. It would really help things if he didn't become a total fruit loop and lose his mind every time he saw a cream bun—"

Athena cleared her throat and Rosemary stopped rambling. "We've been working on something," Athena explained. "It's from an old book about the fae."

Rosemary pulled out the tiny green fabric bound volume that Burk had given her.

"Where did you get this book?" Una asked she flipped through the pages. "I've never seen anything like it."

"I can't say," said Rosemary. "But it's quite rare. I'm not sure if there are any other copies. It's rather outdated, I suppose..."

"It is," said Una. "But there are some things in here that I might find quite useful, if you lend it to me."

"I don't know..." said Rosemary.

"Oh, maybe you can just pop around and read it from time to time?" said Marjie. "I'm sure Rosemary wouldn't mind that."

"No, that would be fine," said Rosemary, smiling. "I just... I'm already borrowing it from a friend and I don't think I can lend out somebody else's book."

"I totally understand," said Una, with a warm smile. "I just got a bit excited there. It's so rare to find any proper information on the fae that isn't just idle speculation or fantasy."

"Like that rubbish about them not being able to lie," said Athena, bitterly.

"Tell me about it," said Rosemary. She filled Una in on some of the details as to why and talked about their recent experiences.

A look of the greatest surprise crossed both sister's faces as they heard the brief story of Rosemary's venture into the fae realm.

"I would have thought it impossible," said Una.

"I remember you being at that ritual," Ashwyn added. "I remember the crystals on the ground, and chanting. And then it all gets a bit foggy."

"Funny how the fae manage to do that, isn't it?" said Rosemary. "Come to think of it, that's another thing I'd like your help with. Do you have any miracle cures or remedies to both protect against the memory altering magic, and also to repel it?"

"We'll have a think about that," said Una. "But in the meantime. This is the spell, is it?" She'd flipped to the bookmarked page.

Rosemary nodded.

"I see. So it's trying to work on the fae side," Una continued. "It's just possible that if we combine what we know from this spell with the one in my mother's Grimoire we might be able to come up with something that works."

"That sounds promising," said Athena.

"Unfortunately it all hinges on something that's totally out of our control," said Una.

"What's that?" Rosemary asked.

"Love," Una replied.

Athena scrunched up her face, looking mildly disgusted.

"What do you mean by that? Asked Rosemary.

"There needs to be love on both sides," Ashwyn explained. It's in our mother's spell, anyway. There needs to be something that he loves more... to have power the addiction. And it needs to be cast by people who love him."

"Sounds tricky," said Rosemary. "They can't be many people who Dain's formed any kind of deep emotional attachment to."

"He did with you, Mum," said Athena.

"That was a long time ago," Rosemary replied. "And while he's very charming. I am not in a position to be able to... do that. You're his daughter, you're probably better placed."

"Err, maybe," said Athena. "He's starting to grown on me... Although I wouldn't go that far."

"We can worry about the specifics of it later, dear," said Marjie. "It's just important that we get the ball rolling on this. I better pop back to the shop, but I'll check on you later at your place."

"I guess we'd better leave too." Rosemary said. "Thanks for your help."

"We haven't done anything yet," said Una.

"Even just a little bit more information is something," Rosemary replied. "We've been totally in the dark apart from the spell in this book. If you'd like, you're welcome to pop around in the next day or two. I'll been home most of the time, keeping an eye on those foundling children and making sure Athena stays out of trouble."

Athena glared at her mother, and then turned back to Una with a smile. "You could come over for a cup of tea."

"That sounds lovely," said Una.

CHAPTER
ELEVEN

Athena left the apothecary with a lingering feeling of warmth. She'd arranged to meet Elise at Marjie's shop for cake a bit later, so instead of going back to Thorn Manor she said goodbye to her mother and wandered across the circular park in the centre of Mytlewood. This park, sometimes called the town circle, was where the village rituals were held. It was surrounded by roads forming a square, lined with shops and other businesses that faced inwards, giving Athena a sense of safety. No one would attack her here, not in broad daylight. Still, as she crossed beneath the hawthorn trees in full bloom, she had the sensation of being watched by someone with malicious intentions.

She looked around, but everything seemed to be in order.

Don't run wild, she scolded her imagination. *I'm totally safe.*

She deliberately drew her attention back to the warm feeling she'd had at the apothecary, the sense of recognition when she'd met Una and the tingling sensation that spread right to her fingertips.

She'd rarely met anyone with such similar heritage to her and wondered if it was something to do with her genetics that inspired the reaction.

Finnigan was the only other person she knew with high fae and human parents, and he was the last person she wanted to see.

This particular reaction to Una was different. It was almost as though they were bonded somehow – connected, like family despite never meeting each other before.

Athena certainly hadn't felt anything like that when she'd met any of the creatures in the fae realm. She tried to push thoughts of that realm out of her mind, along with the guilt that came from her late night activities.

She knew she needed to make friends with Una and spend more time with her. Being in her presence had not only dissipated the uncomfortable, heavy feelings from the physical plane but had also made Athena feel light and safe and contented.

It was a little bit like the feelings she had at night when she cut her way through to the fae realm itself.

Stop it, she scolded. *Focus on the present. There's no point in pining for another world.*

As she neared the tea shop, she recognised Elise's blue hair.

Athena smiled as she opened the door. "You're early."

Elise beamed back at her. "So are you! It must be fate."

"Maybe it's a sign we need to have extra cake."

"That sounds right," said Elise with a nod.

They hugged and made their way up to the counter.

Marjie's new helper, Lamorna, greeted them with a broad smile. Marjie said she had just moved to Myrtlewood from St Austell and came from a magical family. Today, she wore an oversized knitted jumper. Her blonde hair was pinned up into little bundles which Athena thought looked cool in an old '90s sort of way – though she knew Rosemary would have balked at the '90s being considered old-fashioned.

"I'm so sorry about the mix-up earlier," Lamorna said. "I totally forgot about the cream situation."

"That's okay," said Athena, hoping not to sound too uncool. "No big deal."

Lamorna nodded, then gestured to the cabinet. "What will it be?"

"Oooh," said Elise. "I really want chocolate, but I don't tolerate animal products well. I'm pretty sure that one's not dairy free. I wonder if I can handle a bit of cream..."

Athena shook her head. "Not if it's going to make you sick."

"You know what," said Lamorna, with a wink. "We have a fresh triple chocolate cake cooling out the back and I made it with coconut oil instead of butter. You know, I can't tolerate it either. How about I bring some out with cashew cream?"

"Perfect!" said Elise.

Athena grinned and ordered the shortcake and a large pot of her favourite strawberries and cream tea.

They sat down at a table by the window to await their feast.

"She's so cool!" said Elise.

Athena nodded. "There's something unusual about her though. I wonder if she's part fae."

Elise rubbed her chin in thought. "Maybe. Lots of people can't have dairy, though."

"Speaking of part fae," said Athena. "Have you ever met Una at the apothecary? She's awesome."

"I vaguely know her," said Elise with a frown. "She's one of Mum's friends."

"You don't like her?"

"Oh no, it's not that. She seems lovely."

"What is it then?" Athena asked.

"Nothing," said Elise. "I guess I'm just hungry and need an extraordinary amount of cake, right now!"

It wasn't long before their cake and tea arrived. Athena ate and drank, quietly pondering the connection she felt with Una. There was only one person who might have any clue about it who was accessible.

She made a mental note to talk to her father when he'd woken up from his little magically-induced nap.

CHAPTER
TWELVE

That evening, Rosemary opened the door to find a familiar woman standing there, her greying strawberry blonde hair looking as if it needed to be brushed. She was holding a large casserole dish.

"Sherry?"

"Hello," said Sherry. "I just dropped around to bring you some of my famous beef and Guinness stew. I'm so sorry about everything..."

"I understand," said Rosemary, still feeling slightly awkward about the situation. "You lost someone I would do the same thing if I had to.... to get Athena back."

It was true. Rosemary did understand. But she didn't entirely trust Sherry even though she wanted to. It had been invasive. The woman who was supposed to be a friend had stolen a priceless and magical heirloom from Rosemary's bathroom, all so that she could have enough power to go to the fae realm to try to rescue her childhood friend, Mei.

"Can I see her?" Sherry asked.

"Sherry!" a voice called out and little Mei ran towards the front door and wrapped Sherry in her arms. "How did you get to be so big?" she asked.

"I told you this before, Mei," said Sherry. "You were gone for a long time."

"It wasn't really very long," Mei insisted.

"It may not have seemed long where you were," said Athena, following along behind Mei. "But time passes differently here."

Mei giggled, beaming at Athena, clearly star-struck by the teen.

"Won't you join us for dinner, Sherry?" Rosemary asked.

"I don't want to trouble you," said Sherry. "I just thought I'd bring you something to eat since you're so busy looking after all the children."

"Nonsense," said Rosemary. "Come on, stay a little while. It'll give you a chance to catch up with Mei. I'm sure there's a lot for you to talk about after all these years.

Sherry smiled and joined them at the dinner table where they had not only the stew but also roasted vegetables and chicken drumsticks that Athena had already made.

Rosemary smiled at her daughter. "Your cooking is improving. This is really good."

"I suppose I'm getting a lot of practice at the moment," said Athena as she shot little Harry a warning glance across the table. He'd been trying to steal a chicken drumstick from Elowen's plate while she was occupied trying to sneak a piece stewed beef to little Serpentine under the table.

"It's a lot of work to feed so many mouths." Athena continued. "Speaking of culinary tastes, have you made any progress on your chocolate shop – other than looking at derelict old shops, I mean?"

"What's this about a chocolate shop?" Sherry asked.

"Oh, nothing," said Rosemary. "It's just a kind of pipe dream I had. Now I've got the money for it, it's not impossible anymore. I've always wanted to work with food, and being a chocolatier would be amazing. I'd love to have a little shop. But I've been rather distracted lately. Nothing's really happened aside from looking signing up for a bunch of courses and getting deeply confused."

"Well, the two cakes you made while you were still working in my shop were lovely," said Marjie. "I really do hope you make it happen."

"Yes! You must," said Sherry. "That's exactly what we need in town. Everyone loves chocolate. And it's such a mood booster."

"Now that I'm getting better at using my magic," said Rosemary. "I might even be able to something magical with the chocolate. Like little harmless charms to boosts concentration or improve people's emotional state, that sort of thing. "

"What a wonderful idea," said Neve, from across the table. She and Nesta had all but moved into Thorn Manor recently though they still went home sometimes in the evenings, usually taking Mei with them.

They'd turned Nesta's office into a bedroom and Nesta was considering renovating the small cottage in their back yard so she could work from there instead.

"Mum doesn't really know what she's doing, yet," said Athena. "She has started looking at courses and she even found a shop in town that would make a great chocolate shop."

"Is that the one next to Liam?" Sherry asked. "Perfect! You should ask Covvey about it. I'm sure he'll give you a good deal."

"Why Covvey?" said Rosemary.

"Of course," said Sherry. "He's the landlord."

"That's right," said Marjie. "Didn't I mention it?"

Rosemary grimaced. "I don't think I'm in his good books at the moment. I might have accidentally called him a werewolf. "

"Why on earth would you do something so ghastly?" said

Sherry. "I mean, I'm sorry, but there's hardly a worse thing you could have called a shifter."

"Well, I don't know about any of this stuff," said Rosemary. "I didn't grow up in this world."

"I'm sure he'll forgive you," said Marjie.

Sherry gave her a questioning look.

"Well, maybe he'll need a little time," Marjie added. "He is very stubborn."

"Oh bother," Rosemary said. "Maybe I can find another shop to rent, just in case he holds a grudge."

"There's not much around, I'm afraid," said Sherry. "But don't worry. We can help you talk Covvey around. He hasn't leased it for a long while despite people asking."

"Why not?" Rosemary asked. "Surely it's just costing him money without being leased out."

"You'd think that," said Sherry. "He's got some emotional attachments to the bar that he used to have, despite the fact that it was a bit of a seedy dive."

"The mayor shut him down," said Marjie. "Wouldn't renew his license to operate. Said it brought down the whole tone of the town."

"Judgmental," said Rosemary.

"Well, he wasn't wrong," said Neve. "We had to break up so many fights in there."

Marjie tutted, "That's right. The place seemed to draw in all sorts of riffraff, even werewolves."

"Why does everyone hate werewolves so much?" Rosemary asked.

Silence fell around the dinner table and everyone stared at Rosemary, except Athena who looked just as surprised at the reaction as her mother felt.

"If you'd ever met one," said Marjie. "You wouldn't be asking that."

Rosemary shrugged awkwardly. "It's some kind of magical virus isn't it?" she asked with what she hoped was a light and casual tone of curiosity. "Why are people so mean about something that others can't control?"

"It might be a virus. But it seems to have the unfortunate effect of turning people quite rough," said Neve. "They might seem normal for a while, but as time passes they become more and more ragged and rude, quite violent at times."

"Not to mention the fact that on the full moon, they go around attacking and biting people, murdering... and spreading that foul curse," said Marjie.

"Wait, is it a curse or a virus?" Rosemary asked, wondering whether Liam was becoming more aggressive.

"A bit of both, I think," said Sherry. "Sort of like a cursed virus."

"Have you ever wondered whether the reason people might become so hard to deal with is because everyone's horrible to them?" Athena suggested.

Rosemary was pleased that her daughter had asked the question that she hadn't dared to ask. She was worried about accidentally outing Liam by saying too much.

"You would understand people's reactions," said Marjie. "If you've ever come across one of those horrible beasts let alone had a loved one killed by them. Her eyes clouded over."

"I'm sorry, Marjie," said Athena. "Did something awful like that happened to you?"

"My little brother Jowan was murdered by a werewolf," said Marjie, tears welling in her eyes. "I will not abide them!"

"Something similar happened to my cousin," said Sherry.

"Liam?" Rosemary asked, surprised.

"Course not! Liam's still alive," Sherry said, taken aback. "No. He and his brother, Treave, were out walking in the forest one day. Of course it must have been the full moon ... and a werewolf attacked them. Liam was lucky to escape with his life."

"How awful," said Rosemary her mind ringing with the realisation that the event Sherry just described probably led to Liam's present condition, though no one else in the town seemed to be aware of it.

Athena gave her a puzzled look and Rosemary shot her glance, warning her daughter to say stay out of her mind.

There was a sound footsteps in the hallway and Dain entered the dining room looking sheepish and bleary eyed.

"I'm sorry," he said. "It happened again, didn't it?"

"I'm afraid so," said Athena. "Sit down, Dad. Have some dinner."

Dain did as he was told, helping himself to a good portion of food. "I don't think we've ever properly been introduced," he said to Sherry. "I'm..."

"I know who you are," Sherry said, with a little shy smile. "I'm Sherry."

"Of course," said Dain, leaning back in his chair and cradling his arms behind his head.

"We met during that rescue escapade," Sherry said.

Dain's lip twitched. "I was actually going to say, I'm the fae who followed you back out of the realm when you were a child."

The whole table sat in stunned silence.

Sherry gasped. "What? Really?"

"Sure," said Dain. "You probably didn't see me, but I remember you. I figured you were my only hope of escaping Leithrein."

"Leaf rain?" Athena asked.

"Leithrein, the Countess of West Eloria. I hid in the bushes, near the thin part of the veil and I worked my fairy magic to bring down the protections on the inside to let you through. I hoped you had enough magic that you could get past the human protections. And when you did, I ducked in after you."

"You kind of stalked me," said Sherry, sounding slightly uncomfortable.

"Not exactly," said Dain. "I needed to get out of there. I knew the countess was after me. After I played a trick on her and her guards."

"Some fae don't take kindly to trickery," said Sherry, furrowing her brow. "I had some uncomfortable experiences."

"The countess also had a vested interest," Dain added. "She wanted to use me as some kind of bargaining pawn against my mother."

"So that was why she captured you," said Detective Neve. "You didn't tell me that during the police interview."

"I try to keep out of fae politics," said Dain, shrugging. "It's easier that way. And safer."

"You helped me escape," said Sherry, her eyes moonlike. "You helped me get out of there and back home."

Dain flashed her charming smile. "And I do it again in a heartbeat," he said.

"To suit your own interests," said Rosemary, worrying a little at how Sherry was gazing across the table at her ex. He did have a way of charming the ladies, and Rosemary was sure there was some kind of magic at play.

"What do you take me for?" Dain said, raising his hands defensively. "I'm not just out for myself. At least not when I'm sober," he added, apologetically.

"Thank you," said Sherry. "I had no idea how I was able to escape it first time. I just knew I had to get back in there to get Mei out again." She smiled at the little girl across the table who giggled. "I had to do anything that I could to help my friend.

"Well if you ever need any fae magic again, you know who to ask," said Dain, winking.

Rosemary's gut tightened at the obvious flirting. She frowned and Athena gave her a cheeky grin.

"Have you noticed anything strange around here lately?" Detective Neve asked as they cleared up from dinner.

"Stranger than usual?" said Rosemary. "Are you wondering about anything in particular?"

Detective Neve lowered her voice. "I was wondering if you'd noticed any fires?"

With a jolt of recognition, Rosemary replied. "Yes, actually the other day when I went to visit Liam, a fire just burst out of nowhere."

"You told me it was a person who attacked you," said Neve.

"It was, at least at first. I assumed the fire was related to the attacker."

"You didn't think to tell me about the *fire*?"

Rosemary gave the detective an apologetic look. "You know what my memory's like, after everything Granny and Dain did to muddle it. Whether they realised it or not, it seems to have had a long-term effect. The fire slipped my mind. I haven't even told Athena yet, I only mentioned the attack to you earlier because it popped into my head."

"I would have thought you'd have called me straight away." Neve frowned. "Especially after you'd been attacked by somebody in a dark hood... You think it's *them*?"

"I do, actually," said Rosemary. "I'm 99% sure it was the Blood-stones. Anyway straight after I was attacked this fire appeared. So obviously the same person... or people caused it."

"Perhaps," said Detective Neve. "At least that's a potential lead."

"Why do you ask about fires?" said Rosemary?"

"Well, mysterious fires have been popping up around the place. Nobody seems to know why. They're not huge but they might be getting bigger."

"That *is* concerning," said Rosemary, as she rinsed dinner dishes.

"But there doesn't seem to be anything causing them to appear," Neve added. "I've had two reports in the last twenty four hours. At first, I thought it was kids playing pranks. But now it seems like too much of a pattern."

Rosemary nodded. "And besides, kids aren't usually careful enough not to get caught. It could be the Bloodstones starting fires all over the place, though that seems odd."

"It might be tactical," said Neve. "Perhaps they don't have big enough numbers here to go on the offensive. They're just strategically trying to scare people. Throw them off the scent of what they're actually doing."

"Maybe," said Rosemary. "Either way, it makes me uncomfortable."

"What are you talking about?" Athena asked, carrying some more of the dishes to the kitchen.

"Oh, you know, just the usual," said Rosemary. "Mysterious fires and a high chance of a secret magical society attacking me."

"Why didn't you tell me about this?" Athena asked.

"My thoughts exactly," said Neve, putting her hands on her hips.

"Like I said, it's been a busy week," Rosemary said. "And a long day. I'm more than ready for a cup of tea and a good night's sleep."

CHAPTER
THIRTEEN

Athena wiped down the bench and kitchen table, cleaning up after breakfast. She still had an hour before school started. She hadn't had a chance to talk to her father, yet.

She'd been meaning to ask, the night before, about the unusual reaction she'd had to meeting another person with fae heritage. But Dain had gone to bed shortly after dinner, claiming that he was far too tired for someone who'd slept off a magical concussion all day.

Athena didn't blame him, he seemed exhausted. But she kept it in mind for the next morning, after Harry, Elowen and the twins had excitedly woken her up to make them breakfast.

Now, her burning curiosity was enough to overcome any hesitancy she had about trying to have a meaningful discussion.

Dain seemed happy that morning, grabbing a piece of jam toast from the table, he'd immediately begun to chase the restless young children around, making them squeal with delight as they ran out to the lawn.

She waited until he was tired from running around the garden, and had collapsed under the shade of a large magnolia tree. Athena admired it, in full bloom, as she walked over. It's enormous purple flowers reminded Athena, of the fae realm and she felt a pang of longing for that illusive place.

"I wanted to ask you about something," she said, approaching Dain.

"Ask away."

"Yesterday we went to the apothecary and met this amazing woman who was definitely of fae and human descent."

Dain nodded. "There's a few around, although they're not very common."

"Anyway," said Athena. "It gave me a strange reaction... when I met her, a sort of warm feeling. I don't know quite how to explain it, but it's different from when I've met other fae."

"I know you're about as uninterested in fae politics as I am," said Dain. "So I won't bore you with the details. But the different regions within the realm are governed and populated by various fae factions. Each has a unique blend of magic of their own. Most of the fae you would have encountered are likely to be linked to West Eloria, though."

"Because that's the region bordering here?" Athena asked.

"Yes."

"I thought the gates to the fae realm moved around," said Athena. "The one that Finnegan opened in the forest led almost exactly to the same part of the realm as the one that Mum opened from Fin's Creek."

"You're right," said Dain. "It's difficult to explain. You can think of the two worlds, as if they joined together by a kind of string that connects to each realm in multiple places in each region. The fae realm has its own separate pieces of string that connect to different parts of the earthly realm."

"So, you're saying you could go through any of the gates created around here and end up in the same place over there?"

"Yes," said Dain. "There's a complex matrix of probability around each one. But there's also a lot of synchronicity at play."

Athena nodded, not quite understanding.

"Actually," said Dain. "I'm not sure what any of that means. It was just more or less what I was told as a child."

"Good," said Athena. "Because I was just pretending to know what on earth you're talking about. But what does this have to do with Una?"

"Who, now?"

"The woman from the apothecary; that's her name."

"Ah, so more to the point, the different regions and their fae populations have diverging specialities."

"So you think my reaction is to do with Una's particular speciality? I wonder where her father was from.

Dain shrugged. "I couldn't tell you. Maybe if I met her I'd know more."

"That's fair," said Athena. "Why do you have to be so calm and reasonable all of a sudden? I'm so used to you being a rash and irresponsible. I don't know how to adjust to this new version of my father."

"You want to go back to being angry with me?" Dain said, grinning.

"I'm still angry with you," said Athena. "You don't get off scot-free for years of bad behaviour, just because you had a little problem with cream."

Dain shrugged. "That's fair, too."

"Anyway, speaking of little problems," Athena continued. "The women at the apothecary thought they might be able to figure out some kind of magical solution. If they did, would you be interested?"

Dain shook his head and scrunched up his face. "I tried those remedies that your mum gave me. They just made me sick."

"Those ones didn't work," said Athena. "But does that mean you're just going to give up like you gave up on us?"

"Oh, harsh," said Dain. "I guess I deserve that."

"And a lot more, besides," said Athena.

"Of course I'll try," he said. "I'm trying to redeem myself, remember. There's nothing like spending weeks locked up in a mushroom castle, being stabbed and tortured, to make you rethink your life choices."

Athena grimaced. "Was it that bad?"

Dain shrugged. "In a way, it was all worth it."

"What do you mean?"

Dain stared down at the earth around him. He paused for a moment and then said, "Well, if I hadn't gone through all that and had a chance to help you get back here, I might never have been able to spend any more time with you again with no chance to try to redeem myself."

Athena felt her heart soften.

Dain looked up at her. "It's been good, getting to know you as an almost adult."

She smiled. "Tell that to mum."

"Your mother is a tad overprotective," said Dain. "Though I guess I don't have any parental rights to say so."

"No, I don't think you telling her that is going to make any difference at this point. But I do appreciate you trying to stick up for me."

Dain shrugged. "I can understand why she does it. She cares a lot for you."

"Obviously, she does," said Athena. "It's mostly just been the two of us. And Mum never really had to be protective of me before because I never really did very much. I didn't get along with other kids and so we just stayed home and watched a lot of movies and ate popcorn. Now that I have more of a life she doesn't know what to do with herself."

"She's gonna have to figure it out eventually," said Dain.

"That's what I keep telling her," said Athena. "Anyway, I've got to go and get ready for school. Thanks for the chat."

Dain smiled and his eyes held a flicker of hope. "I mean what I said," he called out as she walked away. "I'll do what I can. If there's any way that I can possibly win back your trust..."

"We'll see," Athena called back across the yard.

CHAPTER

FOURTEEN

Athena had just left for school, Dain was playing hide-and seek with the children in the back garden, and Rosemary was putting on the kettle for morning tea when a knock sounded at the front door of Thorn Manor. She went to answer it and was delighted to see the two sisters from the apothecary.

Una came in holding a large old book.

"Good timing," said Rosemary. "I'm just making tea."

"That's sounds lovely," said Una. "How about we do a swap over tea? You can read our book and I'll have a look through yours?"

"Excellent," said Rosemary. She showed them through to the living room and returned a few moments later with a tea tray.

"Before we get started," said Ashwyn, "I had an idea regarding your other request."

"Which one?" Rosemary asked, trying to think back to the conversation they'd had only the day before.

"Your memory," said Una.

"Oh, yes. My memory is atrocious," Rosemary admitted.

"Though it's not entirely my fault. Both fae magic and my granny's binding spell are probably to blame for that."

"Yes, exactly," said Ashwyn. "I was thinking about all that. At least the parts that you told me. And while I could give you a general memory tonic, I don't think that would work."

"That's a shame," said Rosemary.

"It seems like whatever components your grandmother put into the binding spell, she mimicked fairy magic in order to make it stick," Ashwyn continued. "Normally, memory spells don't last for very long."

"You're saying my grandmother was using fae magic?" Rosemary asked.

"I suspect so," said Una. "If only there was a way we could ask her to make sure."

"Well, the next time I see her..." said Rosemary.

Una gave her a questioning look.

"Metaphorically, I mean," Rosemary said. "Or it was a joke? Maybe it was a joke. Yeah..."

The fact that Granny's ghost still inhabited and haunted the manor was a secret Granny did not want them to share with anyone else lest she had more than just her own descendants bothering her for spells, or trying to exorcise or banish her, for that matter. Rosemary gathered that ghostly housemates as stubborn and vibrant as Granny Thorn were rare, and that hauntings were usually much more subtle. She also didn't know if anyone else could see Granny's ghost, or just those wielding the Thorn family magic, and Granny didn't seem keen to test this out, as she was tremendously busy in the spirit world.

Rosemary brought in a tray with tea and biscuits. Ashwyn pulled out a large old book. "Swap you?"

Rosemary handed the small green volume on the fae to Una and grasped the heavy leather-bound grimoire that Ashwyn had passed her. It had the resemblance of a book kept in the family for generations. She found the spell used to stop Una's cream addiction had been bookmarked.

"Oh, and there's this," said Rosemary, handing over a piece of paper. "Athena found it in an old book, all marked up. She thinks Granny might have used it to bind my memory."

"It's just like I thought," said Una. "Fae magic. Look — for the memory issues, there may be an antidote."

"Really?" Rosemary asked.

"I have a tonic that might work," said Una, looking at her sister. "It's a surprisingly simple recipe. Just take some fennel and sage, spring water. In fact, it's coincidentally the exact tonic I use for migraines."

"Seriously?" Rosemary frowned. This seemed like far too much of a coincidence.

"Yes," said Ashwyn. "Actually, it's one we carry with us as part of our herbal first aid kit. Did you remember to bring it, Una?"

"I think so." Una opened an old fashioned doctor's bag and pulled out an emerald green glass bottle. "Migraines work along the same neural pathways as this magic seems to, so it makes sense that unblocking them will solve both kinds of problems. Take a teaspoon of this and see how you feel."

"It's worth a try," said Rosemary. She took the little bottle from Una and retrieved a teaspoon from the kitchen. Returning to the lounge, she sat down on a couch across from the two sisters and poured out a little of the pale green liquid to fill the spoon and then swallowed it.

The taste was aromatic and slightly bitter, leaving an astringent residue on her tongue. "Well, I feel quite normal," said Rosemary, realising quickly that she'd spoken too soon. Stars formed a border around her vision before obliterating everything inside.

Rosemary opened her eyes, feeling woozy, with the dreaded

sensation that she might have been tricked. She blinked, looking up at the ceiling. It took her a moment to get her bearings. "What happened?" she asked.

"I've never seen a reaction like that before," said Una.

Rosemary pulled herself up from the couch, reassured that everything seemed to be in order. She was glad that she'd had a soft landing when she'd evidently passed out. "Oh my goddess!"

"What is it?" Ashwyn asked, sounding concerned.

"My head feels so clear!" said Rosemary. "I feel like I can look right back into the past and see everything, even things relating to Dain."

"Everything?" Una asked.

"Okay, maybe not everything, but before it was all blurry. I couldn't remember specifics at all and now...Wow. Thank you!" A thought struck her. "Do you think this will work on other people?"

Una and Ashwyn gave her a quizzical look.

"I mean, others that have had their memory meddled with by the fae?"

"I don't see why not," said Una. "It worked on you."

Rosemary sighed. "The problem is, how do we get people to ingest something when we don't know them and they're unlikely to trust us? Do you think the formula would bake into muffins that we could leave on someone's doorstep?"

Ashwyn gave her a sceptical look for a start. "Would *you* eat muffins that were left on your doorstep?"

I suppose not," said Rosemary. "Unless I was absolutely sure they were from Marjie. I see your point."

"I don't think that would work anyway," said Una. "It'll have to be in liquid form, otherwise the tannins in the sage will bind to whatever else you combine it with."

"I see," said Rosemary. "What about a fine mist?"

"That could work," said Una. "If somebody could inhale or ingest enough of it."

"Only one way to find out," said Rosemary. "How much of this do you have?"

"I've got a whole supply of it back at the shop," said Una. "You can pick some up tomorrow if you like."

"I think I might just do that," said Rosemary. "Maybe now, with my enhanced memory, I'll be able to figure out this spell and help Dain." She blinked, feeling a whole new mix of emotions where previously she'd just felt only confusion.

Five minutes before, Rosemary would have vaguely recalled that Dain had screwed her over so many times, especially with Athena's many reminders over the years, but none of the specific memories had been able to shine through. Now, after taking the tonic, they stabbed painfully in her chest when she thought of him. Even more overwhelming were the whole wave of happy memories that flooded in. Memories of when they were together and very much in love, memories of them both playing with young Athena.

Now, everything about the cream addiction made a lot more sense. If only she'd known back then what she knew now. She could have asked Granny for help to figure out a solution. Of course she could still ask Granny now, though the old woman in her ghost form had been quite evasive, and that was before she'd up and left them with nothing more than a goodbye note. Perhaps ghosts weren't supposed to meddle in the affairs of the living.

"I think I might have an idea for how this might work," said Una, poring over the small book Burk had acquired on the fae. "If you'll let me copy a few things out of your books, I can examine the basic mechanisms and see if I can come up with some sort of template for a spell to help Dain."

"That would be fantastic," said Rosemary. "Copy away!"

Just then, the children ran in from the back garden, bright eyed, rosy cheeked, and panting, followed by an exhausted looking Dain.

Rosemary wasn't quite ready to confront all the memories and baggage that had re-emerged from Una's tonic, so she tucked that into a side-cupboard in her mind for later, smiled politely, and introduced them all. The children were quite taken with Una and Ashwyn, and convinced them to join in several rounds of ring-a-ring-a-rosy.

Dain pulled Rosemary aside during the second round.

"She's fae, isn't she?" he said, gesturing discreetly to Una.

Rosemary nodded. "On her father's side, I think. But don't get any ideas. I know she's gorgeous, but she's a new friend and I don't want you making things awkward."

Dain's jaw dropped in offence. "What do you take me for?"

"You don't have the best track record," Rosemary pointed out.

"Maybe not, but that's not my angle here."

"Then what?" Rosemary crossed her arms and gave him a pointed look.

"She's just familiar, is all," said Dain. "And I can't recall, but maybe I've met her before?"

"It seems unlikely, unless it was around here. Una never met her father and was raised here in Myrtlewood by her witch mother." She was going to add something about the patterns of fae fathers but was interrupted as Ashwyn and Una approached.

"We'd better get back to the shop," said Una. "If you're sure you're okay after the memory thing..."

"Memory thing?" Dain said.

"I'll tell you later." Rosemary turned back to the sisters. "I'm feeling fine. In fact, I'm feeling a lot better than I have in quite a long time. Everything feels so crystal clear in my head. I've even thought of a few things that I'd forgotten I needed to do."

"That sounds promising," said Ashwyn as Una packed up her things.

"I've copied down the information I need," said Una. "So if you swing by the shop tomorrow I'll have some things ready for you to pick up."

"Wonderful," said Rosemary. "Let me know how much I owe you."

"Oh no," said Una. "This is definitely on the house."

"But you hardly know me," said Rosemary.

"Still, given the involvement of the fae, it's personal," said Una. "I'd feel uncomfortable taking money, especially when it's so rare to come across someone who's like me. Is Athena around? I'd like to see her again."

"She's gone to school." Rosemary was unsure if she should be suspicious of the woman's interest in her daughter. Una and Ashwyn seemed lovely, but she hardly knew them. Then again, Athena had seemed to light up around other fae people, including Una. "But I'm sure she'd love to chat to you sometime about what it's like. You don't have that telepathy thing, do you?"

Una shook her head. "I'm not sure what you're talking about, so probably not."

"Athena hasn't mentioned it recently, but it was bugging her a while ago," said Rosemary. "She said it was kind of like having a radio in her head. She picked up on people's stray thoughts."

"I must have missed out on that ability in the genetic lottery. I haven't experienced anything like that. But I'm sure we have other things in common and I might be able to help with some of them."

Rosemary smiled and showed the two women out. Then, she immediately texted officer Neve, to tell her about the new discovery of the memory tonic, just in case she forgot. She didn't know how long the tonic would hold, and neither did the sisters. Una had explained that people had to take the tonic for every migraine because the neural pathway patterns tended to re-emerge, but with the fae magic, perhaps it would stay gone. Either way, Rosemary was determined to make the most of her new-found clarity. She texted Athena, as well.

We need to fight.

Mum, I'm at school, came her response a few minutes later. *What's this about? What have I done now?*

No, Rosemary wrote back. *I mean, we need to train, we need to practice fighting.*

It was a thought that had occurred to Rosemary after the recent attack by that hooded figure and she'd only just remembered it along with everything else. She and Athena might be getting used to using magic, but they needed combat skills, especially if the Bloodstone Society was coming back.

Sounds great, Athena texted back. *Any excuse to throw you around.*

Rosemary smiled. Despite the sass, it was good to have Athena back.

She went to the kitchen to make herself some toast for lunch and returned her attention to the other topic that had suddenly begun weighing on her mind.

When she'd sipped that sage tonic, other things had become clear in her memory, and one of them in particular was bothering her.

A few weeks earlier, she'd seen Burk at the pub having dinner with an attractive brunette woman, and now that she remembered the details, she was sure it had been Una.

At the time, Rosemary had to suppress a pang of jealousy. She and Burk were just friends, sure. And yes, she had politely turned him down when he'd asked her out to dinner. But that didn't mean she didn't harbour some small and conflicting feelings for him, despite her better judgement.

Burk was incredibly good looking, suave, and genuinely helpful, if a bit arrogant. He'd gone above and beyond to help Rosemary in the short time she'd known him. He might be a vampire and incredibly old, despite still looking like he was in his thirties or early forties, but that didn't mean he wasn't an eligible bachelor, or that he didn't deserve to date other women. Knowing this, Rosemary had done her best not to get in the way, but now that she realised who it was he was dating...What she was...

Una, being of fae descent like Athena, should be kept away from vampires. Rosemary understood that. She wasn't about to leave Athena alone with Burk either. Not that the fae were innocent, but vampires were clearly a threat to them. Despite the fae politics and how freaky they were, and their unsavoury habit of kidnapping young children, they needed protection from vamps who had hunted them for centuries.

Does Una know about all this? Rosemary wondered as she spread butter and raspberry jam on her freshly made toast. She didn't know her father—maybe she was in the dark about how vampires find fae irresistible.

The situation had been so dangerous for the fae that they'd fused protections into their DNA, so that vampires couldn't smell them, or recognise them. Athena said that people couldn't see her face properly, they just saw some kind of projection, something that Rosemary found troubling, as she was sure she could pick her daughter out of any line-up, though perhaps it didn't work on mothers.

If Una was at risk, then Rosemary had to warn her. Burk might seem harmless, but he possessed the preternatural strength and speed of a vampire. Rosemary had only been able to fight them off because of her own magic. She didn't know what kind of magical abilities Una had, aside from clearly being a gifted healer.

If neither of them knew the true nature of the situation they were in, it could be a recipe for disaster. He might not mean her any harm, but if he were to discover Una's true nature, say, if she spilled a drop of her irresistible blood, he might well lose all sense of control.

Rosemary battled with these conflicting emotions as she scoffed down her toast, the understanding deepening in her mind that she had no choice, she had to warn her new friend about the very handsome and often quite considerate vampire.

CHAPTER

FIFTEEN

R osemary gritted her teeth as Detective Neve drove around a tight corner. They were on their way to the house of Elowen's sister again, having picked up supplies from the apothecary just moments before. Una had been busy with other customers so Rosemary didn't have a chance to talk to her about Burk.

Surely she must know. Being a magical person in a magical town, everyone you probably knows who the vampires are. But then again, even if Una knows, maybe she isn't aware of the issues between vampires and the fae. Una was raised by witches and hardly anyone knows much about the fae. Maybe Una doesn't realize what danger she's in if Burk finds out about her true identity.

Rosemary opened the brown paper bag that Una had left on the counter for her. Inside, as promised, was a spray bottle containing the sage tonic, which she could use to create a kind of mist effect that would hopefully help to jog the woman's memory about her missing sister.

There were a few other items in the bag too and some written instructions. Rosemary tried to make sense of them but her mind was in too many places at once.

"This must be something to do with the spell to help Dain," she muttered.

"That sounds promising," said Neve. "Una and Ashwyn are talented. It was good you talked to them. I hadn't even thought of that myself."

"It was a good idea," said Rosemary. "They seem to know a lot."

"I wish they could help me with my other case," said Neve. "Right now, I wish anyone could. We're out of leads."

"The fires?" Rosemary asked.

"Yes, there have been two more since yesterday. The first one we know about was on the old Twig farm, and so far they seem to be fairly random and out in the rural areas, like the one that sparked up near you. They seem to be getting bigger."

Rosemary gulped. "Any idea if they are connected to the bloodstones?"

"There's been no link so far," said Neve. "In fact, I wouldn't have even thought of it if you hadn't mentioned you'd been attacked by somebody wearing a dark hood."

"It seems like too much of a coincidence not to be related though, doesn't it?"

"Anyone can wear a dark hood," Neve pointed out.

"That's true," said Rosemary. "Although the only people that have attacked me wearing them have been involved with that stupid society."

She pondered for a while, looking out the window. "You know, my cousins have some fiery magic, on their father's side. They once set a law office on fire."

Neve raised her eyebrows. "It's worth checking out."

Rosemary laughed. "Although, now that I think of it. Elamina is far too fancy and snobby to be hanging out on the old twig farm.

I'm sure the modest countryside is beneath her and she wouldn't want to get her expensive shoes dirty."

"Well, let me know if you have any other ideas," said Neve. "But witches with a known predilection for fire are definitely on our list to investigate."

They pulled into the driveway of the slightly dilapidated house where little Tamsyn, Elowen's now much older sister lived.

"What's the plan?" Rosemary asked.

"You tell me."

"It's going to look weird if I squirt her in the face with this stuff," said Rosemary. "Maybe when you knock I can try creating enough mist to have an effect when she opens the door."

They stepped out of the car into a strong wind.

"Or maybe not," said Rosemary.

"It's worth a try," said Neve. "But if that doesn't work, you might have to go for the offensive."

"Is that legal?"

"No, but it would be a hard thing to press assault charges for, or even make a formal complaint – a light mist in the face."

Rosemary shrugged. "It's not like she likes me anyway."

They made the way to the door.

"Ready?" Neve said.

Rosemary held up the spray bottle, ready to push the trigger as Neve reached out to knock on the door.

Just as Rosemary sprayed, the door flew open misting Tamsyn right in the face.

"What's the name of..." she cried out.

"Sorry," Rosemary called. "That wasn't my intention."

Tamsyn's eyes glazed over and she teetered on the spot.

Rosemary reached out to steady her, but she managed to stay upright. "What... has happened?" Tamsyn asked. "Everything went white."

"Hopefully we've restored your memory," said Rosemary.

"My... my *memory*? Everything feels so clear. Oh goodness. You weren't lying to me before." A look of utter bewilderment crossed her face. "I had a sister. Elowen. She went missing. It was a long time ago. So clear... now in my mind that it almost seems unreal. Is this a trick?"

"I'm afraid not," said Rosemary. "The trick was whatever memory magic stopped you from remembering your own family member for so long."

Tamsyn shook her head. "She was only four years old."

Rosemary nodded. "You'll find she still seems to be about that age."

"No! Really? How's that possible?"

"Your sister was taken to the fae realm," Detective Neve explained.

"That's right... I think you'd better come in again," Tamsyn, opening the door wide.

Over the next half an hour. She apologized profusely for how she'd treated them the first time they'd come calling. After a while, a look of deep exhaustion crossed her face. When Rosemary and Neve had finally finished explaining everything to her, Tamsyn rested her head in her hands on the table.

"This is all just so surreal," she said. "Please forgive me."

"You didn't do anything wrong," said Rosemary. "I'm sure I would have reacted much worse in your situation. I probably would have blown whoever was on my doorstep to smithereens thinking they were the Bloodstone society—"

"The what?" Tamsyn asked.

"Never mind that," said Detective Neve, shooting Rosemary a warning glance.

"Yeah, don't worry about that," said Rosemary. "I have a rambling problem. It would be best to only listen to at least twenty five percent of everything I say. Anyway. The long and short of it is that you now have a sibling who's still a young child."

"Obviously in a situation where children go missing..." said Neve, "the normal response it to return them to their families. We understand parents passed away quite some time ago."

Tamsyn nodded. She sighed deeply. "Do you know it's funny? I always felt like something was missing. Something I couldn't name. Now it's like the missing part of my life is being handed to me. I probably should be overjoyed but... I... the shock..."

"It'll take you a while to get used to it, I imagine" said Rosemary. "These kinds of situations must be incredibly rare and you probably need to have a good night's sleep and think."

Tamsyn nodded. "You're probably right, though I don't know if I can sleep, knowing what I know now." She looked around at her kitchen, and sighed. "My husband left after the kids grew up. They all live abroad now, and I hardly see them. I felt like I was stuck in a rut here, but I couldn't quite leave. Maybe this is why. I'm sorry. I'm the one rambling now."

"That's perfectly understandable," said Rosemary, patting the woman on the shoulder. "Change is hard, and this situation is exceptional."

"We can leave you to have some time to think. Give me a call anytime," said Neve, handing the woman her card.

Tamsyn shook her head. "No. I need to go. I need to see her now. Can I come with you?"

"Are you sure you're feeling up to it?" Rosemary asked.

Tamsyn nodded, resolute.

"Of course," said Detective Neve. "We can leave straight away."

CHAPTER

SIXTEEN

Tamsyn sat in silence in the back of the car as they drove towards Myrtlewood. Neve and Rosemary kept the conversation to a minimum as well, wanting to give the woman as much peace as possible, considering what she was still processing.

A phone call came through ad they drove. Neve pulled over to answer it.

"Okay, I'll be right there," she said, after a long pause.

She turned to Rosemary. "I just need to make a quick detour. It's urgent. You can stay in the car with Tamsyn; make sure she's okay."

Rosemary nodded. "Has there been another one?" she asked.

Neve raised her eyebrows in a silent 'yes'.

Rosemary could see smoke up ahead as Detective Neve pulled down a familiar road which began to wind up a hill.

"No..." said Neve, looking at the clouds of black wafting through the sky. "This looks a lot worse than I thought. I should have dropped you home before I came.

Rosemary gritted her teeth. "No time. Who's going to put out this fire? Surely the regular fire service can't be expected to deal with magical infernos!"

"Hopefully the Myrtlewood fire brigade will be there by now," said Neve.

"We have a fire brigade?" Rosemary asked. "Why does no one tell me these things?"

"Never mind. Just stay in the car and stay out of trouble." Neve shot Rosemary a warning glance.

"I'm not a child." Rosemary, indignantly folded her arms. "I know how to behave myself."

Neve grinned at her. "Sure you do."

They pulled into a very grand entrance to a driveway that wound up the hill.

Rosemary gasped. "Oh no, It's not..."

"I'm afraid so," said Neve.

Rosemary recognised the driveway from the last trip she'd made to Mr June, the mayor's house. "He's not going to like that I'm here."

Neve shrugged. "Like I said, stay in the car."

She pulled over to the side of the driveway and got out. The mayor's house was alight in flames that covered the whole left side of the building.

"What a shame," said Tamsyn, from the back of the car. "She'd clearly snapped out of her trance."

Rosemary turned back towards her. "Sorry to drag you into this. Neve didn't realize it was a full-on house fire."

"I hope nobody's in there," said Tamsyn.

"I'm sure his lordship will have gotten out quickly, along with his prized possessions," said Rosemary.

"That sounds a bit harsh," said Tamsyn as a siren blared behind them.

"You're probably right," said Rosemary. "I had a bad run in with the mayor last time I was here. He tried to get me arrested. And let's just say his personality leaves a lot to be desired."

Neve pulled over to allow a bright red old-fashioned fire engine to tear up the driveway with, lights and siren blazing. They followed the truck up towards the house, and parked nearby.

Rosemary watched as a muscular black woman emerged from driver side door of the fire engine, strapping on a fireproof jacket.

"Another one!" She called out to Neve, who nodded. "All right then. Let's hope this one behaves just like the last ones did. She pulled out her firehose.

Rosemary watched in awe as the clearly magically enhanced device spirited water all over the building in a way that the no normal hose could manage. The jets of liquid twinkled in a supernatural way as they seemed to seek out each point of flame and extinguish it quickly.

"That's something else..." said Tamsyn, from the back of the car. "I've never seen anything like it."

"I'm glad we have a fire department here," said Rosemary. "Though I wish someone told me these things!"

"Why wouldn't you?" asked Tamsyn. "Oh that's right, I forget how magical this place was. Maybe I need more of that magical spritzer."

"Feel free to take a whole spoonful," said Rosemary. "I'll give you a bottle. I'm not sure if it wears off, or if it's something you only need the once."

I better get my own supply just in case," said Tamsyn. "I still can't believe all that happened to my memory. It breaks my heart that my parents died not remembering little Elowen."

"It's very sad," said Rosemary.

She was distracted by tapping at the car window.

"Returned to the scene of the crime, I take it," said constable Perkins, tugging at his suspenders. His nose was as red as usual, and his stance just as arrogant as the first time Rosemary had met him. "I'm glad that you're already safely in the detective's car, Rosemary Thorne," said Perkins. "I didn't realize, Constantine had so much sense and worked so quickly."

"Oh, you didn't, did you?" said Neve, standing behind him, raising her eyebrows.

"Oh... uhh... Detective Neve. Sorry I didn't see you there," Constable Perkins bumbled.

"Don't you worry," said Neve. "Rosemary is here to help with official police business. And no, she did not have anything to do with setting the fire."

Constable Perkins spluttered and waved his fingers about as though to protest. "Shouldn't you be comforting the mayor and taking his statements?" Neve said, waving him away.

Rosemary smiled apologetically at Neve as the police officer slinked off.

"He's really got it in for you, hasn't he?" said the detective.

"He sure does," said Rosemary. "I don't know what it is about me that rubs him the wrong way. "

"He and Galdie he never got on either," said Neve. "She always bested him in his investigations. That's partly why they brought me on board in the first place. They needed somebody who wasn't always putting their foot in their mouth and getting in the way."

"How is all of this magical law enforcement organized?" Rosemary asked as they watched the fire crew work their magic.

"Orders come from Glastonbury," said Neve.

"I would have thought it was London," said Rosemary. "Isn't that where all the bigwigs are supposed to sit?"

"Not the magical bigwigs," said Neve. "In our community, they all live near the base of the Glastonbury torr. They say it's where the magic is strongest in Britain, anyway. Though the global authorities are in Bermuda, of course."

Rosemary nodded. "I guess that makes sense," she said. "I'm not sure if the bigwigs have a good handle on it given the state of Perkins performance."

"You're probably right," said Neve. "But, just like in any job, once somebody is firmly established it's quite hard to get rid of them."

"That firefighter woman's amazing," said Tamsyn from the back of the car.

Neve nodded and smiled. "Who, Sid? Yes, she is rather..." There was a tightness to her voice. "She's also my ex so we keep things as professional as possible."

Rosemary nodded, wondering why Neve was being so candid despite being at work.

Neve obviously wondered the same thing. Shaking herself, she said "Sorry, I better get back to business."

"Before you go," Rosemary said looking across at the blaze that was very clearly engulfing half the mayor's house in red, orange and bright pink flames. "What's going on with these fires? Any ideas?"

Your guess is as good as mine," said Neve. She walked away, leaving Rosemary to ponder in silence.

Rosemary zoned out a bit, as she sat in the car waiting for Detective Neve to return from whatever police duties were occupying her at the mayor's house after the fire.

She heard Tamsyn cough behind her. "What's going on out there?" Tamsyn asked.

Rosemary shrugged. "I don't know, just some sort of professional emergency response stuff."

"It doesn't look all that professional to me," said Tamsyn. "They look a little bit... *cosy* over there."

Rosemary squinted in the direction of the house to see Neve standing next to Sid, rather too closely. In fact, the firefighter's arms were stretched out and she was stroking her hands down the detectives upper arms.

"I thought she said that woman was her ex," said Tamsyn.

"She did," said Rosemary. "Plus, she's very happily and monogamously engaged to someone else now. Or at least we're hoping they'll get engaged soon."

"And it looks like they're not the only ones getting cosy either," said Tamsyn.

The other smaller firefighter had her hands all over a tall, handsome man that Rosemary recognized is the mayor's husband, Zade.

"Excuse me a minute," Rosemary said.

She got out of the car and sprinted over towards the house, knowing full well that she'd been told to stay put. But she figured that in exceptional circumstances, she had to break the rules.

"Neve!" she called out, approaching the two women. Neve's eyes flicked over to Rosemary. She had a drunken smile plastered over her face.

"Oh, Rosemary," she said, and giggled. "Have you come to join in the action?"

Sid turned towards the interruption. "Aren't you going to introduce me to your pretty friend?" She asked Neve and reached out to towards Rosemary.

"Umm... I'm not sure what's going on here," said Rosemary. "But this is not normal.

That was when she felt it.

A warm wave emanated from the house, drifting over from the smouldering embers on the left side of the building that had now caught alight in a bright pink flame, though none of the firefighters seemed particularly interested in it anymore.

"Oh, said," Rosemary. "It's quite warm, isn't it."

"You're clearly overdressed," said Sid, reaching out to tug at Rosemary's cardigan. Rosemary did indeed feel overdressed. In fact, it seemed like the most natural thing in the world for them to all take off their clothing and frolic naked indulging in all the hedonistic pleasures of the body.

She shook herself. Something was not quite right. But another wave pulsed out from what remained of the fire, loosening her inhibitions and melting her logic like ice in hot water.

Sid pushed Neve up against the fire engine and wrapped her in a passionate embrace.

Alarm bells rang in the back of Rosemary's mind and a little voice screamed out: *Something's not right!*

Rosemary remembered the ancestor with silver hair that she'd met in some kind of void world, and the process she'd gone through to unleash the old Thorn family magic that had been bound. That voice seemed to be communicating with her now.

Stop it at once!

A wave of light gold pulsed out from Rosemary, seeming to freeze the people where they stood.

Clarity returned as the dazed feeling fell away.

It's the fire! It's meddling with people's minds. Put it out!

Rosemary grabbed the hose that was dangling from one of the firefighter's hand, the woman having clearly forgotten her duty to put out the fire in the heat of the moment, too wrapped up in whatever magic had them all spellbound.

Rosemary twisted the nozzle. Turning the hose up and holding on for dear life. The water sprayed out, touching not only the fire, but also the people standing around it. As if dousing the invisible flames of lust that they'd been entrapped in, one by one way they seemed to come out of the daze.

Rosemary continued directing the hose across the fire until nothing remained but smoking embers.

"What on earth is going on. Explain yourself, Rosemary Thorn," said constable Perkins.

He was standing, arm in arm with the mayor. Upon realizing this, he blushed and stepped away.

Everyone else seemed to have a similar reaction, clearly coming to their senses.

"Look, don't blame me," said Rosemary. "I was the one who saved you.

"Trespassing again!" cried Mr June.

"Excuse me," said Rosemary. "Unless you wanted to have a magically induced orgy, you should be thanking me right now! I was perfectly happy to stay in the car. But alarm bells started ringing, and I thought I'd better come over here and stop you from making terrible mistakes."

She gave Neve a meaningful look. The detective appeared to be shell shocked.

"Thank you, Rosemary," she said, her voice wavering a little, her posture stiff and awkward. "I think we'd better be going."

As the two women walked back to the car, Neve asked, "Do you have any idea what happened there?"

Rosemary couldn't help but feel she was being accused of something. "Like I said, I was in the car. Tamsyn pointed out there was something strange going on with you and your ex and I came over to see what in Hades was going on. As far as I can tell it was something to do with those flames. Did you notice the fire had sparked up again from the embers and turned pink?"

"I don't recall..." Neve admitted.

"Well, Whatever it was, it made everyone lose their panties for a minute."

Neve glared at her.

"Metaphorically, I hope," said Rosemary. "Although, you weren't far off."

"Please don't tell Nesta," said Neve. "She's already jealous of Sid."

Rosemary shook her head. "Look, I'm not going to get involved in your relationship politics. But as far as I can see, *you* are the one who should tell Nesta about this, and you should do it soon, because if she finds out some other way, it's going to cause a lot more damage.

Neve sighed. "You're right," she said. "I just need a few minutes and a good stiff drink to do some processing."

Rosemary nodded. "That, I can arrange. Let's get home and I'll bring out the good scotch."

SEVENTEEN

Chapter 17

By the time Rosemary finally got home with Neve and Tamsyn, she was heavy with exhaustion. She opened the front door to find the house empty.

"This is a nice big place," said Tamsyn. "We used to live in a big old house, not quite this big, back when we were in Myrtlewood. We had to downsize when we moved and I always missed living in a place like this—"

"Tamsyn?" Rosemary asked.

"Yes?"

Rosemary smiled kindly. "It's alright. I recognise nervous rambling when I see it. I've had plenty of experience. Take a deep breath and calm down. The kids are probably out back."

"Okay," Tamsyn said, inhaling deeply.

Neve nodded. "You've got nothing to worry about."

"She might hate me," said Tamsyn quietly, as if admitting a secret. "I wasn't the nicest older sister in the world. I'd get jealous when she got attention, and I hated it when she stole my toys."

"Tamsyn..." Rosemary tried to sound reassuring.

"Or worse, what if she doesn't remember me at all? It has been such a long time and I look so different."

Rosemary stopped with her hand clasped on the back door. "Do you need a hug?" she asked.

Tamsyn nodded.

Rosemary held out her arms and gave the woman a big reassuring cuddle. "It's all going to be fine."

"I'm sorry," said Tamsyn. "You hardly know me, and here I am acting like a big baby."

"Totally understandable," said Rosemary.

"Ready now?" Neve asked from behind them as Rosemary pulled away from Tamsyn.

"As I'll ever be."

"Think of it this way, it's not every day you get to meet your abducted baby sister, finding her still alive four decades later. This is a fairly unique experience."

"Not helping," said Tamsyn.

Rosemary zipped her mouth and opened the door.

The children were running and skipping across the backyard, circling a red-and-white-checked picnic blanket where Nesta was sitting cross-legged. Tamsyn looked overwhelmed as she tried to make out their faces.

"Tamsyn!" cried a little blonde girl, skipping over to where they stood. "It is you, isn't it? But how did you get so big?"

"How does she recognise me so easily?" Tamsyn asked Rosemary.

"I have no idea, they seem to pick things up again fairly well after so much time in the fae realm. I'm surprised their memory isn't addled too. Maybe they absorb some of the excess memory that's syphoned away from the people in the earth realm."

"That's not such a bad hypothesis," said Neve. She shot Rosemary a smile as Tamsyn knelt down to wrap her baby sister in a hug.

"Really? It's more of a throwaway comment than a hypothesis," Rosemary said.

"No, really," said Neve. "Magic doesn't work in a vacuum, it's often about altering the polarity of something to shift the result."

"Huh. I really should be going to magic school like Athena."

"Hearing you all talk about this stuff like it's normal is so refreshing," said Tamsyn.

"That's not what you said when you kicked us out of your house," Rosemary joked, and Neve shot her a glance as if warning her to be more professional.

"No, I'm sorry about that. It's just, after Elowen disappeared everything changed. We weren't supposed to talk about magic anymore. It's a shame really. My parents were really talented Rúnsealls."

"Come again?" said Rosemary.

"Rúnseall is a magical specialisation," Neve explained. "They are experts at finding hidden things. Any old witch can perform a seeking spell, but a true master Rúnseall can often find something even if magic has been used to mask it. They can also detect traces of magical intent and figure out which witch cast a particular spell, but that's quite a complex technical process, as I understand it."

"I could have used some of that when my necklace was stolen," said Rosemary. "Or in countless other situations."

"It's a shame, then," said Tamsyn. "Supposedly it's in my blood, and I showed great promise, but true masters work in pairs like my parents. It almost killed them when Elowen disappeared...knowing *where* she'd gone, but they still couldn't get her back. They walked away from everything. It's so sad. I miss all this." She waved her arm around vaguely. "I miss casual conversations where magic is real."

"You can always move back to Myrtlewood," said Rosemary. "We can help you get set up. It will probably be good for Elowen to be in a familiar place close to the other kids she knows. They are all quite close."

"Are you saying I can just...*keep* her?" Tamsyn asked, confused, as Elowen ran off to play with the other children.

"She's your family," said Neve.

"Aren't you even going to do a background check?" said Tamsyn.

"Already done," said Neve. "We completed that before we knocked on your door. We just need to make sure you'll be able to provide her with a safe home where she'll be loved and looked after. That's what children need."

Tamsyn nodded. "I couldn't just up and move, could I?" Her eyes were wide.

"It's up to you," said Rosemary. "Do what feels right."

"I just..." Tamsyn looked around in awe. "I suppose it's something people do. Make snap decisions. Uproot their lives. I just never thought that was me."

Neve smiled patiently. "Take some time and think it over."

Tamsyn shook her head. "No. I don't need time. I know that this is right." She beamed at them.

Rosemary could almost see her transform before their eyes. The downtrodden and worried woman they had met a few days ago in Burkenswood had vanished. Tamsyn stood there, strong and vibrant.

"I might have to take you up on your offer to help me move back here. There's nothing much for me back home, not after my two kids moved to France and Portugal. Just a depressing office job and an underutilised gym membership."

"We'll be happy to," said Rosemary. "Just tell us what you need, and I know someone who will be thrilled to help you find a cottage here. Don't worry, she's not an estate agent, just a wonderful friend."

Tamsyn gave her a confused look, and then returned to smiling.

EIGHTEEN

Athena sat next to Elise in History of Folklore and Mythology class, studiously avoiding Beryl's glare. It had been an awkward morning. Just as Athena had predicted, her snobby classmate was livid after the dynamo incident. Beryl hated to be bested in anything.

It had come as a shock to Athena to hear that the girl she sometimes thought of as her arch nemesis had been instrumental in aiding her return from the fae realm. Beryl had given Rosemary the spell she'd needed in order to get through to help. Although, as Athena kept insisting, she was the one who figured out how to get back on her own, without needing her mother or anyone else.

Still, Beryl had gone out of her way to give Rosemary the spell and Athena felt some mixed gratitude about it. She hadn't even had the chance to properly thank Beryl because every interaction she'd had with her had continued to be so unpleasant.

Athena gazed out the window, longing for the delightful lightness of the fae realm.

"You're zoning out again," Elise whispered. "Listen."

Athena tried to refocus on Ms Twigg, just as she said, "Has anyone heard this passage before? 'When the wheel begins to turn, let the Beltane fires burn.'"

Beryl raised her hand quickly and enthusiastically. Nobody else did.

"Yes, Beryl?"

"It's a quote from the prominent witch, Doreen Valiante."

"Very good," said Ms Twigg. "Beltane is the next seasonal festival approaching in our calendar year. It was customary in the days of the ancients to celebrate fertility in the early summer, so as to bring about a good harvest."

"Eww, gross!" said Felix.

"Yes. Thank you, Mr Lancaster," said Ms Twigg. "As gross as fertility might sound to a group of teenagers, it's also an important part of life."

"And here I was thinking I could escape sex-ed class by going to a magical school," Athena whispered to Elise, who couldn't help but giggle.

"No such luck," she replied.

"Part of the ritual involves lighting magical fires, enchanted with fertility blessings," Ms Twigg continued, ignoring the rowdy class, or at least so it seemed until she slammed a book down on Felix's desk. He tensed.

"Mr Lancaster, would you care to read aloud to the class from the following passage?" She pointed to an open page.

Felix gulped anxiously and then started reading. "It is believed that fire sprites were traditionally involved in Beltane festivities in the rituals of old, bringing with them the potent fertility magic present in the element of fire. Their presence has not been detected for some time since most fire sprites were believed to be chased out of the earth realm by the witching authorities due to their habit of causing havoc."

"Very good, Mr Lancaster. Now, in Myrtlewood, this time of year has always had an interesting significance," she said. "The Beltane fires have granted many fertility blessings. Much more so than in other places."

"Are you saying all this to warn us off getting pregnant?" Elise asked.

"No, Miss Fern," said Ms Twigg. "It occurred to me, recently that something odd is at play. We've had a number of unexplained fires around, including one on my family farm – a rather otherworldly fire, it was."

Athena sparked up and paid attention. Her mother and Neve had talked about the fires.

Ms Twigg continued. "I suspect there might be something magical afoot, and I thought it would pay to prepare you for what might come."

"By getting us to study musty old books?" said Felix, then he stiffened as Ms Twigg's slender forked tongue darted out of her mouth like a frog's and she fixed him with her reptilian eyes.

"Indeed," she said. "We must pay close attention to the lessons of the past so that we do not repeat them. In *A History of Myrtlewood*, written by none other than my aunt Agatha, there is a strong mention of Beltane fires, including the Cavalia."

"What are you talking about?" Sam asked, clearly confused by this unusual diversion from a normally dry class.

Beryl raised her hand. "If I could explain? The Cavalia is believed to be linked to astrological alignments that only occur every two or three hundred years. Last time it happened, in 1763, over one hundred people were killed."

"Doesn't sound very cheerful," said Felix.

"Beryl is correct. It was an enormous fire in Glastonbury and mythical beasts were seen to be involved," said Ms Twigg. "It was rumoured to be brought on by the fire sprites. But as I said before, they were chased off a long time ago, and they can't easily sneak through from the fae realm anymore." She gave Athena a meaningful look before continuing. "And those of us with slightly longer memories or an interest in history have been concerned about the recent fires."

"Why are you telling teenagers about this as if we can do anything to help?" Athena asked, feeling slightly nervous about the way the teacher looked at her. Surely she couldn't know what Athena had been pre-occupied with recently. "Shouldn't you be talking to the police?"

"Rest assured, we've informed the authorities," said Ms Twigg. "Not that that matters a wink."

"Why aren't they taking it seriously?" Elise asked.

"This may surprise you," said Ms Twigg dryly, "but no one takes history seriously enough. That's why it appears we are doomed to repeat the mistakes of the past. People never learn. It's a treacherous flaw. But I fear that our students might be in danger. Young people are especially prone to the magic of fire sprites." Ms Twigg glared around at them all. "It behoves me to warn you and to make this an assignment."

"Aww really?" said Felix.

"Yes, really," said Ms Twigg. "I think it would be in all of your best interests to pay attention. I expect you to write and submit a five page essay on Beltane by next Thursday."

Athena grimaced. Essays were not her favourite thing. She'd had very little assigned work since starting at Myrtlewood Academy and didn't have much experience in the conventions of writing essays about magical things. But something in Ms Twigg's warning was even more disconcerting.

She needed to talk to her mother and Neve about all this, and she needed to do it fast. The class wrapped up, and as the students filed out, Athena recalled another thing she meant to ask her teacher about.

"Erm, Ms Twigg?"

"Yes, Miss Thorn?"

"Do you know anything about fae magic? It's just that—"

"What have you heard? It's all malicious rumours!" Ms Twigg's whole body stiffened, and tiny as she was, Athena took a step back in fear.

"S—sorry," she stuttered.

Athena wasn't sure why Ms Twigg was acting so very strangely, and maybe she never would completely untangle the mystery of the small reptilian-like teacher-librarian, but for the first time she could understand why Felix had such a fear of her.

"I think it's time for you to leave, Miss Thorn," she said sternly.

Athena nodded and scrambled out of the room as quickly as possible.

CHAPTER
NINETEEN

The morning was thick with fog as Rosemary made her way to Liam's cottage. Though the damp air eased some of her concerns about the likelihood of fires, it did nothing to quell her anxiety about potential Bloodstone Society attackers.

She kept her wits about her as she made her way to Liam's front door. She was relieved not to be interrupted by any scary hooded figures.

"You made it!" Liam said, stalking out from behind the house. "Come this way. I've set us up for some practice."

He lead her around to the back garden.

"Are you sure this is the best idea?" Rosemary looked around at the surrounding farmland. "We're so out in the open. People might see us."

"I warded off the area," said Liam. "We should be safe."

"Why do we need to be outside?"

"I want to avoid any collateral damage," said Liam. "Remember how we talked about the fact that I can feel the wolf inside me at all times?"

Rosemary nodded and gulped. "You're not suggesting that we have a practice session where you try to bring it out?"

She wasn't prepared to be faced by an enormous hairy werewolf any more than she was excited about the prospect of a Bloodstone Society attack.

"Not exactly," said Liam. "I just thought you could try shooting me with your magic again and I could see if it has any effect. Only, I don't want to be blown into my bookshelf or break anything else around the house while you're firing off blasts at me."

"I'm not sure this is a good idea," said Rosemary "Last time, I was just protecting myself automatically. I didn't have any particular spell I was doing. I don't think I could replicate it."

"I think it's worth a try," said Liam.

Rosemary agreed, with some trepidation.

"You stand over there," he said. "And I'll stand a few paces away. Just try and blast me with your magic."

"My magic doesn't always comes out the same," said Rosemary. "And I'm still not sure exactly how to control it. I can pull off some relatively complex spells if I try, and I have been practicing, but I think it's going to take years to master."

"Just give it a try," said Liam.

Rosemary held her hands out in front of her and visualised golden magical light. She was trying to recreate what she'd done in the bookshop weeks before. As she connected with her magic, a blast surged from behind her fingers and pulsed out towards Liam, hitting him in the chest and knocking him onto the ground.

He pushed himself up to a sitting position, looking startled.

"Anything?" Rosemary asked.

Liam shook his head. "Aside from the shock, the wolf's still the same. How about if you close your eyes and imagine the scene in the bookshop. Imagine that I'm attacking you in my wolf form."

Rosemary closed her eyes and thought back to the bookshop

where the huge beast was making its way towards her and growling.

She sent out another blast of magic.

"Oh no," said Liam. Rosemary opened her eyes to see that his muscles were bulging right out of his shirt. He was growing taller by the second. And hairier too. His teeth grew long and pointed until standing in front of her, baring its teeth, was a huge wolf.

"I...think I accidentally magicked you *into* a wolf," Rosemary murmured in a low voice. "Uhh, sorry, Liam...Wolfie."

She took a few steps back, but the creature growled and prowled towards her. Rosemary wanted to run, but she knew she could never be fast enough.

Her mind raced through possibilities in panic, but there was nothing for it.

She couldn't out-run an enormous beast like this.

She held out her hands, reaching instinctively for her own survival magic.

Come on...come on...

She blasted the creature with a wave of golden light.

By the time it dimmed, Liam was lying in a heap on the ground with his clothing in tatters, or what was left of it anyway.

Rosemary grimaced, hoping the poor man wasn't badly hurt.

"Sorry, Liam," Rosemary said. "I think that backfired."

Liam blinked and looked around before picking himself up.

Rosemary checked to see he was fine and then stood there awkwardly for a moment. "If you're alright, I think that's enough for the day. I might get going."

"No, wait," said Liam, his eyes widening. "That actually worked! I can feel the wolf inside me, still, but it's diminished."

"Liam, if you didn't notice, that was a total disaster," said Rosemary. "I made you turn into a werewolf *outside* of your normal cycle, and then blasted you to the ground."

"You did," he agreed. "But you also made me change back!"

"It seems like I can turn you back just out of my will to survive," said Rosemary. "But I don't know how to replicate it."

"It's progress," said Liam. "I'm tired now, but maybe we can try again in a few days."

"I'm not sure."

"I didn't mean to attack you," said Liam apologetically.

"I'm aware of that. It's just, it's quite dangerous, and not just for me. I don't know if it's also hurting you as well. You look a wreck."

"You promised to help me," Liam said.

Rosemary felt a stab of guilt, and perhaps something else akin to duty or loyalty. In werewolf form, Liam terrified her, but as much as she wanted to run away, she also cared about him.

"I will help, if I reasonably can." Rosemary clenched her hands together. "But for now I think I need some time and space to process all this. I'm not convinced that turning you into a werewolf and then blasting you back into human form is a good way forward. And I hope you're not expecting me to make a house call every full moon."

"That would be something," said Liam.

Rosemary narrowed her eyes at him.

"Okay, fine," said Liam. "We've got another week and a half until full moon. You can take a few days to process, but maybe then we can regroup and come up with a plan."

Rosemary nodded, still feeling shaken and unsure.

TWENTY

osemary opened the door and entered Marjie's teashop. It had become a regular occurrence that Marjie would drop off morning tea for the children, and anyone else who was around at Thorn Manor. Today, she'd asked Rosemary to stop in and pick it up instead, as she was too busy to make the delivery, herself. It was the least Rosemary could do, considering how helpful Marjie had been.

The teashop was bustling with activity. There were plenty of customers and Rosemary felt a little pang of emotion in her chest when she saw Lamorna, the new employee, behind the counter. If Rosemary was completely honest, she'd been avoiding the shop, recently. It didn't quite make sense, rationally. Since the foundling children had moved in and Rosemary was signing up for courses towards her chocolate business, she hardly had time to help Marjie out anymore, but she still felt a twinge of emotion seeing her young replacement with the lush blonde hair.

Rosemary had quite enjoyed working at the teashop when she was first settling into Myrtlewood. It had given her, not only a sense of independence, but also a sense of purpose and helped her to feel like part of the community. Seeing the new girl in her place some-times had the effect of making Rosemary feel a bit dislocated, somehow.

Lamorna seemed lovely, and reasonably competent apart from a few mix-ups, but Rosemary couldn't help but dislike her for some reason.

"There you are love. Take a seat," said Marjie. She strode out from behind the counter wearing a floral apron in her usual style.

"I don't need to stay along. I don't want to trouble you," said Rosemary.

"Nonsense. Sit down. I'm going to bring you something."

Rosemary sighed and did as she was told. Marjie returned with a tea tray.

"Really, don't bother about me. Go and help your customers," said Rosemary.

"My customers are perfectly fine. Mind your own business," said Marjie with a grin.

"You know, I didn't mean it that way," said Rosemary. "I just don't want to be any trouble."

"And that is part of your problem," said the older woman.

"What do you mean?"

"You've been doing everything to help out everybody else. And nothing for your own self. Here, sip this tea — yes, it does have some of my special remedy in it — and think about what you want to do for yourself and for your *own* future. You've been spending so much time looking after the children, helping Neve, looking out for Dain and supporting Liam with whatever it is you're doing for him. Your whole life is helping everybody else."

"You're one to talk. You're always helping other people."

"That's because I figured out what makes me tick a long time ago. It took me a few false starts, mind. But after the fiasco with the recyclable toilet paper business I realised what I really like doing is nurturing people, feeding them, making them smile. You, on the other hand... well, you're not a natural nurturer, dear. No offense or anything."

"None taken," said Rosemary. "You're right. I'm surprised I've kept Athena alive all these years. I'm more interested in making food – and eating it – than giving it to people

Marjie smiled. "You still have your whole life to live. You need to be the main character, not just a supporting role. You've told me about the chocolate shop dream that you've had. And I've taken a few liberties..."

"You've *what?*" Rosemary's eyes widened.

"I just made some inquiries on your behalf. That's all."

"Oh no... really?" Rosemary said. "I've already got so much to think about with trying to get the children re-homed and Dain's addiction, not to mention trying to keep Athena out of trouble and everything else. I don't think I could start a business right now."

"Take it from somebody who's learned this the hard way," said Marjie sagely. "Helping other people is a lot easier than helping yourself."

"Says the woman who spends most of her time helping people."

"Not at my own expense," said Marjie. "And what can I say, it's a calling. But for the longest time I resisted it. I wanted to save the world with my inventions, despite the fact they often backfired on me. It's an ironic truth of life that doing what you really need to do can be the hardest thing. Meeting your own needs and dealing with your own issues is much, much harder than trying to save other people, but it's also far more important. If you don't do what you need to do for your own dreams, then you'll wither inside. And then you'll be no real help to anyone else."

"Oh Marjie," Rosemary said, giving her friend a frustrated look.

"Now don't protest, you know that I'm right."

"You *do* sound right," Rosemary admitted grudgingly.

"Alright then. It's settled."

"Settled?" Rosemary asked.

Just then, the bell tinkled above teashop door, and a tall, gruff, older man walked in, complete with scars on his face and a grumpy demeanour.

"What's all this about," Covvey barked. "You tell me to come down here, old woman and here I am."

"Speak for yourself," said Marjie. "I'm not that old."

Covvey grunted.

"I have someone here who wants to do business with you," said Marjie.

"What kind of business? What are you talking about?" said Covvey.

Rosemary balked as Marjie gestured to her table. "Take a seat," she said.

"What's *she* doing here?" Covvey asked, suspiciously, clearly reminded of the last run-in he'd had with Rosemary when she'd inadvertently accused him of being a werewolf, which, to Rosemary's mind was only offensive because everyone was so prejudiced about the poor cursed beings.

"Yes, Rosemary's interested in leasing your vacant shop,"

Covvey down and folded his arms. "It's not on the market."

His words were spoken with a decisive finality that made Rosemary's heart sink, but Marjie was having none of it. "Don't be silly. It's not like you planned to do anything with it. And I'd say you have a good sweet tooth on you."

Covvey's brow furrowed. "What is it you want to do with it?"

Rosemary let out the breath she'd been holding. "Look," she said. "I'm not quite ready yet, but I would love to have a chocolate shop one day."

"A chocolate shop," said Covvey. "Well, I'm sorry the premises is pretty much condemned. That mayor won't let anyone near it with a 10 foot pole."

"That's not what I heard," said a familiar, silky voice.

"Mind your own business ye blighter," said Covvey.

Rosemary glanced around to see Burk approach approaching. "The premises are sound," said Burk. "The reason that the mayor won't let you operators is because he didn't like your previous establishment."

Covvey growled and Burk raised his hands. "I'm not one to judge, *believe* me, but as it stands, you're just wasting money, having to pay rates while the shop still sits empty. You might as well lease it to someone else, at least that way you'll get rent."

"What makes you think I'd take advice from one of your kind?" Covvey barked.

"Do you mean a lawyer?" said Buck, with a slight raise of his eyebrows.

Rosemary suppressed a giggle.

Burk continued. "Look, I'm happy to throw in the legal work you'd need on both sides for free."

"Why would you do something like that?" Covvey voice was tense and suspicious.

"It's a shame to see that shop sitting vacant. And I'd quite like to see what kind of chocolates Rosemary can make." He flashed her a stunning smile that Rosemary pretended not to react to.

"I do like chocolate," said Covvey, slowly, raising his hand to his chin and pondering. "And old Galdie would have liked it... Your idea. She was a fierce one. And we didn't always get along. But she was loyal, a good strong woman. We had history, we did."

Rosemary nodded. "Look, I'm sorry if I caused you offence the other day."

Covvey raised his arms dismissively. "No. It's all forgotten all in the past." He began to stand up to leave. "I'll think about it. But I'm not making any promises."

He stomped out of the shop and Marjie beamed. "See, I told you I'd made some inquiries. "There'll be nothing to it."

"It didn't sound too positive," said Rosemary.

Burk flashed her a soul-melting smile.

Rosemary turned away and looked at her phone, hoping to avoid a conversation. She reminded herself that Burk was dangerous, especially to the fae. She needed to keep Athena away from him, along with anyone else with similar heritage.

She'd been planning to call in to see Una after the tea shop. She needed to warn the fae woman about associations with a vampire.

"Rosemary," said Burk, his voice slightly strained. "Is something the matter?"

"I've got to go."

"I insist," said Burk.

"Please don't," Rosemary said, aware that her tone was cold. "I need to make sure we keep out interactions at a professional level." With that, she got up from the table and left Marjie's teashop, forgetting about the treats she'd gone in there to collect.

Rosemary crossed the town circle towards the apothecary only to find it shut up. There was a note stuck to the door saying that the shop was closed for personal reasons and that it would reopen next week.

A tingle of warning ran through Rosemary's nervous system.

"For personal reasons," she muttered to herself. "That doesn't sound good."

She went back to her car to find Marjie waiting there with a box of freshly baked ginger biscuits and a puzzled expression.

"What?" Rosemary asked.

"What happened back there?" Marjie asked. "With Perseus?"

"I forget his name is Perseus," said Rosemary. "I always think of him as Burk."

Marjie shrugged. "Don't change the subject. You're acting rather off."

"Marjie, I'm worried about Una."

"What's the matter with Una?" Marjie asked. "She seemed All right when I saw her earlier."

"You saw her today?"

"O'course I did. Her cousin Matilda's just had a baby. She and Ashwyn have gone out of town for a few days. They stopped to pick up some cakes for the family."

"Oh," said Rosemary. "I wondered what the personal reasons for the shop being closed were..."

"Is that all you're worried about?" Marjie asked her, a little suspiciously.

"No," Rosemary admitted. She looked around to make sure nobody was watching. "Marjie, the other day, when I had the tonic from Una, a whole lot of memories came back to me."

"That's excellent news!" Marjie said. "Finally cleared out all those fake cobwebs in your head."

"Exactly," said Rosemary. "Only, it took me a little while to realize that Una was having dinner with Burk at the pub a couple of weeks ago."

"And?" Marjie raised her eyebrows.

"Well, okay, to be honest, Burk and I... well there may have been at little spark between us at one point."

"So you might be jealous," said Marjie. "But that doesn't explain why you'd be worried."

Rosemary folded her arms. "I might have been a little bit jealous. But then it occurred to me that Una being fae... Don't you think she should be staying well away from vampires?"

"Oh, I see," said Marjie. "This is really about Athena."

"It is *not*," said Rosemary.

Marjie shook her head and smiled. "You're projecting your fears for your daughter onto Una, because you know they have similar parentage."

"I never thought of it that way," said Rosemary, crossing her arms. "Isn't it dangerous though?" she asked, lowering her voice. "I thought fae blood was irresistible to vampires."

Marjie shrugged. "Burk isn't one to lose control, though, is he? I'm not saying you shouldn't warn Una. She may well be unaware of all that. All I'm saying is Perseus Burk is a perfect gentleman. I've never once seen him lose his composure, or fly off the handle or attack anyone who didn't deserve it."

"But you have seen him attack people?" Rosemary said.

"I've seen you attack people, too, including Dain," Marjie pointed out. "And you don't do it with quite so much composure or rationality."

Rosemary frowned. "Okay, fine. Maybe it is a little bit to do with Athena. I don't know. Everything's so complicated at the moment."

"That's because you've been trying to help too many people, like I said. Why don't you go home and have a nap and daydream about the chocolate shop. You could even have a go at making some chocolate. Do something for yourself, you know?"

Rosemary tried to protest but the more she thought about it, the more she realised Marjie was right. She'd been putting off looking after herself at her own expense, to distract herself. Worrying about other people was far easier than dealing with her own problems. "Alright, you win," said Rosemary. "I'll see you later."

TWENTY-ONE

"Mum!" Athena called. "Mum!"

"What is it?" Rosemary's heart raced at the urgency in her daughter's voice. She grabbed hold of the porcelain sides of the large bathtub, trying to push herself out but underestimating the slipperiness of the sides. Water slopped over the floor. "I'm in the bath," she called out.

"Oh, don't worry then," said Athena. "This can wait until you're out."

Rosemary sighed, slipping back into the warmth of the bathtub, but she couldn't relax until she knew whatever it was that Athena was clearly concerned about.

"Can't you just tell me through the door?"

"Not really," said Athena. "It's too awkward. Besides, you might need a cup of tea for this."

"Okay, give me a minute. I'll meet you downstairs."

Rosemary got out and dried herself off, putting on the first clean clothing she could find. She'd been trying to take Marjie's advice and do something nice for herself, but clearly fate had other ideas.

"What's going on?" she said, making her way out to the kitchen where Athena was making tea.

"What on earth are you wearing?" Athena asked, her eyes boggling.

Rosemary looked down to see she had on a sunshine yellow top over forest green pants with a hot pink cardigan. She frowned. "I *thought* you had something important to say. You sounded worried."

"I did, but your outfit is also disturbing."

"Leave my outfit out of this," said Rosemary. "It's my new look. I'm calling it clashing Titans."

Athena giggled. "Okay, let's sit down."

"Now I'm really worried," said Rosemary.

"It's not bad news...exactly," said Athena as she carried the tea tray over to the window seats. "It's just that I learned something at school and I think it might be a clue as to what is going on."

Rosemary gulped. "Don't tell me you've been studying werewolves?"

"No," said Athena, looking confused. "Why would you guess that?"

"Erm...nothing," said Rosemary, feeling foolish for the slip-up. "It's just, I'm scared of werewolves after what Shelly and Marjie said."

Athena gave her a strange look as if she wasn't quite convinced. "Anyway," she said. "Today in Folklore and History, Ms Twigg – that's Agatha's daughter."

"Yes, I remember that," said Rosemary. "It's so nice to have my memory back."

"Pay attention, Mum," said Athena.

"I'm sorry. What did Ms Twigg say?"

"Wait." Athena crossed the floor and pulled out her note-book from the schoolbag she'd carelessly flung on the floor earlier. "Here it is," she said, making her way back to the window seats.

Just then, Detective Neve burst into the room. Her was clothing singed and the scent of smoke drifted across the house towards Rosemary.

"What happened" Rosemary asked.

"Another one," said Neve. "And they're getting worse." She slumped down next to them on the window seat."

"Another *heated* scene?" Rosemary asked.

"Fortunately we got this one early," said Neve. "But that reminds me. Is Nesta out back?"

Rosemary nodded.

"I still haven't told her about...that other thing." Neve groaned.

"I'm sure you'll have plenty of chances," said Rosemary, trying not to begin rambling, as Neve clearly didn't want to air her dirty laundry in front of the teen. Instead, Rosemary changed the subject. "Athena was just in the middle of telling me something."

"Was it another fire?" Athena asked. "Where was it?"

"It was out by old Briar castle," said Neve. "They seem to happen either in relatively powerful places, or around groupings of two or more highly magical people. That's the only pattern I can detect."

"None have happened here," said Rosemary.

"You're lucky this place has been warded up to the nines by old Galdie," said Neve. She turned to Athena. "What were you going about to say?"

"I was just about to tell my mum something that they said at school. Only, I'm not sure if you'll take it seriously," said Athena.

"Try me," said Neve.

"Well, Miss Twigg told us all about the Beltane fires and the fire sprites and how in previous times they were involved in worshipping the god Balanus."

Neve nodded.

"Anyway," Athena continued. "Miss Twigg seems to think all that has something to do with these fires happening the moment. She set us all assignments on it and I've been doing some research. One source I read said that every few hundred years the planets align in a special way with Uranus and Jupiter in Aries, and Mars joining them. It sets the scene for something called the Cavalia. It hasn't happened in a long time, but that might be because there aren't enough fire sprites to instigate it. I read that fire sprites used to be involved in the old rituals of the Cult of Belamus. But you don't see many of them around these days. My guess it they all got sealed in the fae realm when the veil borders closed."

Neve shook her head. "Why's she telling schoolkids about all this and not the police?"

"Well, she said that lessons in history are important." said Athena. "And apparently she did tell the police, though I'm not sure if anyone listened."

Neve sighed. "I'm gonna have to have words with Perkins about this. Not telling me things that notable people in the community have said is definitely along the lines of obstruction of an investigation."

"He probably didn't take her seriously," said Rosemary. "He doesn't seem to take much seriously apart from himself."

"Harsh but true," said Neve. "If you'll excuse me, I have to go and make a very grumpy phone call."

Rosemary looked at her daughter. "It was good you told us. Nice work, kid."

"I'm surprised either of you took me seriously," said Athena. "People don't usually listen to teens."

"You're not just any teenager," said Rosemary. "You're my daughter. I know you're incredibly clever. And you don't suffer fools. I'm sure if you thought the teacher was having you on you wouldn't have spared them a second thought."

The two Thorns sipped the tea their tea in silence until Neve returned a moment later. "Perkins wasn't happy about that," she said.

"What was his response?" Rosemary asked her.

"He complained that if he had to relay every half-brained thing the ridiculous townspeople told him he'd never get on with any of his other more important work."

"It sounds like something he'd say," said Rosemary. "Anyway, I'm glad we have you on the case. At least you've got plenty of brains."

"Thanks. I might pay your teacher a visit later," she said to Athena, and then turned back to Rosemary. "But now, I'd better go and talk to Nesta. Wish me luck."

"What's going on with them?" Athena asked as Neve left the room.

"Hopefully nothing," said Rosemary.

"Oh, fine," said Athena. "But tell me, what was it you said about fighting you?"

CHAPTER
TWENTY-TWO

"You'll pay for that!" Athena drew energy into her hands. It sizzled, a white blob of light flecked with green. She raised it above her head and lobbed it at her mother. "This is really helping me to work out some anger issues."

Rosemary ducked, spun and hurled a golden ball of light back. Athena only just got out of the way. The ball landed on a nearby tree, burning a charred mark into the bark.

Dain and Marjie were out shopping and Nesta had taken the foundling children inside so that the Thorns could use the back lawn for training purposes. Though the excitement had meant there now were a row of very interested little faces peeping through the back windows of the house.

Rosemary and Athena stood five meters away from each other, crab-walking slowly around in a circle as they practiced both attacking and defending with magic.

"I'm glad you found an outlet for your anger," said Rosemary, shooting a fireball.

"Hey!" Athena dropped to the ground to avoid it. "At least give me a chance to retaliate."

"Our enemies won't do that."

"Fair point. That was heavy one," she said as she got to her feet again.

"I'm glad you noticed," said Rosemary. "I constructed out it out of my rage at the all the injustices in the world."

Athena smiled. "You know, we also need to practice close range combat." She lunged towards her mother and kicked out.

Rosemary raised her hands, and a blast of white light shot out, blowing Athena back across the lawn.

"How did you do that?" asked Athena.

Athena's magic had come in much more strongly since she'd left the fae realm. It was even stronger on the mornings after her night time escapades that had continued, recently, where she tried to cut a door through to the other world.

She knew she shouldn't, but she couldn't help it, just to get that sensation of feeling warm and connected in at home in her own body.

Of course, Rosemary didn't know anything about it and Athena wasn't about to tell her mother. Rosemary was only just starting to relax a little after the fae realm debacle. Athena was doing all she could play the sympathy card of Finnigan's betrayal even though it made her feel sick to her stomach to do it.

"We can't just fight with magic," said Athena. "Our attackers might have weapons."

"Let's try hand to hand combat before we add in dangerous weapons, shall we?" Rosemary jumped forward and threw a punch towards her daughter.

"That was terrible," said Athena, leaning back. "Even if I'd stayed perfectly still it would have hardly hurt at all."

"Well, forgive me for not wanting to hurt my own child," said Rosemary.

"If you're not going to properly attack me this is not really going to work."

"You're right," said Rosemary. "We need a proper trainer. Only, I don't know anyone who fits the bill."

"Maybe Marjie will know someone," said Athena. "Or you could always ask your vampire friend."

Athena watched as her mother visibly stiffened.

"Stop that."

"I will, if you stop denying it. You definitely got jealous when you saw him at the pub with another woman."

Rosemary looked uncomfortable. "feelings don't always make sense as you well know," she said.

"Sure thing, Mum," said Athena. "It seems like you've moved on with Liam now, anyway."

"That's *not* what's going on, and you know it." said Rosemary.

"It's a shame though," said Athena. "It would probably make you less wound-up."

Rosemary shot a huge ball of a sizzling electric purple light towards her daughter.

Athena blasted it out of the way with her own magic. "I guess I deserved that." She caught a glimpse of her reflection in the windows of the house. Her hair stood up on end from the near miss. "How did you do that? I want to play with electricity."

"I think it's a mixture of elements, but I have no idea," said Rosemary. "That's part of the problem. And if you must know, I'm try to help Liam with the medical issue, one that I'm not privy to discuss."

"Oh... *Oh!*" said Athena. "I see. Is it gross?"

Rosemary narrowed her eyes.

"You're right," Athena continued. "I don't want to know if it's gross."

Rosemary laughed and Athena made the most of her mother's

distraction by lobbing another ball of pale green light. It hit Rosemary in the chest, making her fall straight back.

"You got me," she said, staring up at the sky.

"It's not fair that I can only do balls of light and you can do fire and all sorts of weird stuff," said Athena.

"I'm just playing with my emotions," said Rosemary. "Maybe if you weren't so closed off about yours you'd be able to make cool stuff too."

"Touché." Athena lunged towards her mother, kicking and punching before being blasted back again by a ball of energy that was big and fluffy and baby-pink. It wrapped her wrap in the air, and held her, hovering above the ground.

"Not fair!" Athena shouted from the giant pink bubble. "Put me down!"

"You're protected by my love," said Rosemary, laughing.

Athena closed her eyes and imagined a dart of magic, shooting out. The bubble popped, with a bang, and she collapsed to the ground in a disgruntled pile.

"Had enough for the day?" Rosemary asked.

Athena lay there, on the ground grumbling unintelligible noises, not bothering to pull herself up.

"Marjie dropped over some homemade lemonade," Rosemary coaxed.

"Sure," said Athena, her voice a whimper.

Rosemary helped her up. "We can try again tomorrow. But I do really think we need a trainer, otherwise we're not going to get very far. We need to be on our game if these creepy things keep showing up and attacking us."

As if in answer to her words a deep crackle like the sound of thunder shocked the air around them. They turned to see three figures appear at the side of the house. They were all shrouded in dark hooded cloaks.

"Oh no. No you don't!" Rosemary crouched down, already on the offensive. She threw her arm to the side and a silver disc of light shout out, taking out one of the enemies at the rear.

"Uh... Mum... What's going on here?" Athena felt a flutter in her chest as she realised the danger their unexpected guests posed.

"My guess is it's the Bloodstones," muttered Rosemary, as the figure at the front raised her hands in the air. Lightning sizzled between her palms and the hood fell back revealing long silvery blonde locks. Her face remained concealed behind a butterfly mask that gleamed, iridescent. All Athena could see of her face were her eyes which flashed blue in the sunlight.

"Who's that?" Athena asked. "She looks familiar."

"Whoever she is, I don't think she's entirely human," said Rosemary.

Athena looked at the woman, her limbs were slender like the fae, but there was something different about her.

"Join the club," Athena replied. "I've got this." Her hands trembled a little as she held out her arms, creating an enormous ball of magical light energy, and then gave it a huge shove, pushing it towards the woman, who dived out of the way.

One of the woman's cronies ran at Rosemary. Athena watched as her mother's super strength kicked in. She threw the attacker to the ground, but the other crony was close behind. Athena was prepared to attack but Rosemary was faster, blasting magic, instinctually. It burst out as light and air in a wave of energy, stripping the hood back from the attacker. For a moment they saw that he was a dark-haired man with pasty skin, before he burst into dust.

"Didn't your mother ever tell you to wear sunscreen?" said Rosemary.

Athena cringed at her mother's cheesy line and laughed at the same time. "Seriously, who brings a vampire to a daylight fight?"

"I see you're not unprepared," said the masked woman in a gravelly voice. "No matter. I'm merely here to relay a message."

"What's the message," Rosemary asked.

"We're here, all around you. We are coming for you. There is no way you can run or hide. We're bringing our leader back."

In a flash of lightning, the hooded attackers were gone.

"Holy Hades," said Rosemary. "Well that was bloody unexpected."

"You're sure it's the Bloodstones?" Athena asked, her blood running cold.

"It must be said," Rosemary. Especially with their penchant for wearing black robes."

"But didn't you kill their annoying little vampiric leader?" Athena asked.

"Well, I thought so," said Rosemary. "Unless..."

"Unless what?"

Rosemary made a dash towards the house, Athena following close behind. They got inside to find the place ransacked. Chairs were strewn around and shattered porcelain littered the floor. The children were hiding underneath the couch, Nesta to huddled close by, trembling.

Athena gasped. "What happened?"

How did the Bloodstones get through the wards, Athena wondered. *They must be packing some pretty powerful magic.*

"It was a distraction," said Rosemary. "They wanted to keep us busy. So they could get *something* from inside the house."

"Any idea of what?" Nesta asked.

"I have a hunch," said Rosemary. She and Athena looked at each other and then took off towards the library.

The door had been flung open. Books lay strewn around the room, and the little box that had once held the thorn family magic had vanished.

CHAPTER
TWENTY-THREE

Rosemary tried to slow her breathing. She and Athena, stood in shocked silence, looking at the spot on the desk where the box had once been.

Athena gasped. "She was still in there? All this time?"

"At least, that's what her followers think," said Rosemary.

They turned towards the sound as the front door of the house swung open.

Dain and Marjie had returned from their shopping expedition. Rosemary noticed that Dain was already dressed in some new jeans and a crisp white shirt. He beamed at her, and then he took in the carnage around him and his expression pressed into concern.

"What happened?" He asked.

"Did you try that spell again and mess up the house?" Marjie asked.

Athena shook her head. "No, we were attacked by the Bloodstone Society."

Dain ran forward, sweeping both Rosemary and Athena into a ferocious hug.

"My girls," he said, his voice cracking, in a gesture that was both caring and protective. "Are you alright?"

"We're fine," said Rosemary, her body stiffened in awkwardness as her ex continued to hug her. "It was just a distraction. They attacked us outside when we were training, but what they really wanted was in here."

"What was it, dear?" Marjie asked, she stepped around the group hug, surveying the damage.

"The box," said Athena. Rosemary was surprised her daughter was continuing to allow her father to hug her. "You know the one that used to house our family magic."

"But the magic's not in there anymore," said Marjie. "Surely they know that."

"We suspect they think Geneviève is still in there, somehow," said Rosemary, wondering about the best way to pry herself out of this awkward hugging situation was. It had clearly gone on for far too long, but there was only sweetness and concern in Dain's demeanour. She thought back to what Una said about the spell for the cream addiction.

It requires love.

It was quickly becoming clear to Rosemary that despite Athena's long-held resentment towards her father, there was definitely a more positive attachment there too. And now that Rosemary's memories had cleared up, she could remember the good times and the bad. It gave her a new perspective, coupled with the knowledge about Dain's addiction.

She finally managed to extricated herself from the hug with the knowledge that there was definitely a feeling of warmth between them... she wasn't sure if it was romantic but it did feel a lot like love.

Rosemary turned towards Athena, who had a slightly over-whelmed expression on her face. "It's time to try the spell."

CHAPTER
TWENTY-FOUR

"These notes are quite complicated," said Athena. "Are you sure we're up to doing this?"

They were standing in the lounge an hour later, after cleaning up from the attack, in which the house helped a great deal. They'd had lunch and begun preparations for the spell.

"It's nothing compared to the spell I had to do to create a temporary warp in space in order to try rescue your silly arse from another dimension," Rosemary replied.

"How long are you going to keep reminding me about that for?"

"Probably until you're retired," said Rosemary. "That'll give me a good few decades of ammunition."

Athena sighed.

Rosemary rubbed her hands together. "Alright. Let's start."

"Don't you think we should wait until Una comes back from her family thing? She might be able to help."

"We could do," said Rosemary. "Although, I don't think we need her here to do the spell. Her notes say it should be cast by the people closest to the fae in question."

"No, that's not what it says," said Athena. "It says we have to love him. I don't think that we qualify."

"I wouldn't have said so either, Rosemary said. "But I think something has changed. Or maybe whole lot of things have changed over time. You can still be angry at someone that you love. You can even hate them sometimes. In fact, sometimes the reason that feelings are so strong is because of the love."

"Sounds like a self-help book," said Athena. "I don't mind Dad. In fact, he's kind of growing on me a little bit. But that doesn't make up for the facts."

"It doesn't make up for it," said Rosemary. "You're right. And it's not about making up for it. We just have to deal with the situation... wherever we are. And this is where we are right now."

Athena narrowed her eyes. "Why are you so focused on this? Don't you have a million other things to worry about? Like Liam's little health disorder and all these fires and the children still run wild around the house, not to mention getting your own life together, setting up your business?"

"One thing at a time," said Rosemary. "I've just got to tick this off my list. The less I have to worry about Dain, the easier it will be sort out those other things. It makes me nervous having him around when we never know if he's going to lose the plot. It seems even more dangerous to kick him out."

Athena shrugged. "Okay. Let's set up, then."

They gathered together the ingredients for the spell: Amethyst crystals to be placed at the four direction points; a bundle of sage and another of rosemary; three sprigs of time in one of vervain, and nine cardamom pods. They applied the anointing serum to their temples that they'd made out of the essential oils of thyme, black pepper and juniper. It smelled wonderful.

They pushed the couches out of the way in the lounge and lay the herbs and the crystals in a circle and said the basic blessing to cast a sacred space. Then they called Dain in. He'd been waiting in the kitchen, blindfolded and the instructions said that he had to enter the ritual space that way. He stumbled a little bit, tripping on the arm of a chair that had been pushed a little too close to the doorframe.

"Can we help?" Athena whispered.

Rosemary nodded. They stepped forward and led Dain to the circle.

"Sit down," said Rosemary.

Dain did as he was told, sitting cross legged on the floor. Athena and Rosemary stood above him, joined hands and began to chant.

By the power of our love for you, we bind you.

We shackle you to free you.

We bind you so that which would tear you from us now only sickens you.

We bind you, Dain, in our love.

We bind you to free you.

A burst of light emanated from the centre of the circle, above Dain's head.

It radiated out in between where Rosemary and Athena stood. It shone out in an intricate paisley-like pattern and then contracted around the three of them.

Rosemary felt something shifting.

It was as if a new lens had come over her way of seeing.

The world stilled for a moment, then her vision went blank.

There was a heavy darkness and Rosemary realised she must have passed out. She tried to open her eyes, only to find everything different. She was still standing, holding onto Athena's hands, but she was also somewhere else entirely, in her mind.

A reel of memories ran through her head, but they weren't Rosemary's.

It was Dain's perspective, as a young fae, peeking through the veil, leaving behind everything he knew, entering into the human realm.

Rosemary felt the extreme heaviness of emotion, and the disconnection he'd experienced. He'd been running from something big and terrifying and found himself in another world, a much harder, heavier world where nothing made sense.

She watched and he as he was picked up by the authorities, not understanding anything about the way the world operated. She watched his memories stream past as he was passed from foster home to foster home, often to be beaten and yelled at and threatened.

She watched through his eyes as he saw her for the first time.

Rosemary, beautiful and young, her red hair blowing in the breeze on a crisp spring morning as she stopped to pick a bluebell on her way to high school.

He could see the magic all around and inside of her, even though she couldn't see it herself. It was the magic that drew him in. It was her personality that kept him anchored to her.

Rosemary felt the deepest love swim through her. Only it wasn't her emotion. It was Dain's. It was a beautiful sensation that gripped her heart, only to be interrupted by shame and failure.

No matter what he tried, Dain could never do things right. He kept going back, to the cream bottle over and over again because it made him feel good when nothing else was right. He couldn't stop himself from being reckless. He kept doing things that seemed outside of his control. Wasting every chance he got.

The memories faded and she heard Athena sob. Rosemary

pulled her closer, only, Dain was in the way. They tripped and fell into a pile of family on the floor.

The ridiculousness of the situation made them laugh, even though Athena and Rosemary were both tears.

"What... what happened?" Dain asked.

"It was so sad," said Athena, not bothering to get up from the floor. "I mean, you told me you had a rough life. You told me bits and pieces, but it was like..."

"It was like we were there," said Rosemary, beginning to move in an attempt to extricate herself from the puddle. "Like we went through everything you did, although, obviously the Reader's Digest version."

"Well, I didn't come here to get embarrassed," said Dain, pushing himself up. "I'll just show myself out."

"No, it was important," said Athena. "We needed to see all that. It means something."

"It does," said Rosemary. "Our lives might have been tough, and you are probably the cause of most of that to be quite frank."

"Thanks," said Dain in a caustic tone. "That makes me feel so much better."

Rosemary gripped his arm. "But we didn't know what you'd been through."

"I've been angry at you for so long," said Athena, shaking herself. "You didn't know any different."

"That's right," said Rosemary. "In some ways, I understood that, intellectually. But to experience it is a whole other thing."

"Great," said Dain, still sounding unimpressed. "Did it actually work?"

"We'll find out," said Athena.

CHAPTER
TWENTY-FIVE

"Is this really necessary?" Dain asked.

Athena laughed at the absurdity of the situation. "Yes, Dad," she said, wrapping the rope around him one more time before fastening it to the chair he sat in. "You might not remember it very well, but you totally lose your head when the cream comes out. We need to make sure you're restrained and are no danger to yourself or others."

Rosemary nodded. "It's really a surprise you've lived this long."

"What can I say? Fae are resilient creatures."

"That does not give me much hope for us when the Countess figures out how to get her revenge," said Athena.

She had been thinking about this possibility a lot lately. Every time she cut another door through to the fae realm there was a risk that fae could push their way through. It seemed like they hadn't figured out how to do it yet. Something came through when she sliced into the veil, but it wasn't solid.

She hoped that the Countess had no idea what she was doing, and considering Finnigan could go back and forth between the worlds as if he had dual-passports, the Countess could probably mount her own attack without Athena accidentally enabling it, though that thought wasn't exactly reassuring.

Worse still, it was a far greater risk that she'd encounter her infuriating ex crush, and she did not want to think about him.

"Stay very still," said Rosemary, strapping Dain's hands down onto the arm rests with duct tape.

"This is all a bit much for a little cream," Dain protested.

"Quiet, you," said Athena. "Marjie will be here any minute with cream buns or something. It will all be over soon enough and we'll see if the spell worked."

THE DOOR OPENED and Marjie came in, brandishing a bottle of cream. "Are you sure this is a good idea?" she called out, hesitating in the doorway.

"Don't worry, we've got him restrained," said Rosemary.

"And the kids are all out at the park with Nesta, just to be safe," Athena added.

Rosemary watched as Marjie took a deep breath.

"Right then," she said, entering the room.

It had been a few days since they'd cast the spell. Dain had been exhausted afterwards and had spent most of the elapsed time sleeping.

Una's instructions said to let him rest and wait two to five days before they tested it by carefully allowing him near high fat dairy products.

"Are you ready," Rosemary asked Dain.

"As I'll ever be," he replied. "But if it doesn't work, please knock me out gently and forgive me for anything stupid I do."

Athena smiled. "Happy to. We know it's not your fault. At least you're trying Dad."

Dain's eyes lit up with hope.

Rosemary smiled. "It warms my heart to see my daughter getting along with the father who had always been such a thorn in her side."

Athena glared at her.

"What? Animosity wasn't doing either of you any good. And though we won't forget the past, it's about time we stop living in its shadow."

"All right, here goes," said Marjie. She cracked open the bottle of cream and peeled back the foil seal.

They all watched Dain, nervously.

Instead of lighting up gold, as they usually did in reaction to cream, his eyes had a greenish tinge. In fact, his whole face looked rather pale. All of a sudden he coughed and then wretched.

The chair rocked backwards as his whole body convulsed.

Athena turned away as Dain was violently ill, all over himself on the floor. Rosemary tipped the chair to the side so that he didn't choke on his own sick.

"I wasn't prepared for that," she said.

"Disgusting," said Athena. "I wish I didn't have to see it."

"Well, the spell did something," said Rosemary as Dain continued to vomit on the floor.

"Not exactly what we bargained for," said Athena.

"He was sick the last time he tried the remedy from that old book," Rosemary pointed out. "This time, maybe it will actually work, if cream makes him sick in the long term."

"But the point is, Dad should be able to get over his problems, and function in society, regardless of what dairy products are being served. We can't have him curling over and making a mess every time he seems a cream cake."

Rosemary sighed. "At least he's not going to take all my money and gamble or give it away."

"Wait a minute," said Marjie. "I'm going to get Una on the phone."

"Isn't she away?" Rosemary asked.

"Haven't you heard of cell phones?" said Marjie.

Rosemary blushed. "It's not like I know her all that well."

"Look, here you go. It's ringing," Marjie said, holding up the phone.

Rosemary raised her hands in protest not quite sure what to say.

"Oh fine," said Marjie. She spoke into the receiver. "Hello dear. Yes, I'm perfectly fine. Look, we've got a situation here. The Thorn girls tried the spell and they thought it worked but Dain was violently ill. Oh, I see."

Marjie raised her eyebrows and Rosemary gave her a questioning look.

"Here," said Marjie. She handed the phone to Rosemary.

CHAPTER
TWENTY-SIX

"Uh, hi," said Rosemary, grabbing the phone reluctantly.

"Oh, Rosemary. I'm sorry," said Una's voice. "I should have warned you that this might happen. It wasn't so severe with me, but I can see how things could have been a lot worse."

"What do you mean?" Rosemary asked.

"Cream made me nauseous," Una explained.

"Are you saying he's going to continue to be sick like this every time he smells cream?" Rosemary asked.

Athena frowned.

"I don't think so," said Una. "The nausea wore off after a few weeks, so don't worry. Hopefully the same will happen with Dain. Then you'll be able to take him out in public without fear of cream buns."

"Thank you," said Rosemary. She sighed with relief, feeling the exhaustion of the past few weeks catching up on her. "So you're saying the spell worked?"

"It sounds like it worked rather well," said Una. "He wouldn't have had such a reaction to cream if the magic wasn't potent. You must really..." Her voice trailed away and Rosemary interrupted her.

"Oh, there was something I wanted to tell you." Rosemary was thinking about the situation with Burk, but then she hesitated. This probably wasn't the appropriate time and place with Athena, Marjie, and Dain all listening in.

"Yes?" Una asked.

"Never mind," said Rosemary. "It can wait until you get back. When are you back, by the way?"

Tomorrow morning," said Una. "Maybe we can catch up for a cup of tea in the next few days."

"That sounds perfect," said Rosemary. "Thanks again, for everything." She hung up the phone. "Good news," she announced. "The spell worked and Dain's not going to be sick forever, though he won't be wanting to be around dairy any time soon."

"Fabulous!" said Athena. "We can probably untie him now."

"I was gonna ask when you were going to remember that," said Dain. "I'm quite uncomfortable here, tied up in a pool of my own vomit."

"Well, it's not the best situation for the rest of us either," said Athena as Rosemary got started on the rope.

"Una thinks the extreme effects should wear off after a few weeks," said Rosemary. "And then you'll probably just be left with a mild dislike for dairy products. You can tell people you're lactose intolerant."

"True enough," said Dain. "It might not be the lactose, but I don't tolerate nausea well." He was out of the chair and looking rather dishevelled. "If you'll excuse me, I'm going to go and have a shower. Don't worry, I'll clean up when I get back."

"How considerate," said Athena as Dain wandered towards the bathroom. "He's not too bad to have around, after all."

LATER THAT DAY, Rosemary, Athena, and Marjie sat in the window seats, watching as the children played with Nesta outside. Marjie had insisted on staying to clean up the mess.

"Thank you for everything," said Rosemary.

"It's no trouble, my dear." Marjie patted her arm. "I know Dain had offered to do it when he woke up, but that seemed both unfair on him, being sick and all, and unfair on you for having to deal with it until he got himself in order."

"I was hoping the house would do it for us while I got changed." Rosemary said.

"Actually, you're right. Most of the mess was gone by the time I got to it."

Rosemary smiled. "As long as Dain doesn't get too used to Thorn Manor picking up after him."

"Don't worry, Mum," said Athena. "There will be plenty of opportunities for him to help around the house in the future. Hopefully none of them will be quite so gross."

Rosemary rested her chin in her hands in thought.

In future sounded like some kind of commitment. Sure, Dain had been hanging around for weeks after being rescued from the fae realm, and sure, they had plenty of room at Thorn Manor. It *was* nice that Athena was building a healthier relationship with her father. Dain had helped out a lot with the foundling children and Rosemary didn't mind his company, now that she seemed impervious to the fae magic that previously kept her swooning over the guy, though she wasn't sure whether that was to do with the memory tonic, her magic being unbound, or the complex set of charms and wards that Athena had insisted on setting up.

This arrangement can't be permanent.

Rosemary had assumed Dain would just drift off eventually, like he usually did. But perhaps this time it would be different. He hadn't asked her for money, nothing had noticeably gone missing from the house, and given the spell they'd just performed, perhaps he would settle down. Rosemary just wasn't sure she was ready to think about a situation where her very troubled ex was settling down *in her house!*

"You need to relax, dear," said Marjie, clearly troubled by Rosemary's expression. "After all that...I have a present for you."

"Oh no. No you don't," Rosemary said. "You've done quite enough."

"When are you going to come to your senses and stop resisting my way of showing I care?" Marjie asked, and there was a cutting edge to her tone that shocked Rosemary out of her resistance. "You and Athena are family to me now, and I'll spoil you as much as I possibly can. That's the truth, whether you want to accept it or not."

Rosemary sighed and smiled sheepishly, not wanting to disrespect her very generous friend, who was indeed starting to feel more like family.

"Rosemary, I'm serious. Stop trying to take on the world by yourself. You're used to being alone, but you're not anymore. You've got us now. And goodness knows we have to take care of our family, wherever we find them."

"Thank you," said Rosemary, as Marjie's words warmed her heart.

"Not yet. I haven't even given it to you."

"What is it?" Athena asked.

Marjie fished in her handbag and pulled out a cream coloured envelope. "This is for you, both. Take it and relax. You need it. And stop apologising for being yourself. You're a strong determined woman and you've been looking after everyone else for too long.

Now that you've sorted out Dain's cream addiction, take a little breather."

Rosemary opened the envelope to find a voucher for a local spa. "Oh Marjie, how thoughtful! I've never been to anything like this before."

She gave the older woman a big hug.

Rosemary might have resolved Dain's problems, at least for now, so he didn't need babysitting so closely, but Liam was still wanting her help, and there was still the looming issue of the mystery magical fires, and the attacks from hooded figures, but overall, it seemed like a relatively good time to take a little break from it all.

"You can enjoy a whole day of pampering. Take Athena, the voucher will cover it."

Athena's eyes lit up in excitement. "We'll be just like film stars with cucumbers on our eyes, Mum."

Rosemary laughed. "That actually sounds perfect."

CHAPTER
TWENTY-SEVEN

The plants outside seemed greener than usual, lush from the heavy rain the night before. Rosemary left Thorn Manor relatively early for a Saturday morning and drove towards the spa. She followed the directions from her phone. Nesta was going to drop Athena off later, as the teenager didn't feel comfortable with Rosemary's first planned activity of getting a nice long relaxing massage. It seemed like heaven to Rosemary, but Athena was squeamish about the idea of strangers touching her.

The spa was a little off to the west side of the village, further up the coast from Thorn Manor. Rosemary drove along the seaside road. It was soothing to see the ocean waves rolling in.

Despite living relatively close to the sea, they'd barely spent any time at the beach. It was often too windy, but now that the weather was warming up perhaps that would change. She needed a day of relaxing, especially since she was now training with Athena every day, with Dain sometimes helping. They were quickly improving, but the magical fight practice took its toll.

As Rosemary drove, she glanced up towards the hill on her right to see the mayor's house peeking through the trees from a distance as she passed by. It looked slightly different, though she couldn't see the details from this far away. Perhaps it was scaffolding for the repairs, following that fire.

Thinking about Mr June left a bitter taste in Rosemary's mouth. He had not been happy to see her and she was more than happy to avoid him for the foreseeable future. She only hoped that their little run-in a while back where he'd accused her of breaking and entering into his house hadn't dampened her chances of getting a license for the chocolate shop.

She was more determined than ever to go ahead with the business, especially now that Covvey had agreed verbally to lease her the building, but she felt a frightened flutter in her heart every time she thought of it. She didn't know the first thing about running a business.

She'd found numerous online small business courses alongside the chocolatier qualifications that she was still trying to decide between.

Marjie was right. It was much harder to think about herself and get on with the things that she wanted to do in life than it was focusing on other people's problems and trying to sort out their issues.

But today, she didn't have to worry about any of that. Not the children, not Dain. Not Liam, not even the police investigation into the fires, or the Bloodstone Society, touch wood. She reached out to knock on the polished wood panel in the dashboard of Granny's Rolls Royce.

Today was about relaxing. First of all, just by herself as a person in her own right, and then later Athena would be joining her for facials and footbaths and manicures and pedicures and all sorts of other cures.

It sounded almost too good to be true, despite the fact that Rosemary had never done any of this stuff and had a sneaking anxiety that it might actually be rather awkward and uncomfortable.

She pushed away her fears as she drove into the carpark of an exquisitely landscaped area with little rock gardens dotted around the outside. The building itself had enormous gates made of wood up front. It looked like a luxury resort and Rosemary wondered who in the modest magical village of Myrtlewood was keeping a place like this going.

An engraved silver placard on the door read that the Myrtlewood Spa was a treat for magical people from across the world.

"That would explain it then," Rosemary muttered to herself as she continued to read.

Enjoy the exquisite luxury of the spa, complete with magical treatments such as you've never seen before. We have everything required to put your mind, body, and spirit at ease.

"That sounds lovely."

She rang the bell, and a smaller door opened from within the gate. It seemed to move all on its own. Rosemary wasn't sure if it was through magic or some kind of electric-powered mechanism.

Through the door, a smooth cobbled path wove along more elaborate gardens with ornamental rocks and tropical plants.

As Rosemary began to wander along she heard the sound of trickling water from a small stream which flowed to her right. She took a moment to admire the water feature bubbling out of some rocks forming a tiny waterfall. Being there was already relaxing.

She made her way up to reception and entered to see a familiar face behind the counter.

"Ferg?"

He was wearing a brown pinstriped suit, suitable for a Saturday by his standards. He looked up from the book he was reading. "Ah, Ms. Thorn," he said. "I see you're right on time for your massage."

"You...work here as well?" Rosemary asked. She was used to Ferg as an event organiser, taxi service, and sometimes gardener. She wasn't expecting him here as well.

"It's my weekend job," said Ferg, sounding proud. "Got to keep busy! Please take a seat and we'll be with you shortly."

"When do you sleep?" Rosemary asked.

"I've never found sleep to be particularly interesting," said Ferg.

"Oh, sorry," said Rosemary. "I didn't mean to ask personal questions."

"Personal how?" Ferg asked.

"Never mind," said Rosemary. She took a seat in one of the plush purple velvet chairs in the waiting area and picked up a magazine. She'd expected it to be a regular women's magazine, or even one of those nice, healthy lifestyle ones with the thicker paper. She was surprised to find it was titled *Magical You*. On the front there was a picture of a pixie-esque woman with a bluish tinge to her skin and pointed ears.

"Can't escape unrealistic body standards even in the magical world," Rosemary mumbled.

"What was that?" said Ferg.

"Nothing." Rosemary smiled warmly at him.

Ferg gave her a stern look and walked away.

Rosemary looked back at the image of the blue woman on the magazine. She was surrounded by various fonts of text that read: sixteen ways to charm him with spices, the secret magic of cinnamon, harmless garden hexes to keep the pests at bay, and fire up your love life – advice from a rare fire sprite.

Rosemary giggled and began flicking through the pages. "Where do I subscribe to this? It's hilarious."

Ferg approached again, carrying a tray laden with objects.

"Ms Thorn, I'd appreciate it if you kept your voice down, please."

"But we're the only ones here," said Rosemary.

"The spa is a peaceful place."

"Ferg, what are you, a librarian?"

Ferg gave her a serious look. "I thought we discussed this. I work here in the weekends. And please call me Mr Burgess while I'm here. It's more formal."

"Okay," said Rosemary shrugging. "I didn't realise this was a formal place. I thought it was supposed to be relaxing."

"Formalised relaxing," said Ferg, straightening up the paisley-lined collar on his blazer. "Now, I've brought you some artesian spring water from a sacred well in the north of Ireland. Its properties help to ease your worries and strengthen your essence."

"Uh, sounds lovely," said Rosemary, looking at the tray that Ferg was holding.

"And also an assortment of fruit," said Ferg.

"Does that have any special properties?" Rosemary asked.

"No, should it have?"

"Just ordinary fruit then?" said Rosemary.

"I can go and check if you like." Ferg looked concerned and slightly bothered.

"It's okay," said Rosemary, but Ferg had already stomped off after placing the tray down in front of her.

Rosemary sighed, hoping that Ferg wasn't going to be doing the treatments too. If he was, this could be quite a long day.

After a few moments and a good slug of the artesian spring water, which made Rosemary feel all sparkly and happy inside, she managed to eat a few strawberries and a piece of kiwifruit before a petite woman with blue hair came to collect her for the massage.

"You look familiar," said Rosemary.

"I think our daughters know each other," said the woman. "I'm Fleur. Elise's mum."

"That's a clever play on words, like the song," said Rosemary.

Fleur gave her a quizzical look. "I'm sorry, I don't understand."

"Never mind," said Rosemary with an awkward smile. She followed Fleur down an ambient passageway and into a candlelit room with ocean sounds.

"Where's that noise coming from?" Rosemary asked, not seeing any kind of speaker or stereo system in the room.

"From the ocean," said Fleur.

"Oh, I see," said Rosemary. "Why didn't we hear it out in the lobby?"

"The sound in here is magically enhanced," said Fleur.

"That's pretty clever," said Rosemary. "I wonder if I can do that with my magic."

Fleur smiled at her. "You're very unusual." She said it in a friendly way that Rosemary chose not to take offense to.

"I'm just going to slip out of the room," said Fleur. "Just get yourself ready and get on the massage table."

"Oh...okay," said Rosemary. "How?"

Fleur gave her a quizzical look.

"I've never had enough money to get a proper massage before," Rosemary explained.

"Just remove your clothing and get under the sheet," said Fleur.

"That's not usually what I do for my daughter's friend's parents," said Rosemary, blushing as she realised she'd put her foot in her mouth again and made the situation unnecessarily awkward.

"Well, it's a fairly ordinary situation for me to be in," said Fleur, taking it in her stride. "I can assure you it's not as racy or exciting as one might be led to believe from the way you just phrased it."

"Given how racy and exciting my life's been lately, I'm rather pleased about that," said Rosemary. "Excitement is not all its cut out to be."

"Thank you for helping my daughter get back to the earth realm," said Fleur. "I just needed to say that. I would have thanked you before, but I didn't really know how to approach you."

"That's okay," said Rosemary.

"I warned her not to go. But you know what teenagers are like."

"Do I ever."

"She hasn't been quite the same since." Fleur sighed. "I'm sure you know what I mean."

"What *do* you mean?" Rosemary asked.

"Oh, you know. The fae realm does things to people."

Rosemary gave Fleur a quizzical look. "What kinds of things?"

"It might not be the same for you, as you're not of fae heritage, are you? And you weren't there long. But, you know, if Athena has been quiet and drawn lately, it'll just be that she's missing home."

"Home?" Rosemary asked, feeling her shoulders tense. "She's *at* home. I went and got her and brought her home. That was the whole point."

"Of course she's at her earth realm home," said Fleur. "That's the way my mother explains it. The fae realm is different for us who are biologically natives of that place. It calls to us. It sings in our bones, like we're part of it."

"Athena hasn't mentioned anything," said Rosemary. "Maybe it didn't affect her that way."

"Maybe," said Fleur, though she didn't sound convinced. "I've never been, so I wouldn't know exactly what it's like. Elise has been a little quieter lately. Anyway, I'll leave you to it."

Fleur left the room, and Rosemary stood for a moment, pondering the conversation. Had Athena been quieter and more withdrawn than usual? She didn't think so. It was hard to tell with a surly teenager. She slipped out of her clothes, leaving them in a pile on the chair, and got under the silky sheet on the massage table. Lying there in the warm candlelit room, listening to ocean sounds was relaxing enough in itself, but when Fleur returned and began to knead at Rosemary's back, using magically enhanced oils that smelled like frankincense, it seemed to lull Rosemary into a kind of healing trance. All of the worries slipped away from her mind, at least temporarily.

She was finally doing something that was just for herself and it actually felt ridiculously good.

AFTER THE MASSAGE, Rosemary hardly knew herself, in a very good way.

She couldn't remember ever feeling this relaxed before and was tempted to schedule in regular massages, at least every month for the foreseeable future.

She put on the fluffy white and purple bathrobe which was heavenly soft, along with matching slippers and went out to the lobby to wait for Athena.

She was surprised to find that a lot more people were milling about.

Must be rush hour.

Athena wasn't there yet, so Rosemary sat down in the waiting room, reading the pamphlets and leafing through other magazines, while also discreetly ogling the various guests who walked through.

She read in one of the brochures that people came and stayed in the various bungalows around the main building, to restore and replenish their energy. It was a destination for magical people from all around the world.

A woman with flaming red hair and a bright red dress, who

looked like she was almost on fire herself, sauntered through the lobby. Rosemary wondered what kind of creature she was.

A large man wobbled in looking as if he was almost made of jelly. He became increasingly less human though kept on his bowler hat as he approached the reception area. Ferg ushered him into a room at the side.

There are all kinds of creatures out there that I hardly know anything about.

It was hard to believe that a few months ago she'd thought magic was something entirely confined to fairy tales and fiction, and now she found herself heavily immersed in a fantastical world.

A group of people in lime green business suits walked through. It looked as if they were all part of the same club or on a business trip. Rosemary caught a glimpse of someone walking away, down the passageway behind them, in pastels with a familiar black bob cut.

Rosemary stood up and began to walk after her, heart hammering in her chest, and the palms of her hands beginning to itch.

Despina!

She hadn't seen the woman since the Bloodstone Society's thwarted attempt to steal the Thorn family magic, months before. Rosemary had put a stop to it, including destroying the leader, a young looking but ancient vampire who had been masquerading as Despina's niece. The very same niece who may well somehow still be alive and trapped in the little wooden carved box that had been stolen from Thorn Manor recently.

Rosemary hadn't seen Despina since. The woman disappeared down the hallway and Rosemary ran after her but was stopped by an arm catching her shoulder.

"Mum! What are you doing?"

Rosemary turned to find her daughter there.

"Despina was just here. We've got to stop her."

Athena gave her a strange look. "Are you sure?"

"Of course I'm sure," said Rosemary. "My hands were itching and everything."

"Mum, we've discussed this. Your allergy to realtors is completely psychosomatic; it's not a real thing."

"A little while ago you thought magic wasn't a real thing," Rosemary reminded her daughter. "How is an allergy to realtors any less bizarre? Anyway, we don't have time. We have to go after her."

Athena shrugged and followed her mother down the corridor, but the woman had disappeared. Rosemary tried to go into a few of the rooms, but after getting yelled at by a few unusual creatures she decided she'd better not create any more disturbances.

"Did you even see her face?" Athena asked.

"Not exactly," said Rosemary. "But she was in pastels."

"Mum!"

"We should go home. It's not safe," said Rosemary.

"On a hunch? You must be joking. I thought you were supposed to be here to relax."

"I was totally relaxed until a moment ago. And now, I don't think I can afford to be."

"No," said Athena. "No way."

"What is it?" Rosemary asked.

"There is no way that you're ruining this. Not for you and not for me. Even if you glimpsed the back of someone who really was the estate agent vampire involved in attacking us, we've got no reason to believe that she knows we're here. And even if she does, we are way more powerful than we were before. The Bloodstones have been keeping relatively quiet, aside from a few weird little attacks. But if they came after us now, this would be the worst place to do it."

"Why is that?" Rosemary asked.

"Look around," said Athena. "We're surrounded by powerful magical beings and I'm pretty sure most of them aren't in league with a particular almost disbanded magical secret society."

Rosemary shrugged. "Okay, fair enough. You have a point."

"This way," Ferg called, motioning them towards the front desk. "Your lunch is being served by the pool. And then your facials will follow."

TWENTY-EIGHT

Athena sighed she let her feet sink into the foot spa and relaxed back into the unnaturally comfortable reclining chair. "I told you. This is just what we needed."

"Lovely, isn't it?" said Rosemary. "How sweet of Marjie to look after us like this."

"Aren't you glad you didn't go running off after an estate agent vampire look-alike?"

"I suppose so. But I'm still worried."

"Look," said Athena. "You've got to leave things like this to the authorities. I know you think you're some kind of detective now. But really this isn't something you should be sticking your nose into. You've already called Neve and told her your wildly paranoid theories. Now let her deal with it."

"You're probably right," said Rosemary. "It's just that the authorities haven't exactly had a great track record. Don't get me wrong. Neve's smart and I'm sure she's good at her job. But she has the habit of disappearing when things get gnarly. And I haven't exactly seen proof of her effectiveness yet. I know she's smart and I don't mean to speak ill of a good friend..."

"But Mum, you haven't exactly let her show off her effectiveness because you keep meddling in everything and getting in the way."

"Who knows what would have happened if I just let things take their course?" said Rosemary. "We would probably have been killed by the Bloodstones, and even if we'd managed to survive their attack you'd be stuck in the fae realm."

"It's also possible your meddling made things worse before you made them better."

Rosemary sighed. "Maybe. Marjie keeps telling me off for getting involved in everyone else's problems instead of solving my own."

"Well, Marjie is absolutely right." Athena glared at her mother.

"Time for your facial," said the spritely attendant whose name Athena had already forgotten, though with a shock of orange hair and baby green eyes, her appearance was certainly memorable. "Here's your facialist, now."

"Thank you," said Rosemary. The door opened and a familiar face peered in, shrouded in long wavy light blonde hair.

"Ashwyn!" said Rosemary. "What are you doing here?"

"I come here in the weekends, and sometimes do special treatments during the week," said Ashwyn. "It helps to keep our business in the black, to have a few additional income streams on the side."

"But aren't you supposed to be out of town?" Athena asked. "Mum said something about your cousin's baby."

"We just got back this morning." Ashwyn took out her phone and showed them a few photos of a very chubby newborn with a squished up face.

"Why do newborn babies always look like aliens?" Athena asked.

Rosemary nudged her gently with her elbow. They were seated far enough apart that she couldn't reach to have any jarring impact and Athena was grateful for that.

"What? It's true," she continued.

"You're right," said Ashwyn with a musical laugh. "Newborn babies do look rather odd, don't they? Anyway, I had to come back this morning in time for work. Now, tell me, is there any special kind of effect you want from the facial?"

"What do you mean?" Athena asked.

"Well, sometimes people want more luminous and glowing skin and other people want to look a bit younger. We get all sorts here. But they mostly fit into two camps. The ones going for health and the ones going for more 'special effects' shall we call them?"

"Is it a little bit like magical plastic surgery?" Athena asked, feeling awkward.

"Something like that," said Ashwyn. "Though it only lasts for about a month before the glamour starts to wear off."

"Well, I don't think it matters too much for me," said Athena. "Apparently, no one can see my true features anyway, unless they're fae."

"That's a good point," said Ashwyn. "My sister has the same thing. People can tell she's gorgeous. But it's like they don't really *see* her. They can't recall the specifics."

"So strange...the fae magic," said Rosemary.

"Tell me about it," said Athena.

"I don't want to go overboard," said Rosemary. "I mean, I still want to look like myself. Just, you know...make me look like I've had a few good nights of sleep and a lot of adequate hydration. That should do the trick."

Ashwyn laughed. "I'll give you our classic skin healing and hydration treatment then." She went about mixing together various items from tubes and bottles into a little bowl before she started applying it to their faces.

"Are you going to do the thing with the cucumber?" Athena asked. "I've always wanted to have that."

"Then of course," said Ashwyn. "Everyone always wants that. I think because it's so popular in the movies."

"I certainly feel like a celebrity," said Athena.

A few minutes passed, and Ashwyn finished applying the healing face masks and the cucumber slices over their eyes, then she left them to relax.

Athena took a deep breath, feeling more tranquil than she had since she'd entered the fae realm. "My skin's all tingling. It feels nice."

"While you're a captive audience," said Rosemary.

"Oh no, Mum. This is not the time to start heckling me about anything. It's bad enough that I can barely leave the house these days."

"I wanted to talk to you about something that happened earlier."

"We've already talked about that," said Athena.

"No, not that," said Rosemary. "I mean, before, when I first arrived. The woman who gave me the massage was the mother of your friend Elise."

"Oh," said Athena. "It's funny. I've never met her. And now you have. It seems a bit weird, doesn't it? I know, maybe it's because *you never let me go to my friend's houses!*"

"Something like that," said Rosemary. "But Elise and her mum do seem lovely. I might be comfortable waving that rule for a special situation, especially seeing as it seems you've learned your lesson for now."

"Really?" said Athena, with a spark of excitement. "You'd let me go and visit Elise's place?"

"As long as you don't go doing anything stupid. Anyway..."

"Oh, I see," said Athena. "Now, having dangled the carrot, you're going to give me the stick."

"I just wanted to ask you about something," said Rosemary. "Fleur was telling me her daughter seemed quite tired and withdrawn lately. She said it was something to do with going to the fae realm."

"Mum," Athena started. She didn't want her mother to pry into her personal experiences, but she knew it was inevitable.

"Fleur seemed to think that anyone of fae type heritage, who went into that realm, felt like they were much more at home there. She said it felt so good there they just wanted to return, and that was what was making Elise feel so low."

Athena was silent for a minute, mulling it over. What could she tell her mother that wouldn't just stir her worries and make things even more challenging at home? She didn't want to lie about this, mostly because she didn't think she could get away with it.

"I have felt a bit like that," Athena admitted.

"Why didn't you tell me?" Rosemary asked.

"Why do you think, Mum? This is a situation that you've constructed. You're so paranoid, and I can't do anything. You're so worried about me that it doesn't exactly make me want to reveal the whole truth to you, does it?"

"I thought we were over this," said Rosemary. "I thought we were done with secrets."

"You just make it so hard," said Athena. "I can't tell you everything because I'm scared you're going to overreact and make my life even worse."

"I thought you were *glad* to be back."

"I was," said Athena. "I am. It's just...I can't help the way I feel. When I went there, it was like...well, sure it was weird and strange. You were there. You understand. But the thing is, I kind of lit up like

I belonged there. I'd never felt anything like that. It's like that place stripped away a whole lot of my worries. In comparison to being there, this world feels so heavy. I'm still getting used to it."

Her mother was silent for a moment and Athena wondered whether she was getting herself into even more trouble.

"Okay," Rosemary said eventually. "Thanks for telling me."

"You're not going to confine me to my room?"

"Of course not. That's hardly going to help the situation is it?" Rosemary sighed. "I guess I'm just realising that I need to build back your trust, just like you need to build mine."

Athena felt a stab of guilt. She hadn't told her mum the whole truth. She certainly wasn't about to start talking about how she'd snuck out at night several times over the last week to cut a hole to the fae realm in her nightie just to get a hit of that good feeling again. She wasn't going to risk losing what small freedom she currently had, even if it was something she had to steal in the middle of the night.

"It helps, hanging out with people like Elise," said Athena, hoping her mother would give her a little more freedom. "And even Una. It gives me a little bit of that feeling again without having to go anywhere."

Athena wasn't lying, even if she was angling for a particular outcome.

"That's good to know," said Rosemary. "We can work with this. Maybe...maybe you can see more of your friends. And I'll let you go to Elise's house if that's what you want to do. Just promise me—"

"We'll be careful. I promise," said Athena. Her guilt was only intensifying.

CHAPTER
TWENTY-NINE

Rosemary and Athena the left the spa feeling calm and relaxed, after all the pampering.

"I haven't felt this good in a long time." Rosemary checked her glowing reflection in a window as they headed to the car. "Thanks for making me stay."

"Anytime you need somebody to boss you around, you know who to call," said Athena.

Rosemary smiled. It was wonderful to see her daughter in such a good mood. She thought back to the conversation they'd had earlier over the comments that Fleur had made, and realized that Athena had seemed reasonably reserved lately. In comparison to how she was now, at least, with her eyes sparkling.

Rosemary started up the engine and they began to drive. "You know, I haven't seen you light up like this in quite a while. How was your morning anyway, what did you get up to, before you came to the spa?"

"It was nice," said Athena, cheerfully. "I just played with the kids and the kitten, and did some work on my essay for folklore and mythology. Granny's got some really good old books. I have to be careful with the pages."

"Find anything interesting?" Rosemary asked.

"Actually, I think I did. Beltane is supposed to be named in honour of one of the very old gods, and there's not much information about him around. There's plenty on Brigid and Cerridwen and Cernunnos and all of those younger ones. They've only been around for a few thousand years."

"Spring chickens then," said Rosemary, wondering exactly how old Burk was.

"Exactly," said Athena. "But the old gods... well, It's really hard to know what they were all about. Beltane is named after the ancient god Belamus, who was also called Belli."

"That's kind of cute," said Rosemary. "It reminds me of a dog. You know, when they roll over and they want belly rubs."

"I'm pretty sure that's offensive Mum," said Athena. "And I don't think he was cute, exactly."

"That's a shame," said Rosemary. "A cute god sounds much more palatable than most other forms of god I can think of."

"Yeah, well, we might have a problem," said Athena. "The books hint that if the Cavalia happens again, we might have a very, very old God on our hands."

"What do we know about him?" Rosemary asked.

"Well, it was a cult that worshiped him all the way through Italy," said Athena.

"Not so cute sounding," said Rosemary, she looked out on the countryside as they drove, checking for fires. "What did they do?

Athena shrugged. "That's kind of the problem. Nobody seems to know. In fact, the only thing that I could find out about him was that he's thought to be the grandfather of many of the gods from around here. And he's something to do with light..."

"Light?"

"Yes, God of light," said Athena.

"Love and light," said Rosemary, weakly. "It sounds kind of hippy dippy, and I'm not a fan of toxic positivity but surely light is better than carnage or something?"

Athena made an uncertain sound. "Granny's books have some details about how he would ride across the sky on a great golden chariot."

"Subtle guy," said Rosemary.

"Oh yes, quite flashy, and I think he's got horns on his head or antlers or something," Athena continued on babbling away enthusiastically about the tidbits she had pieced together from the old books.

Rosemary smiled warmly. It was so nice to see her daughter really happy and enthusiastic about something.

She felt proud, not only that Athena was getting into her schoolwork for a change, but that she was coming into her own. She could certainly hold up against Rosemary's magic the other day, which gave her hope regarding future attacks.

Athena would be able to look out for herself.

Rosemary wasn't sure about this Belamus character and she hoped he wasn't about to show up on a flaming chariot and turn the town into soup or cinders, but she didn't want to worry too much in this moment. She just wanted to enjoy listening to her daughter.

After everything they'd been through over the past few months, all the ups and downs, and all the arguments they'd had, they seemed to have found a new even keel.

Rosemary felt like she just might be ready let go of the reins a bit more, to let Athena demonstrate her sense of responsibility, and have a little more freedom, along with it.

THE SUNLIGHT WAS BEGINNING to fade as Rosemary pulled up in Myrtlewood town. It was part of their gift from Marjie to have afternoon tea at her shop after the spa, though the pampering had taken so long that it was almost closer to dinner time. Fortunately the tea shop stayed open later on Saturdays in case people wanted to stop in for Marjie's signature pies and pasties.

"You both look so radiant, you're practically glowing!" said Marjie as Athena and Rosemary walked into the shop. "And just in time for tea!"

"Oh Marjie," said Rosemary, giving the older woman a big hug. "Thank you so much. We had a wonderful time."

"Yes, thanks!" said Athena.

"I hope you haven't gone to too much trouble over afternoon tea," said Rosemary, as she surveyed the table Marjie gestured them over to, heavily laden tea with delicious looking things.

"Oh," Marjie blushed. "I might have prepared with special versions of your favourite cakes," she said.

"These are the two cakes we had the first time we came to the tea shop," said Athena. "You remembered! I had chocolate and Mum had lemon sponge."

"How sweet of you," said Rosemary. "And there are the strawberry tarts I can't get enough of."

"You're so wonderful," said Athena, giving Marjie a kiss on the cheek.

"Oh, It's nothing," said Marjie. "You know I enjoy fussing over the two of you. You're the family I never managed to have. And giving you a special day of pampering is exactly the kind of thing that brings me joy, followed by a late afternoon tea – my treat."

"Marjie, you're exactly the kind of person I want to be when I finally grow up," said Rosemary with a laugh.

Athena shot her a wry look.

"Don't grow up too soon, mind," said Marjie. "You've still got your whole life to live. You might as well look and feel radiant while you do it!"

"I do feel like I'm glowing," Rosemary said. "Or at least I'm rather relaxed. I don't even need any of your special remedy this time."

"No," said Marjie. "I'm afraid if you had some of it now you might drift away and float right out of the tea shop."

They ate their cakes and sipped tea in silence, enjoying the good feelings soaking in, post-spa. As they sat there, the bell above the door tinkled and Una walked in, her shiny brown hair falling in perfect ringlets.

"Good to see you," Athena said, as Una approached.

"I've so been looking forward to catching up!"

"Come and join us," said Rosemary, remembering what Athena had said about feeling even better around other fae. She swept a cream cake to the other side of the table and gestured for her new friend to sit down.

Una smiled. "I can only stay for a minute. I need to go and sort of few things out at the shop before we reopen again tomorrow. I'll have my usual," she said to Marjie who returned moments later with another pot of tea and some bliss balls.

"I take it you don't go in for chocolate cake?" said Athena.

"I'm afraid to say it doesn't agree with me," said Una. "Which is a shame because it looks delicious." She glanced longingly at Athena's plate. "I can't really have dairy."

"Oh, of course," said Athena. "I'm sorry."

"No, no, it's fine," Una replied. "I'm used to it, and wheat gives me a rash as well. It's not really ideal either way. But Marjie does a lovely job of accommodating me and makes me these very delicious, healthy bliss balls. They're not quite the same as cake. Now... there was something you wanted to talk to me about?" she asked Rosemary.

Rosemary looked at Athena, wondering whether this was an acceptable topic to broach in front of her teenager, then decided she might as well. It might be good for Athena to hear the conversation anyway, considering what she *was*. Rosemary just hoped she didn't get teased too mercilessly about it afterwards.

"Well, a few weeks ago..." said Rosemary. "I didn't realize that at the time, and in fact, I didn't remember until after I'd had your special memory tonic. But anyway, I saw you sitting at the pub with Perseus Burk."

Athena coughed and Rosemary could tell she was trying not to giggle.

"Oh, yes. He and I are friends," said Una.

"Okay then," said Rosemary. "That's... that's nice." She shot Athena a warning glance. It looked as though the teen was teetering on the edge of bursting out with something inappropriate.

"The thing is," said Rosemary. "I just wanted to talk to about it because..."

"'cause Mum likes him!" said Athena. "And she's obviously jealous."

"No, it's not that at all," said Rosemary, blushing. "We've covered this a billion times before."

Una was blushing too.

"No, the reason I wanted to bring it up," Rosemary continued. "Is because you know what he is... uh... you know what he is, don't you?"

Una raised her eyebrow. "Uh... a Capricorn?"

Rosemary stuttered, knowing that it was considered very rude to *out* vampires without their consent. "Not exactly."

Una laughed. "I'm joking. I know what he is."

"Oh, good," said Rosemary. "But do you know that... 'Capricorns'..."

"You can say it, Mum," said Athena. "It's not like we're in the fae realm and no one else is around."

"Okay," said Rosemary, feeling a ramble coming on. "Vampires. They... they have a sort of long and sordid history where they hunted your kind to the brink of extinction in the human realm and I just wondered if you knew about that and whether it was safe for you to be hanging out with them because I'm just trying to look out for you."

"Oh," said Una. "I see what you mean."

"Sorry, if it's patronizing," said Rosemary. "It's just that... I thought since you weren't raised around your own kind, and you don't necessarily know very much about it, I worried that you might not be aware and it might be dangerous. And I wanted to warn you."

"I get it," said Una.

"Mum, you can stop talking now," said Athena, stifling another laugh.

Rosemary cleared her throat and took another sip of tea to try and quell her own instincts which inevitably led to her babbling uncontrollably in any possible awkward situation.

"Yeah. I know a little bit about that," said Una. "But there's nothing to worry about. The thing is with, with Perseus he's... he's not like that. You know as vampires age they often get more refined and controlled."

"But his brother," said Rosemary.

"His brother was a bit of a deadbeat," said Una, sadly. "But anyway, Perseus is a perfect gentleman. He's lovely."

"And do you think he knows?" Athena asked.

"Knows what?" Una asked.

"Knows what you... we... are?"

"I think so. I mean It's not something we explicitly talk about."

"I thought you said you were friends," said Athena, pushing her plate away and crossing her arms.

"We are friends," said Una, looking slightly embarrassed.

Rosemary had a creeping sense of jealousy again.

"And I I'm sorry, I didn't realize you had feelings for-"

"It's not like that," said Rosemary.

"I can assure you it's not like that with us either," said Una. "We just catch up from time to time and have dinner. Believe me, you are in safe hands with Perseus he wouldn't hurt a fly. Well, okay, he would hurt flies and probably other vampires and demons..."

"Demons?!" said Rosemary, her eyes widening. "Demons are real too?"

"Of course they are," said Una.

"I was kind of hoping they weren't," Rosemary admitted.

"What kind of world do you think we live in?" Una asked.

"I'm wondering that more and more every day," said Rosemary.

"Anyway," Una continued. "I'm Perseus wouldn't hurt any of us. He's really a lovely person. Athena's in safe hands around him. In fact, I bet he'd protect you both, no matter what, even if it was putting himself at risk."

Rosemary felt her shoulders soften as she visibly relaxed, surprised at how relieved she felt that Athena would be safe around Burk.

"See Mum? I told you there was nothing to worry about," said Athena. "I'm safe. We're fine. We can carry on with our lives now."

Una smiled. "You know, it's so lovely being in your presence," she said to Athena. It's refreshing."

"Umm, thank you?" said Athena.

"You're welcome to come and visit us again sometime," Rosemary said.

"I'd like that," Una replied. "How about tomorrow afternoon."

"It's a date," said Rosemary.

CHAPTER

THIRTY

The sky was darkening outside but a red flash caught
Rosemary's eye thought the window of the tea shop.

"No!" she gasped.

"What?" asked Athena, turning around.

They watched as bright flames flared from the town square,
growing higher.

"Oh gross," said Athena. "This isn't one of those magical fires
that makes people get all icky, is it?"

"I'm afraid so," said Rosemary, watching as the red and orange
fire became tinged with pink. "Stay in here."

"Mum!"

Rosemary shot her daughter a concerned look. "Seriously. You
do not want to go near this."

"Fair enough," said Athena. "This is one dangerous situation I
really don't want to get involved in. But do you ha—"

"I'm glad you see it my way." Rosemary ran towards the door
before Athena could stop her.

"Don't lose your head or your panties!" Marjie called out,

waving from the kitchen as Rosemary stormed past the counter. "There's a fire hydrant outside if you need it."

"Thanks." She pushed open the door and stalked out.

"Run away!" she yelled towards the people gathered in the town square who'd stopped to look at the sudden appearance of fire. They didn't seem to respond. "It's not safe!"

"There'll be an explosion if that builds up," said Ferg popping up out of a hedge to Rosemary's left.

"No, they certainly will not," said Rosemary. "Listen, just get as far away as you can, and take people with you."

"Roger that!" said Ferg taking off at a gallop. He began moving the dazed bystanders along, seemingly unaffected by the blaze. Rosemary recalled what Sherry had said about Ferg not being a romantic or sensual sort. In this situation it seemed ideal!

Rosemary needed water. Unfortunately she didn't have the first idea of how to open a fire hydrant. She could see the sign and the little square tile on the ground in yellow. But obviously she didn't have her own fire hose and she was... feeling rather warm as she stood there in the fires glow. Warm and melty.

She pushed through the carnal flush from the flames and was grateful that nobody else was around to see it as she reached down and tried in vain to open fire hydrant to turn it on. Nothing happened.

"Desperate times call for desperate measures," she muttered to herself, feeling her legs press together in a rather pleasurable way. She focused on the hydrant, trying to push the seductive feel of the magic away.

"Stop it, Rosemary," she scolded herself. She needed to concentrate. Just then, she remembered something that Athena had told her about automancy, the kind of automatic magic that the Thorn family apparently specialised in. That was exactly what she needed.

"Come on then," Rosemary said to the fire hydrant. "Come on. I know you're in there."

She focused down on it.

"There's something in you that just wants to spill water everywhere," Rosemary said, encouragingly. "Wake up. You know you want to!"

"What are you doing?" said Ferg.

Rosemary jumped.

"Magic," she grumbled. "Go away."

"It's not like any magic I've seen before. It seems like you're just talking to an inanimate object. Haven't you noticed the fire's getting bigger?"

"Ferg," said Rosemary with a warning in her voice. "Unless you're also a part time firefighter who knows how to—"

"Okay, okay," said Ferg. "I know when I'm not wanted. I'll just go and check on the those folk who were in the square. They're all acting a bit weird."

Rosemary ignored him and focussed back on the fire hydrant, willing it to life.

A moment passed and she had the strange sensation that she was staring right into the heart of object.

Something clicked in her mind and it sparked to life.

There was a clunking sound and then a gurgle. Water burst forth, showering Rosemary, but not going anywhere near the fire.

"Good," she said to the hydrant. "That was the first step, now..."

"Rosemary! Get out of there!"

Rosemary turned towards the familiar voice to find Burk careening right into her.

"*You* get out of here!" she yelled, gripping his the arms of his suit which were quickly soaking with water.

Burk was the absolute last person she wanted to see when she was feeling like this.

"Rosemary?"

She grimaced. "It's bad enough having to sort out my own dramas involving you, let alone you actually being here in person."

"What are you talking about?"

"Listen. I've got the situation under control. You can leave," said Rosemary, though Burk did seem awfully tantalizing standing there in is crisp white sign a shirt and expensive looking drenched suit.

Rosemary knew she had other more pressing matters to attend to. But surely they could wait just a few moments...

She reached towards his starched collar.

"Rosemary, what do you think you're doing?" he said.

"Less talk, more action," she said, and pulled him into a kiss.

Something in the back of Rosemary's mind screamed at her. This wasn't the time or the place.

She pulled away.

Burk stared at her in stunned shock and Rosemary came to her senses.

"Oh no... Oh no, no, no! What have I done?"

A growl sounded behind them and Rosemary tuned to see Liam standing at the front of his bookshop staring daggers.

Burk cleared his throat. "This is..."

"You're obviously not affected by this magic," Rosemary muttered, pushing Burk away. She was battling desire, confusion, embarrassment and social awkwardness all at the same time.

Morbid embarrassment, perhaps was a better word as she realised Athena, Marjie, and countless others were watching the whole fiasco from a safe distance.

Liam lunged towards Burk.

Rosemary sensed a blast of her magic automatically coming out of her hands in some kind of defence mechanism.

Liam fell backwards.

Another growl sounded, this time not from Liam but from the fire itself.

"*What...* was that?" Rosemary asked.

She turned to see a beautiful, delicate creature looking at her through the flames.

"You growl?" she asked the creature, before noticing that behind it was a great horned beast.

"Oh no you don't," said Rosemary. She flung her hands towards the fire hydrant, willing the water to spray in the direction of a fire. The effect was a little bit like putting a thumb over top of a running hose.

The water spurted out sideways, not only blasting the fire, but also hitting Rosemary, Burk and Liam, covering them all with water.

Rosemary ducked out of the way of the strong spurt and then pivoted around to aim it more directly towards the fire.

The flames grew brighter and it began to sizzle, then a great cloud of steam rose up and the entire blaze disappeared, creatures and all.

Rosemary shook herself. "That was a close call," she said. She wasn't sure if she was talking about the situation with Burk and Liam, or the fire itself.

"Oh my *goddess*," said Athena as she emerged from the tea shop.

"I don't suppose there was a chance that you happened to miss seeing all that," said Rosemary.

"Not a chance in Hades," said Athena. "In fact, I think the entire town saw."

Rosemary looked around to see that indeed, many of the town's people were standing around, ogling her.

"I'm just gonna go home and hide in my bed for the next forty odd years," said Rosemary. "If you'll excuse me."

"THAT'S some love triangle you've got going on, Mum," said Athena as Rosemary drive them back to Thorn Manor. "I mean, I knew it was bad, but I didn't realize it was *that* bad."

"It's not a love triangle," Rosemary argued, gritting her teeth as she drove. "It was merely... a misunderstanding."

Athena laughed hysterically for several minutes. "I love how you kissed that very old, but also very-attractive-for-an-old-guy vampire in the middle of town, in front of your ex-boyfriend who you happen to be spending a lot of time with lately for 'medical reasons.' And you call it 'merely a misunderstanding'."

"It was the magic of the fire," said Rosemary. "I told you the spell or whatever it is makes people go wigity."

"Wigity?" Athena asked.

"Okay then frisky," said Rosemary.

"Gross!"

"Well, how would you explain it in ways that I won't be uncomfortable for you?"

"Look," said Athena. "I'm just saying it's obvious that there's something going on there. And then if you add Dad into the mix—"

Rosemary laughed. "You're dreaming."

"Come on! There's something there."

"Stop with your obsession with my romantic life," said Rosemary. "It's time for you to think outside the box."

"Yuck!"

"That's not what I mean," Rosemary grumbled. "All I'm saying is you're treating this like some kind of romance novel. We're not in Jane Austen, or one of those godforsaken paranormal romances I sometimes catch your reading."

"They're good books!" Athena insisted.

"Be that it as it may, it's not reality is it?" said Rosemary. "I have a lot of feelings..."

"Eww!" said Athena. "Please keep them away from me. I do not want to hear about your feelings."

"You're a walking paradox sometimes," said Rosemary. "The point is, none of my feelings make very much sense at all. And it doesn't help, that you're teasing me all the time."

"What else am I supposed to do for fun?" said Athena. "It's not like you're letting me out on the town much these days."

Rosemary sighed. "Oh, I haven't told you the worst part yet."

"There's a worse part than my mother making an absolute fool of herself in front of the entire township."

"I'm afraid so," said Rosemary, grimly.

"Out with it," said Athena.

"So, I'm pretty sure nobody else was close enough to see them," said Rosemary. "But there were creatures..."

"Creatures?" asked. "What do you mean? Did creatures cast the fire? It wasn't the Bloodstones?"

"Who knows?" said Rosemary. "They might well have been responsible, but the creatures I saw were actually in the fire?"

"Oh no! Do you think they're okay?"

"They seemed more than okay. In fact, I think they were part of the fire. It was more some sort of pixie-ish thing and a big beastie with horns."

Athena inhaled sharply. "This is not good. Do you think it could be *him*?"

"Who?"

"You know, Belamus, the Old God."

Rosemary shrugged. "Honestly, I have no idea. It could've been a Satyr for all I know or some other mythical beast. But maybe it is the old god dude."

"Okay then," said Athena. "My guess is it's one point for Ms Twigg and zero to Constable what's-his-face."

"Perkins," said Rosemary. "And yeah, I suppose if you don't actually have any theory about what's going on you're not going to get any points at all. We have to tell Neve!"

Fortunately, Detective Neve was at Thorn Manor when they arrived. Nesta had made a giant pot chicken soup with her grandmother's recipe. The children were all sitting around the dining room table. Tamsyn was there too, sitting next to little Elowen.

Tamsyn had been visiting the house a lot over the past week, and Elowen had been spending time at the small cottage in Myrtlewood that Marjie had helped Tamsyn to find. Marjie had all the connections. Clearly she was a good person to know. Rosemary wouldn't hesitate to call her the backbone of the community.

Elowen was happy alternating between the two homes but was transition towards living in the cottage.

Over a bowl of hearty and satisfying soup Rosemary and Athena filled Neve and Nesta in on the details of what had transpired that day. Athena, took pains to describe the scene of Rosemary's morbid embarrassment, making the children giggle about kisses.

"But other than that you had a good day?" Nesta asked.

Rosemary smiled. "I guess so. It's hard to remember now. But yes, the spa was lovely."

"It was," said Athena. "In fact, it was probably a perfect day. And then it was

made even more interesting. Mum is never going to live this down, although I'm slightly mortified of what my friends are going to say at school."

"It could have been a lot worse," said Neve.

Nesta gave her an uncomfortable look.

They'd obviously had the talk about what had happened at the mayor's house with Neve and her ex-girlfriend.

"That magic is incredibly powerful," said Rosemary. "Despite all my supposed magic, I really struggled to resist it. Although Burk seemed impervious."

"That makes it so much worse," said Athena.

"It does make it more embarrassing," Rosemary conceded. "It was kind of a one-sided thing."

"But he let you kiss him?" said Nesta.

The children giggled again.

"I think he was just shocked, actually," said Rosemary. "He didn't seem particularly enthusiastic. He asked me what on earth I was doing."

"Still, vampires move incredibly fast, don't they?" said Athena. "He could have pulled away at any time. And in fact, he could have stopped you from even getting close to him."

"What are you implying?" said Rosemary, narrowing her eyes. "Never mind, I know exactly what you're implying. This is not a romance book, for the millionth time!"

"No, you're right," said Athena. "In a romance book there would be far more kisses!"

Rosemary had the feeling that Athena had said that just to make the children giggle again, which of course it did.

"Alright, enough about me," said Rosemary. "How are you settling in?" she asked Tamsyn.

"Well, thank you," said Tamsyn. "I mean, things have been a little bit strange, but overall, it's great. It was wonderful of Marjie to connect us up with a cottage to rent. Elowen seems to be adjusting well to living with me. Though she still thinks it's funny that I got so old."

Elowen giggled.

"There is far too much giggling here tonight," said Nesta with a grin, which of course made the giggling even worse.

"I'm glad you're settling in well," Rosemary continued.

"Everyone's so lovely here," said Tamsyn. "I can't believe my family ever left this place. It already feels like home."

"Tell me about it," said Rosemary, though she noticed Athena had a sad look in her eyes at those words.

Rosemary reached out to pat Athena's shoulder. "Why don't you invite Elise over Next weekend? Or... I suppose you could go to her house. If that's okay with Fleur."

Athena smiled. "Thanks, Mum, I'll message Elise."

With her daughter's sadness averted, Rosemary focussed her full attention on finishing the delicious hearty soup, pushing all worries of fiery beasties out of her mind.

CHAPTER
THIRTY-ONE

Rosemary was just finishing up her soup when she noticed that Dain had a serious expression on his face. He'd been sitting at the table but had not joined in on the conversation. She hadn't been paying much attention, but as the giggling died down, Athena also seemed to notice something wasn't right with her father and abruptly changed the subject.

"Anyway, Mum. What's the next step for your chocolate shop?"

"I suspect it's mountains of paperwork," said Rosemary. "Plus, I need to learn how to run a business and how to professionally make chocolate. It seems a bit ridiculous doesn't it? What on earth am I getting myself into? I don't know the first thing about being a chocolatier."

"I'm sure you know the first thing and the second," said Nesta. "Probably the third and fourth too. You might not know everything, but you've got a lot of life experience."

"It does seem like a frivolous thing to be focused on," said Rosemary, "when there's so much else going on here. That fire today, Neve, it was something else. Athena was excited to tell you

195

about how I made a fool of myself. But there's more. Before I put the flames out, I saw creatures staring out at me from inside the blaze."

"What creatures?" Neve asked.

"It was some sort of fae or pixie-like thing."

"Inside the fire?" Neve said incredulously.

"It sounds a bit ridiculous, I know," Rosemary admitted.

"It sounds like what Athena was talking about the other day, actually," said Neve. "We need to look into this. I'm going to ask your teacher to come into the station and give a proper statement."

"I'm really glad that none of your records get transferred to the regular police stations," said Athena. "Can you imagine what that statement would look like?"

"Even the magical authorities are going to have a hard time with this," said Neve. "They might know magic, but this is something else, something ancient."

"That's what I was thinking," said Athena. "I've been working on my essay for folklore and mythology and I can hardly find anything about Belamus even though everyone's heard of Beltane."

"I hope you don't mind sharing the research you're doing with me," said Neve.

Athena smiled proudly. "I don't mind at all. It might not be all that helpful, though."

"There must be someone casting the spells or doing something to summon the fires," said Nesta. "These things don't just happen willy-nilly. Something different is going on here."

"We can try and find out," said Neve. "Of course we are already following our usual processes, but nothing's coming up. If only we had a real Rúnseall. It would make a huge difference if we could track down whoever is causing this."

"It's sad that my parents aren't around anymore, they were expert Rúnsealls," said Tamsyn. "But I could give it a whirl."

"Doesn't there need to be two of you?" said Rosemary, recalling a conversation they'd had earlier.

"There are two of us," said Tamsyn, reaching out to take Elowen's hand on the table.

The two sisters smiled at one another.

"I didn't realise a four year old was up to advanced magic," said Neve.

"Of course she isn't," said Tamsyn. "But I've been looking through my parents' old spell books. I found some of them in boxes in their attic after they passed away. And having the two people there isn't so much about them both needing to be advanced. It's more creating a kind of channel. Elowen has our same genetics, so hopefully she's inherited gifts, too. I know I can do some of the magic, but I haven't gotten into too much of it. Mum and Dad were always trying to get me to stay away from it after we moved. I think it was too painful for them."

"But it's worth a try," said Neve, looking tired. "You might not come up with anything, but I don't have any leads at the moment. Every single one that's cropped up so far has been a dead end."

"Okay," said Tamsyn. "It's the least I can do after everything you've all done for me...for us. I'll need a few days to practice and memorise some parts of the spell."

"Great, how about we reconvene on Tuesday?" Rosemary suggested. "And see what happens."

"Sounds good." Tamsyn was practically beaming. "I'm actually quite excited. I've been so looking forward to doing magic again."

Rosemary noticed a strange look passing across her daughter's face and Dain still seemed oddly serious, but she pushed her concerns away. She'd had enough to think about for one evening.

Rosemary was looking forward to curling up in bed, perhaps after a hot chocolate or two. She was on her way to the kitchen when there was a knock at the door.

She answered it, curious about who the night-time caller might be.

Liam was standing there, looking slightly dishevelled.

"Rosemary, I'm sorry to come so late. I just wanted to apologise for...*before*. I didn't mean what happened. It was sort of instinctual."

Rosemary gave a him a strange look. "It's instinctual for you to try and attack people?"

Liam nodded. "Unfortunately, the moon is waxing," he said quietly.

"Full Moon is not for another week." Rosemary was unimpressed. "I've been keeping an eye on it in the witchy calendar Marjie gave me."

"I know that," said Liam, lowering his voice and looking around to make sure no one was listening. "My wolf grows stronger in this part of the month, as the moon waxes."

"I have a right mind to wax you!" Rosemary said.

Liam gulped, but looked slightly excited by the possibility.

Rosemary blushed. "Oh, you know what I mean! You can't just go around attacking people. It's not socially responsible."

"I thought I had him under control."

"Him? Your wolf?" Rosemary asked in a horse whisper. "Do you have a name for him?"

"Fluffy," Liam admitted.

Rosemary was torn between laughing out loud and slamming the door in Liam's face. A rogue werewolf named Fluffy was the last thing she needed.

"Anyway," said Liam. "What you did the other day worked, or it seemed to for a few days...but clearly it hasn't stuck. When I saw you—"

"That's just great," said Rosemary. "Well, it's time for you to go home and tend to Fluffy yourself. Sorry I couldn't be of more help."

"Don't tell me you've given up," said Liam. "Rosemary, I need this. You can't just—"

"Hey. I'm not the bad guy, here," said Rosemary, feeling frustrated. "If there's something in you that goes around attacking people in town for no good reason, even in your human form, you can't make that all my problem."

"It's not like that," said Liam. "The only reason I attacked the vampire was because he had his hands..."

"On me?"

"Yes. I felt..."

"Possessive? Jealous?"

"I couldn't contain myself," said Liam.

"That makes it slightly more awkward," said Rosemary.

Liam looked downcast. "I can't help the way I—"

"Look," said Rosemary, feeling bad for him, but also desperately not wanting him to talk any more about feelings, especially when Athena could appear at any moment and listen in. "You're right. It's not your fault you have this...virus."

"It's not your fault either," said Liam. "I'm sorry for making it seem like you had to take responsibility for me and my problem. I don't expect anything of you, I just hope...This is the closest I've come to a cure. If there's anything you can do to help in the next few days...I'll do anything to return the favour."

"I'll see what I can do," Rosemary said. "But don't expect too much."

Liam's gaze moved from Rosemary's face to a point just behind her. She turned back to see Dain, standing with his arms crossed.

"Oh, I'm sorry," said Liam awkwardly. "I didn't realise you had company."

"No, no," said Rosemary. "He just lives here. Liam, this is Dain, Athena's father. Dain, this is my friend, Liam."

She expected them to reach out and shake hands, but instead

they both stood there, staring at each other like a couple of staunch tomcats.

"Really?" said Rosemary. "What is with this?"

"What?" Dain asked.

"This territorial behavior," she said, looking back and forth between the two men. "This is ridiculous!"

When neither of them budged or said a word, Rosemary turned back towards Liam. "Thank you for visiting," she said. "You should go now."

"Yes, it's time to go now, Liam," said Dain, waving to him with a smile.

Rosemary fixed Dain with a glare. Liam was also glaring at him when she turned back.

"Rosey, I'm sorry for bothering you." Liam had clearly decided to ignore Dain and focus on her instead. "And I'm sorry for my behavior before. You've done a lot to help me. I mean it, if there's anything I can do to help you, anything at all, just let me know."

"Thanks, Liam. Have a good night," said Rosemary, closing the door.

"Yeah, have a good night, Liam," Dain called, smiling even more broadly as he waved again and the door clicked shut.

Rosemary elbowed him. "That wasn't necessary."

"I'm just having a little fun," said Dain. "You seem to have a lot of suitors lately, *Rosey*."

"Rosey was a childhood nickname, and I don't have any suitors, thank you very much." She folded her arms. "Why doesn't anyone believe me?"

"Maybe because a beautiful woman such as yourself shouldn't be single. It's a crime."

"I'm sure that's sexist," said Rosemary. "I don't need a man to complete me – or a woman, or any kind of romance. Also that sounds like a pickup artist line."

Dain raised his arms in innocence. "I can't do anything right, can I?" he said. "I'm just the guy who lives here and has no life."

Rosemary smiled sympathetically. "You've actually done a lot of good things lately."

Dain looked at her questioningly.

"It's been nice to see you getting on so well with Athena and you've been great with the foundling kids. So, as weird as it is to have my ex living here, it's been good to have you around."

A big grin spread across Dain's face. "I'm glad you think so. I can think of a way you can properly thank me." He winked, and Rosemary felt the slight draw of Dain's fae magic, or perhaps it was just his natural charm. Either way, she was far too strong for it to get the better of her.

"Nice try," she said. "But I'm not falling for it."

"Pity," said Dain. "But you're right. It's been so good us being back together again."

"*We're* not back together," Rosemary insisted. "You know that. 'Us' was never going to work."

"Wasn't it?" Dain asked. "Or was it just that my problems were always ruining everything?"

"Your problems had a huge role to play," Rosemary admitted. "But we can't go back in time. It's too late for us. I'm not the young, innocent girl you met all those years ago."

"I don't want you to be innocent," Dain said, his lip curling.

"Dain, so much has changed since then. I need you to know that we're not together, okay? We're not going to be together. Athena needs you in her life—if you're going to be a good influence, anyway. She's been having trouble."

"What kind of trouble?" Dain said. It looked as if a storm cloud crossed over his face. "Is it that guy again?"

"No," said Rosemary, smiling at his reaction. "I think she misses the fae realm."

Rosemary explained the conversation she'd had earlier with Fleur.

"It makes sense," said Dain. "This world is a lot heavier. It's one of the things that I struggled with so much in coming here, why I was so prone to weakness when I couldn't give up my addictions."

"And now?" Rosemary asked.

"I'm stronger now," he said. "I was tortured for weeks, Rosemary. When you've been right to the brink of your own experience, you've been so far that you didn't know if you'd ever survive, and you've come back from that, you know what you're capable of. And you know what matters to you. You and Athena are what matter to me. I've been through hell, but I'd do it all again in a heartbeat."

Rosemary felt warmth spreading through her chest. "I appreciate the sentiment." She was going to continue with some kind of statement like 'but it doesn't matter' or 'but it's too late' or 'but that doesn't change anything', but nothing came out. So she left her previous words hanging. She didn't need to ruin the moment.

"How about some dairy free hot chocolate?" she offered and continued on to the kitchen.

CHAPTER
THIRTY-TWO

As was tradition in Myrtlewood, the school was closed in the week leading up to the seasonal festivals. Beltane was to be the following weekend. Yet that didn't mean all the work had to stop. Athena still had her essay due on Wednesday, but it did mean no classes, which also meant that Rosemary allowed Athena to visit Elise's house, even though it wasn't a weekend.

A sleepover; it was actually something Athena had never done before. She'd missed out on slumber parties with friends when she was younger because she never really had any close friends, only a few acquaintances who she spent time with at school. Besides, Rosemary and Athena had never really lived anywhere nice enough before to bring company, so if she had been invited over, she wouldn't have been comfortable returning the favour.

Now, however, things were different. Rosemary was dropping Athena off on the condition that she got to meet the parents, despite the fact that she'd already met Fleur.

"As long as you don't embarrass me," Athena said as they drove into the dense forests northwest of Myrtlewood.

"I'm surprised anyone lives out here at all," said Rosemary.

"Why not? It's lovely," said Athena. "All these green trees."

"What's wrong with our trees?"

"There's nothing wrong with trees," said Athena. "That's kind of the point. Besides, it's not a competition. It's not like they've asked me to move in or anything. I'm just saying. It's nice."

"It's nice where we live, too." Rosemary had been oddly defensive since the conversation at the spa where Athena had admitted to missing the fae realm, making Athena's other secret even harder to share with her mother.

The road became narrower and more gravelly as they continued on.

"I hope there's some way to turn round at the end," said Rosemary.

"She would have mentioned if there wasn't," said Athena. "I doubt you're the first person to drive down here. It is a road, after all."

"I suppose you're right," said Rosemary. "I'm just feeling nervous. I've never had to deal with anything like this before."

"Just relax, Mum. Why don't you go home and book in for another massage?"

"Ohh, maybe she offers them from home," said Rosemary.

"No, Mum. Absolutely not. You're not crashing my sleepover."

"That was a joke," said Rosemary. "Sort of."

"I'm serious," said Athena. "Don't you dare ask for a massage while I'm visiting my friend."

"Fine," said Rosemary. "Look. Here we are."

The little wooden house was almost camouflaged in the trees in front of them, painted green and brown and hoisted above the ground on stilts. Athena noticed little bridges made out of rope and wood running between the trees.

"It's adorable," said Athena.

"It's kind of like in that Star Wars movie with the bear creatures," said Rosemary.

"Mum," Athena said with a warning in her voice.

"What?"

"You're being weird – weirder than usual. Perhaps it would be better if you try to keep your mouth closed as much as possible. And don't stay long."

"All right, all right," said Rosemary. "I just want to meet them."

They got out of the car and made their way up a rickety wooden staircase towards a bell-shaped front door.

"It's like a fairy house," said Rosemary.

"Shush. Don't say things like that. It might be offensive. Remember, they are fae folk."

"Well then, it shouldn't be offensive," said Rosemary.

Athena shot her another warning glance and made a motion for her mother to keep her mouth shut.

The door opened before they could knock. A pretty blue-haired woman stood in front of them.

"You must be Athena," she said. "I'm Fleur."

"Hi," Athena said.

"Mum!" Elise called out, coming to the door. "It's okay, I've got it."

"Nice to see you again," Rosemary said, smiling at Fleur as Elise grabbed Athena's arm and pulled her into the house.

"Bye, then," Rosemary called out.

"Remember what I just told you," said Athena, hoping her mother wouldn't embarrass her.

Rosemary waved dismissively.

Athena pushed concerns about Rosemary's behaviour out of her mind as she followed her friend. "Your house is awesome."

"It's not enormous and fancy like yours," said Elise as they passed through a small cosy living room complete with quilts and crocheted pastel rainbow coloured doilies. "But it's quite nice here. This is my grandma, Ambrosia."

"Hello," said a woman who didn't look a day over fifty, smiling at them from a rocking chair where she sat knitting.

Athena barely had time to reply before Elise whisked her out of the room again.

"I thought your grandmother was supposed to be over a hundred years old," said Athena.

"She is," Elise replied.

"She doesn't look anywhere near that old. You've got good genetics."

Elise smiled. "Come up here. This is my room." She climbed up a wooden ladder. It was painted bright blue, almost matching Elise's usual hair colour.

Athena followed her to a kind of loft space. The ceiling fell in a triangle. There wasn't much room, just a reasonable sized bed, low to the ground, and little bookshelves lining the walls.

"It's lovely," said Athena. "What a nice space."

"It's not much," said Elise. "But it's home."

"You don't sound very enthusiastic when you say that."

"Oh, you know. When I say that word now it just reminds me of—"

"The fae realm," Athena said. "I totally understand."

"It's nice to have *you* around, though," said Elise. "When you're not here, I feel kind of drained and tired."

"I know the feeling," Athena admitted. She wanted to share the secret she hadn't told anyone else about, but now wasn't the time. "Things have been weird, recently. I didn't want Mum to know about it. Turns out she knows now though. It didn't help that your mother talked about it when she was giving Mum a massage."

"I'm sorry," said Elise. "Parents are so weird."

"That's the understatement of the century," said Athena.

"Never mind. It's okay now. It's probably for the best. At least Mum will let me out of the house to see you more often because she knows that it makes me feel better about being here in this world."

"That is a fortuitous turn of events," said Elise, folding her arms. "Now, would you like some tea?"

The rest of the afternoon passed in an enjoyable blend of tea and cake and conversations, followed by a supper of roasted fern roots and chestnuts which Athena found surprisingly delicious.

Later that evening, as they lay in Elise's bed, Athena felt inspired to let her friend in on the secret that she hadn't shared with anyone yet.

"I want to show you something," she said. "Just promise you won't tell anyone."

Elise gave her a look that was both excited and suspicious. "What is it?"

"Can we get outside from here? Without anyone noticing?"

"Of course we can," said Elise. "This way." She opened the window and showed Athena how to climb down the sturdy vines that grew up the side of the house. They scrambled down until they reached one of the rope bridges and made their way across to a little platform between three big old trees.

"This place is so awesome," said Athena. "I can tell why you like living here."

Elise smiled. "What is it that you want to show me?"

"Something you're going to like," Athena replied. She held out her index finger and took a deep breath before she began cutting a door in the air, just like she had the other nights recently.

"What are you doing?" Elise asked in a slightly panicked whisper.

"You'll see," said Athena.

A light glowed in the air, making a trail behind her finger. Elise gasped as whisps of fae realm magic flowed through. "Oh my goddess!" she said.

"It's feels good, doesn't it?"

"Yes," said Elise. "It feels amazing. It's wonderful!"

Athena beamed at her.

"Have you been doing this often?" Elise asked.

"Most nights," Athena admitted. "I probably shouldn't. It's dangerous, I know, but I can't help myself. It just feels like...like I'm meant to be there. Even though everything important in my life is here."

Elise nodded and took Athena's hand.

Just then, a large reddish coloured whisp in an almost human shape flew through the veil with such speed and force it pushed the two friends apart.

"What was that?" Elise asked.

"I don't know," said Athena. "That happens sometimes. I wonder if I'm letting things through that shouldn't be in this realm, but no high fae have tried to come through yet, so that's something."

"It's concerning, though," said Elise.

"I know."

"No...I mean like really concerning."

"Why?" Athena asked.

"Because I think sometimes when things pass between the realms, they do it in an incorporeal kind of way. That's what my Grandma said used to happen, back when the realms were more open. It was like she'd dissolve a bit when she came through and re-form on the other side."

"So you're saying—"

"You could be letting anything in!"

"Even fae?" Athena practically choked the words out.

"I don't know," said Elise. "I'm just a bit worried."

"Why, though?" said Athena. "I mean, aside from that nasty countess and her henchmen, it's probably fine. There's plenty of faery type creatures in the earth realm. What's wrong with a few more? Your grandmother seems harmless."

"You should see her in a temper. But anyway, plenty of us *are* harmless. The real reason I'm worried is that I got a sense...from whatever it was that just drifted through that it could potentially be something dangerous."

She reached for Athena's hand again and the light faded.

"You're really that worried?" Athena asked.

"I am." Elise gave Athena a knowing look. "I have a feeling that could have been a fire sprite."

"Oh...Oh, no," said Athena. "Are you sure?"

Elise shook her head. "I'm not a hundred percent sure. I just got that kind of vibe from it."

"Have you met one before?" Athena asked.

"In passing," said Elise. "But obviously not in this kind of situation. I've heard that the fire sprites who've been here for generations are quite different from the wild creatures in the fae realm."

"Do you think it's possible that I'm the one responsible for all the fires?" Athena asked, her voice rising in panic.

"I don't know," Elise said. "And part of me doesn't want to find out."

THIRTY-THREE

Rosemary joined roughly two hundred other residents of Mytlewood as they crowded town hall. Some faces were familiar, some were rather odd.

Marjie had phoned her early on Monday morning to tell her about the special meeting that night, called by Mr June, the Mayor. Rosemary hadn't wanted to show her face after the recent interactions with his highness, lord of pompousness, as she liked to call him inside her head, but Marjie had insisted that it was important.

The town hall was an old Edwardian building with high ceilings. Rosemary had never been inside before, and was relieved by the strong turn-out. She hoped it meant the mayor and his charming husband wouldn't notice her.

Ferg stood up first, and did a sort of blessing, thanking the elements of the four quarters and the town's patron goddess, Brigid. Next, it was the Mr June's turn to speak. He approached the podium with his black hair gelled back, wearing a long black and purple cape, edged in gold and draped over a three piece suit in matching colours which Rosemary thought was a rather dramatic choice of outfit.

"My dear townsfolk," said the Mayor. "I'm sure you understand the gravity of the situation we face, at least in part."

There was a murmur of concern from the crowd.

Mr June had a gleam in his eye as he continued. "There have been no less than sixteen fires around town over the past week or so."

Movement caught Rosemary's eye. She turned her head to see Detective Neve, clearly a late arrival, excusing herself as she slipped down the row to take an empty seat next to Rosemary.

Mr June cleared his throat and glared in their direction.

So much for not being noticed, Rosemary thought.

"What's happened?" Neve asked in a whisper.

"Nothing yet."

"If. I. may. *continue*," said Mr June, emphasising every word in a way that was laboured and unnecessary. "I'm sure you are all concerned for your safety, and the safety of your families. We understand that the fires are both real and also magical. That is, they can burn like an ordinary fire, but they also have some quite... unexpected effects."

"That's an understatement," said Neve, under her breath.

"I will allow our Chief Fire Attendant to come up here in a moment to give you more details on what to watch out for, but first, I must make an announcement. It is with a heavy heart that I must officially cancel the Beltane festivities."

A murmur of surprise and disappointment rolled around the room.

"But... that's outrageous!" said Ferg, standing up, clearly unable to hold himself back.

"Please sit down, Mr Burgess," said the Mayor. "You can ask questions later."

Ferg sat down, but Rosemary could still see the look or outrage on his face.

"I'm aware that this is almost unprecedented," Mr June continued. "We haven't had to cancel a ceremony in my entire time as mayor, though we did postpone the winter solstice once due to a stray banshee."

The audience laughed, though Rosemary didn't get the joke.

"In fact, no ceremony has been cancelled in this town since the fae troubles of Nineteen Twenty. But, in the interests of your own safety and the wellbeing of the town, we cannot risk a large gathering at this time. Not until we are clear of the dangers posed by the fires. Therefore Beltane will be cancelled, with a possibility of rescheduling it, if, and only if, this fire business is cleared up forthwith, though I'm afraid our local law enforcement are clueless as to the culprit."

He glared at Neve and then panned the room, his eyes narrowing in suspicion.

"If you have any information at all on these fires, please come forward to the authorities."

The audience broke into conversation as the Mayor finished up and passed the microphone over to the Chief Fire Attendant, who also happened to be Neve's ex.

Neve had a slightly uncomfortable expression as they watched her speak about the risks posed by the fired, something they already knew rather a lot about, from personal experience.

"What is it?" Rosemary asked.

"We're going to be overrun with hearsay and rumours for days, after what he just said. I'd bet on it. Besides, it's not going to help."

"The rumours?"

"No. Cancelling Beltane. It won't reduce risks. In fact, I think it will only make things a whole lot worse."

And that... Rosemary realised. *Is exceptionally suspicious!*

CHAPTER
THIRTY-FOUR

Athena paced her room, late into the evening hours. She'd been so stressed since she came back from Elise's house earlier that day.

She'd tried to hide it from her mother but had failed miserably. Thankfully, Rosemary had bought the excuse that her anxiety was over the essay on Beltane being due on the next day.

It was true that Athena had spent hours researching it, though she still wasn't very happy with the lack of information and how she'd tenuously tried to thread it together. Athena had never cared so much about school work before, and had never wanted to do well, but she loved Myrtlewood Academy, and besides, she wanted to beat Beryl just to wipe the smirk off her face.

It was slightly stressful, and the Beltane-related school work was only the tip of the iceberg. She hadn't been able to sleep the night before, not after realising that all of the problems happening around town with the fires might well be her fault. Rosemary already seemed overwhelmed with all the magical danger posed by their new life. Athena hadn't voiced it, but she was scared that one more disaster might push her mother over the edge and make her move them both out of town, and back to the mundane world where nothing made sense anymore.

The last thing Athena needed was for her already over-protective mother to find out that she might be the one responsible for the fires.

There might be no way to hide it if Tamsyn was able to do the finding spell...Unless Athena could come up with some kind of magic powerful enough to contradict it.

She had poured over Granny's most potent books but hadn't been able to find anything of use, until she came across a spell in one of the old Thorn spell books in the tower room.

The spell did look promising. Athena was hoping it would do the trick and that her now-functioning Thorn family magic would be able to get it to work well enough to mask her presence.

She couldn't risk Rosemary finding out and lose her freedom again.

She felt guilty to hide something as big as this, but she needed to stay hidden long enough that she could figure out how to fix what she might have done. That was a whole other mystery that she hadn't figured out how to solve yet.

Perhaps some kind of summoning spell would work. She could call all of the fire spirits or sprites or whatever they were and lead them back through the veil.

Rosemary wasn't exactly going to get on board with anything like that. Especially not if it involved Athena going into a different world again. So even though she did feel terribly guilty, she pushed it down, suppressing it.

"I have to figure out how to solve this on my own," Athena muttered to herself. "If I've created the mess, I'm going to clean it up."

She crossed her room, back to the old spell book that she'd brought down from the tower, and read over the spell again.

It looked complex at first glance and Athena had had to use a special book on old British runes to decipher some of the symbols. Though the more she looked at it, the more the magic intuitively made sense to her, apart from one perplexing piece – how could the tiny quantity of ingredients fill an entire cauldron?

Once she was sure Rosemary was fast asleep, she took the spell book back up to the tower room, grateful that it had been accessible to them ever since Granny had apparently vacated the building.

Athena needed to use the large cauldron and some of the ingredients up there that she'd previously catalogued in case they were of use.

It was a strange spell and Athena couldn't quite figure out how it all came together. There didn't seem to be enough liquid involved to fill the cauldron by any stretch. She sprinkled in the dry belladonna leaves and said the ignition charm to light the cauldron.

The leaves started to smoulder and she added in river stones, acacia bark, and four crushed dried hornets from Granny's supply cupboard, along with a spoonful of honey. The next step was to prepare a glass of enchanted spring water. Rosemary never bothered with expensive over-priced bottled water, but fortunately Thorn Manor prevailed. The fridge must have heeded Athena's mind's call. She found it stocked with dozens of bottles of water, complete with labels saying it was from a local spring. This was simple enough for Athena to enchant with an easy spell, though she did hope the remaining water disappeared before her mother saw it.

As the spell instructed, she began to slowly pour the glass of enchanted water into the cauldron at a trickle, while stirring with her other hand.

To Athena's astonishment, one small cup of water managed to fill the entire enormous cauldron.

Athena chanted the words that she didn't entirely understand, with the intention of hiding herself.

A scent a lot like lavender filled the room, along with billowing clouds of steam.

Satisfied, Athena took three drops of the potion on her tongue. It tasted like raspberries and had the unnerving effect of emptying the entire vessel so the cauldron became completely dry and clean as if she'd never put anything into it in the first place.

She felt an odd sizzling sensation inside her, and then a thudding like the beat of her heart, only heavier.

She checked herself in the mirror, but she looked quite ordinary. She stood for a moment longer, observing her reflection. She almost jumped as four large tendrils of light, like the legs of an octopus, sprang out from her back and wrapped around her, tucking her in like a new born baby into a blanket.

It would have been terrifying if the sensation wasn't so comforting.

As she stood there, the light faded away to nothing.

"Well," Athena muttered to herself. "Hopefully that worked and I'll be protected for a few days. If not, I suppose I'd better have a backup plan."

She offered a small prayer to the goddess Brigid and then slipped back down the stairs and into bed.

The next day, Athena woke feeling rested after a good night's sleep. The spell seemed to have the side effect of making her feel far more relaxed than she'd previously been.

She went downstairs for breakfast to find that Rosemary had already made pancakes.

Dain and Nesta were sitting around the dining table with the foundling children. Thea and Clio were staring determinedly at a fork as it levitated between them and Harry was cheering them on.

Definitely not normal children.

"I'm afraid we're not going to be here for too much longer," said Nesta to the children.

"Aww." They sighed. "Why not?"

"Well, Mei's mummy is well enough to travel. She's arriving soon," Nesta explained. "Mei and Neve are going to spend more time in our house with her. She's a little bit older and she needs some extra care."

"It'll be a shame not to have you around much," said Rosemary.

Athena nodded, although she did wonder whether it would be easier to keep a secret without having a detective in the house all the time.

The past few days, Neve had occasionally given her funny looks and Athena was worried that she might be found out.

"So that's the plan for today, then?" said Athena, trying to put a jolly tone in her voice.

"Yes," said Nesta. "Neve is picking her aunt up from the airport soon and is going to bring her here. We'll hang around for a bit while we get to know each other, which will give Tamsyn plenty of time to try the finding spell."

"Isn't it a bit much to do all in one day?" Athena asked, hoping to delay the inevitable.

Rosemary shrugged. "There's plenty of us around. If Neve has to go off for a little while to investigate anything, I'm sure we can hold the fort."

"But wouldn't we want her to be here for support?"

"Maybe," said Rosemary. "If that's the case, then we can do a bit of digging and report back."

Athena gulped. She hadn't even started eating her pancake yet.

She squeezed some lemon juice over it and sprinkled on sugar, though she barely paid attention to what she was doing.

She tried to think it over in her mind. She barely noticed the tangy, sweet flavour of her breakfast as she ate it.

"Oh look, here they are now," Nesta cried, getting up and going over to the doorway. Moments later, Neve and Nesta led in an old woman wearing a big grey coat, her black hair streaked with grey.

"Where is this you've brought me?" she said.

"Aunty, these are my friends, Rosemary and Athena," said Neve. She introduced them all.

"What is this house, Constantine?"

"This is Rosemary's house," said Nesta.

"No...this house. I recall...this is the house of Galderall Thorn."

"Yes, it was," said Rosemary. "I'm her granddaughter."

"Connie, where is my little girl?"

"Mummy!" Mei cried, running over and wrapping her arms around the legs of the old woman. "You got so old!"

The older woman laughed. "Yes. Yes, I did...I did get old. And you stayed so young."

It would have been enough to bring tears to Athena's eyes. And indeed, she noticed a few in the eyes of those around. She couldn't properly enjoy the moment as she was feeling too anxious about what was to come.

"You there!" Meng called out, pointing at Athena. "You. You are evil! You don't belong here."

Athena's eyes widened and her pulse quickened.

"Auntie, now, now," said Neve. "We've been over this. I'm sorry, Athena, she's still suffering from dementia, I'm afraid."

"Come on, come outside," said Nesta. "It's a lovely day." They led the old woman away.

Athena stood still, mortified.

"Sorry, love." Rosemary put her arm around her daughter's

shoulder. Athena didn't even shrug it off. Her heart pounded in her chest and she didn't know what to do. "Don't worry," said Rosemary. "You know she doesn't know what she's saying."

Athena tried to smile and nod and shrug casually, all at the same time. The problem was the old woman knew exactly what she was saying. She knew far more than anyone else seemed to about the real nature of the situation.

"I think I might just go to my room," said Athena.

"Wait," said Rosemary, turning back towards the front door. "Tamsyn's here."

Tamsyn came in with little Elowen. They were both dressed in red T-shirts with blue jeans.

"Elowen is excited about matching outfits," Tamsyn said with a smile.

Rosemary beamed. "Adorable!" She turned to Athena. "Put some tea on, will you love?"

"Okay," Athena replied weakly.

She went to the kitchen and started making tea as if on autopilot, trying not to think because thinking wasn't doing any good. She could hear the conversation nearby between her mother, Neve, and Tamsyn, which only made her feel worse.

"How does the spell work?" Rosemary asked.

"It's based on what we know about the fire sprites being involved," said Tamsym. "Whoever is behind that should be revealed to us."

Athena's hands trembled and she put in too many tea leaves. She poured them all out and then she realised, on her second attempt, that she was putting tea leaves into the kettle instead of the tea pot. She had to wash the whole thing out and start again.

On the third attempt, she finally made tea and carried it into the living room, only to find that her hands were shaking so much when she was pouring it that she slopped it all over the tea tray.

"Go and get a cloth," Rosemary said, not seeming to realise the state that Athena in. Rosemary could usually tell things like that and Athena wondered whether the binding spell was indeed protecting her, not only from spells, but also from her mother's perfectly ordinary intuition about what was going on with her.

She went to the bathroom and washed her face, then to the kitchen where she found a cloth to wipe up the mess. By the time she got back to the living room after giving herself a pep talk in the mirror, the spell was already underway.

Athena was trying to think of an excuse to make herself scarce when her mother said, "Come in and close the door."

Athena's heart shuddered in her chest. *Does she know?*

But Rosemary's expression seemed perfectly normal.

Athena wondered whether she could get away with closing it, but it was too late. She tried to press herself up against the wall, making herself as invisible as possible despite the fact that everyone could see her perfectly clearly.

If only I had found an invisibility spell, if such a thing exists. Then they wouldn't be able to find or see me.

Tamsyn moved her hands in a particular and unusual pattern, saying an enchantment that sounded Latin, or maybe French. She took hold of little Elowen's hands while they walked around in a circle over a map of Myrtlewood that had been placed on the ground.

"Here it goes!" said Tamsyn as a tiny spark of light shot up from between them and hovered in the air then plunged down towards the map, spinning around in circles over the township.

The spark vanished into the air in front of them.

"Did it work?" Rosemary asked.

Athena realised she was holding her breath.

Tamsyn shook her head. "It seemed like it was going to," she said. "But I can't see anything on the map that wasn't there before."

Athena let out the breath she'd been holding, grateful that nobody was paying any attention to her in all the confusion and excitement of the spell.

"I'm sorry," said Tamsyn. "I was sure we'd got it sorted. We've been practicing on my cat all morning."

"You've been doing spells on your cat?" Rosemary asked.

Elowen laughed. "Dixie! His name's Dixie!"

"Kind of," said Tamsyn.

"We had to find Dixie on the map," said Elowen, smiling.

"That's very clever," said Rosemary. "It sounds like a useful spell for when we can't find Serpentine, or someone else I know." She looked over at Athena, who tried to smile and shrugged.

"Hey, you pretty much always know where I am anyway, and I'm not a cat."

"You do have some cat-like tendencies," said Rosemary. "But we won't go into that now. It's a shame we don't have any leads on whoever is summoning these fires, if that's what's happening."

"Never mind," said Athena. "I'm sure we'll figure something out."

"I can try again, or maybe use another spell," said Tamsyn. "I'm not sure what happened, but it really should have worked."

"The other finding spells didn't work," said Athena.

"Most finding spells aren't that powerful," said Tamsyn, sounding confused. "But the ones in my family that fit with our magic...they should be able to find almost anything. I just...maybe it's my fault. I'm not as good as my parents."

Athena felt guilty, but she couldn't very well reveal that the spell would probably have worked perfectly well, had she not put in adequate protections against them.

"Never mind. You did your best," said Rosemary. "That's all any of us can really do."

Athena nodded and smiled and felt terrible.

221

CHAPTER
THIRTY-FIVE

Rosemary stirred the bubbling pot of porridge on the stove as the cooked breakfast for the remaining three children, herself and Dain. The house was quiet, though she occasionally heard squeals and laughter from the back yard. Neve had promised that good foster parents were being lined up, though Dain still wasn't sure that was the best idea, given his bad experiences, and the paperwork was taking so long to process that Rosemary wondered whether the children would be teenagers by the time things were all organised.

Athena had left early for the day, despite Rosemary's protests. Since Beltane was officially cancelled, so was Athena's school break. The teachers had taken an extra day to organise themselves and then expected everyone back at school as if the seasonal festival had already happened.

Mr June obviously thought this was the best way to return to 'normal', Rosemary disagreed. She didn't really want her daughter trudging off into the fiery wilderness when Neve thought it was only going to get *more* dangerous.

More fires have been reported across Cornwall since the Mayor's announcement, two with serious injuries requiring hospitalisation.

Rosemary had tried to get Athena to stay home, even promising that she'd be able to help with the investigation by rifling through Granny's books, but Athena had other ideas. She clearly didn't want to stay cooped up at home and Rosemary could hardly find a good enough reason for Athena to miss more of her education. She had already skipped a few weeks while stuck in the fae realm, besides it was refreshing to see Athena so interested in school work for a change.

There was a knock at the door and Neve let herself in. Rosemary had insisted on keeping the revolving door policy for her select closest friends, mostly because it saved her from having to open it so often.

Tamsyn followed close behind Neve with little Elowen in tow.

"Welcome," said Rosemary, as little Elowen caught site of the other children outside and ran out to join them. "Tell them breakfast is almost ready," Rosemary called out after her. Then she turned back to Neve and Tamsyn. "Would anyone like some tea?"

"Yes please," said Tamsyn.

"I could do with something stronger," said Neve. "My aunt has been quite a handful. But as it's still morning, and I'm technically on duty, I'd better stick with tea."

"I have some of Marjie's special tea tonic," said Rosemary.

Neve waved the offer away. "I'll be fine. I just need a moment of peace."

"How is Mei adjusting to the change?" Tamsyn asked.

"Mei is fine," said Neve. "In fact, sometimes I worry about how fine she is. Time in the fae realm sure seems to make children docile and easy going."

"I only wish it had that effect on teens," said Rosemary. "Of even on me! I'd love to feel relaxed and easy going."

Neve and Tamsyn laughed.

"She does miss the other kids. That's the only thing that seems to upset her," Neve continued. "It's the worry I have about fostering out the other three kids. What do they really know of this world apart from us and each other?"

"Hopefully we can keep them close enough to visit," said Rosemary.

"That's the problem," Neve said. "All the available foster homes are in Burkenswood or further afield."

Rosemary sighed. "As adorable as they are, I really don't think I'm cut out to foster three more children. I can barely cope with Athena, sometimes."

Neve smiled. "We never expected them to stay here in the long term. Don't worry. We'll figure something out. You've already done more than enough to help, and it pains me to ask you for anything else, but—"

"I take it this isn't just a social visit, then?" Rosemary asked, her voice tightening in concern.

"I called Neve because I think I've figured out how to cast the finding spell differently so that it doesn't rely on a map. For some reason, that didn't work last time."

"From what Tamsyn told me on the way over," said Neve. "We should be able to just follow the spell and find out who is letting all those fire sprites into this realm."

"Where's Athena?" Tamsyn asked. "Does she want to help with the spell?"

"She went off to school early today," said Rosemary. "Now that the holidays for Beltane have been cancelled, she can't wait to get away from me."

"Teenagers are so surprising sometimes," said Neve. "It's like she doesn't want to have a holiday at all."

"I suspect she just wants to see her friends," said Rosemary, smiling.

They drank their tea, quietly, while Rosemary multi-tasked, finishing off the children's breakfast. They'd graciously slept in that morning, leaving the adults to get a bit of extra well-needed rest.

"Alright then. Shall we get started?" said Tamsyn.

Rosemary turned the pot of porridge off. "I'll just check with Dain to see if he's okay to feed the kids breakfast and look after them while we do the spell."

She went out the back and called out to Dain. He looked exhausted from running around with the kids, and was perhaps a little emotionally distant, but happily agreed to mind them for an hour or two.

"What would I do without you?" Rosemary said.

"Find a new man slave," said Dain, with a grin.

Rosemary couldn't help but smile at his teasing, though it also made her want to throw something at him. There was no time for theatrics. She went back inside to find Tamsyn and Neve setting up in the lounge.

"All right," said Tamsyn. "Technically, this is a simpler spell. But I'm hoping that the way I've worked it will make it more powerful than the last one. I'll just go and get Elowen and then we can begin."

Neve looked at Rosemary. "Thank you for helping so much with this," she said. "I have to say I'm in over my head with all of these magical investigations, lately. Not being terribly magical myself, I feel kind of at a loss."

"Well you're heck of a lot more competent than Perkins, at least," said Rosemary.

"Low bar," said Neve's. "There's something about this whole

situation that doesn't make sense. But hopefully, we'll figure it out soon enough."

Tamsyn returned with Elowen in tow. "I think it'll help if you join us this time," Tamsyn said to Rosemary. "I'll be able to draw on your magic as well. You can join in too, Neve."

"Oh no. I'll probably just dilute things," said Neve. "My mother always said my magic was like tepid dishwater."

"That's a bit harsh," said Rosemary.

"I used to think I made up for it with my cleverness, you know, being a good detective was a way that I could help out even though there wasn't much else I could do when things went wrong. Anyway, enough about me."

"I think it will help," said Tamsyn, firmly. "Come and join us."

"If you insist," said Neve.

It only took a few minutes to set up for the spell using rosemary and onyx for protection with ginger and tiger's eye crystal to reveal the truth.

The four of them held hands, Rosemary crouched down one side to reach Elowen's tiny little hands, the soft little fingers reminded her when Athena was small. She missed those days in some respects, but in other ways she relieved to be free. Of many of the struggles of raising a small child, other than all the children she seems now be swamped these days.

"Alright, Elowen," said Tamsyn. "Remember the poem we practiced?"

They began chanting.

ESSENCE OF WILL. *Let us be still.*

Reveal to us the source. As a matter of course.

What is hidden, let us see. So mote it be.

. . .

ALL WAS SILENT. Rosemary wondered if the magic was working at all, and then she felt a little tug. It was as if her magic was being pulled downwards.

She could see it coalescing like gold dust in the air in front of them, forming a kind of small cloud of light.

"Alright," said Tamsyn. "Now just focus on the light with our intent to find the source of whoever is creating the fires."

They all focused in on the gold dust floating in the air. It began glowing and sparkling, forming the shape of an arrow. Rosemary thought it looked like a slightly translucent hood ornament.

"Now we just have to follow it," said Tamsyn.

"Okay," Rosemary said. "Wait, it's moving fast!"

The arrow flew right through the wall, leaving trails of gold sparkles in its wake.

"We've got to go," said Rosemary. "Come on, quick!"

"Elowen, you stay with the other kids," said Tamsyn.

"Okay," Elowen said and skipped off as the three woman dashed out to the front of the house.

Rosemary could see the arrow headed down the driveway.

"It should stick to the roads, at least," said Tamsyn. "I didn't think about walls!"

"We should have cast it outside," said Rosemary.

"With the car running," Neve added. "Never mind, we can still make it. Get in!" she gestured towards her police vehicle.

They all jumped in and took off, following the arrow as it zoomed towards the village and then hooned around the streets of Myrtlewood, only slightly above the speed limit. Neve popped the sirens on so they I could legitimately drive a little faster.

"It seems to be heading past the town centre," said Rosemary.

"Maybe it's going to someone's house," said Tamsyn, as it continued on into a suburb.

"Wait a minute," said Rosemary, as they turned down familiar street. This is close to Athena's school. I hope there's nothing terrible going on here that could affect all those kids.

"I think it's worse than that," said Neve, as the arrow stopped right outside Myrtlewood Academy, hovering in the air next to the old stone buildings.

"I think we have a problem," said Tamsyn.

"At least now it's being patient," said Neve.

The arrow seemed to be waiting for them, so they parked and got out of the car. They followed it as it moved, much more slowly now, right into the school grounds.

"This is bad," said Rosemary. "I wonder if it's one of the teachers... or one of the students."

"Shush," said Neve. "We don't want to give ourselves away. Stay quiet and walk as if you're just going about an ordinary task."

"I think I've forgotten what it's like to have ordinary tasks," said Rosemary.

She followed Neve through the courtyard, between several buildings, trying not to look too suspicious. The arrow moved in an organic kind of way, almost like a little dog. It seemed to be looking around for something.

Rosemary's phone buzzed. She glanced quickly at the screen to see that Liam was calling.

That's right. I was supposed to meet him today to help with this little problem, Rosemary recalled. *That will have to wait.*

They followed the arrow through an entrance way and along a corridor until it stopped outside the closed door of a classroom.

"Ohh, this is going to be awkward," Rosemary muttered. "If Athena catches me here, she will be so mad!"

She hoped like anything it wasn't Athena's classroom they were standing outside.

Neve knocked on the door and poked her head in. "Excuse me," she said.

Rosemary craned her neck but she couldn't see much through the slither of open door.

"Yes?" said a voice of someone who must be the teacher. "Oh... Detective. Can I help you?"

"I just need to come and ask someone a few questions," said Neve. "Nothing serious."

"Who do you need to talk to?" said the teacher.

"We'll see in a moment," said Neve. She opened the door wide so that the now-very-patient arrow could move in.

It hovered around the room, above the heads of the students.

Rosemary, standing in the doorway, saw Athena sitting there with a look of absolute horror on her face.

Oh no, Rosemary thought. *She's going to kill me!*

She continued to panic until the arrow came to rest right above Athena's head.

"Miss Thorn," said the teacher. "I believe the detective here wants to have a word."

"Come with me, please," said Neve.

Athena stood up.

"There must be some mistake," Rosemary mumbled, as she looked at her daughter. "Maybe it was looking for the person missing from our house. Yes... that must be it."

She chucked, awkwardly.

Just then there was a sound of gasps and screams coming from the other students in the classroom. Rosemary turned back and looked across the room. Out the window, enormous orange and red flames burned.

"Oh, no. Oh, no, no, no! This is the last place we need *that* to happen!"

Rosemary ran outside. "Get back!" she cried. "Get all the kids as far away from the fire as soon as possible."

"Obviously!" said a teacher with pink plaits and orange robe.

"Line up class. Get away from the flames this instant." The teens didn't seem to listen, though.

"The school had things well under control," the teacher said. A blast of air emanated out from her hand, knocking the students back, away from the flame. A further blast, scooping them up and escorting them all to a designated area.

"It's just protocol," said a the teacher.

"Yeah," said Rosemary. "Well this is no ordinary fire, and you'd better stay away too because I don't think you're my type."

Neve followed close behind as Rosemary dashed towards the flames.

She knew that she could at least handle a little bit of their beguiling magic. The fire seemed to start in the front entrance to the school, but it had quickly spread all along the corridor.

"This is bad," she muttered to herself.

"I'm going to go and find a source of water," said Neve, leaving Rosemary alone, facing the flames.

Rosemary caught sight of a very tiny teacher and a very large bearded teacher canoodling nearby.

"Get away!" Rosemary called. They didn't pay any attention to her. She blasted them with her light magic, and they flew back. She could only hope that the rest of the school had been evacuated as far away from the flames as possible.

She felt a warm, relaxing sensation coming over her, but this time she wasn't going to be fooled. She knew how to fight it. She used her protective light energy to coat her entire body so that she was impervious to the seductive lure of the flames.

I need water.

She attempted to summon the feeling of water to see if that worked, but nothing came out of her hands.

It was a relatively clear spring day but even so, she tried to reach for the small tufts of clouds floating in the sky, pulling them down towards the fire with her magic.

They did nothing but sizzle in the extreme heat. The fire grew bigger.

A flaming beast emerged, seven feet tall and horned with gleaming red eyes.

"This is what I was worried about," Rosemary muttered. She glared at the beast, adopting her best mum voice. "Get back in there, you freaky flaming thing!"

"You could use some help with your swearing," growled the beast.

"Oh really? Are you some kind of God, then?"

"Ha, ha, ha," laughed the beast. "I'm merely a minotaur. My master will be here shortly."

He stalked towards her through the flames.

"Oh no you don't" said Rosemary. She hurled a ball of lightning towards the creature blowing him back several meters.

The lightening had no effect what so ever.

He laughed again and then lunged at her. There's wasn't any time for punches and kicks. She could feel the heat coming off his body from metres away. One touch could melt her or burn her to cinders. So she fortified her magical protections and concentrated with all her might, pouring her magic forward, like a steady stream of water.

She felt it, flowing through her hands emanating the very elemental feel of a river. This was the element Rosemary struggled with the most. She was mostly fire and air, as Athena had pointed out with her Sagittarius Sun and Gemini rising. She wanted action and quick thinking, but water was slower. To connect with elemental water, she needed to relax and let go.

She closed her eyes. All she could hear was her own heartbeat, pumping blood around her body. Her body made mostly of water.

It shouldn't be this hard!

Rosemary struggled against her own instinct for control.

Relax, came the intuitive voice of the ancestor. *Let it come to you.*

Against her own instinct, Rosemary let her shoulders slump. Her breathing slowed.

Water came gushing through her as if channelled from another place entirely. It spurted against the beast, causing a cloud of steam to rise up.

"Impressive," he growled. "But you are no match for me."

He continued to march towards her. Rosemary bolstered herself and blasted him back with more ferocity this time. The Minotaur fell back into the flames just as a great burst or water came forth from behind Rosemary.

She turned to see Neves ex-girlfriend, Sid, standing there.

Reinforcements had arrived, just in time.

Rosemary sighed with relief and stood back as the firefighters took over, blasting the flaming school buildings with their magical hoses. It gave her a moment to take stock of the damage which was far more extensive than she'd realised, but at least the students and staff had all been evacuated to the far lawn and there had been no casualties. Rosemary overheard Sid talking about this with her colleagues.

As she watched, the fire slowly died down at the hands of the six magical firefighters possibly all of the crew they had in town, certainly more than had arrived at the mayor's house.

"Amazing," said Sid, as she turned off her hose and walked towards Rosemary. "I've heard legends of fire-dwelling creatures connected with the old gods, but I didn't believe it until now."

"Alarming, wasn't it?" said Rosemary.

Sid nodded. "This fire was a big one. Much worse than the others. It's just as well you were here to hold it off. he school is going to be out of commission for some time."

"Oh," said Rosemary. "Can't it just be magically repaired?"

She shook her head. "No. The properties of this fire seem to withstand that kind of magic. The magic is old and complex. It seems to withstand out contemporary reparation spells. The mayor's house is being rebuilt the old fashioned way and he keeps complaining that it's taking such a long time."

"That's a shame," said Rosemary. Where will the kids go?"

"That's a worry for another day," said Neve. "Come on, we better go and find Athena"

Rosemary followed Neve to the lawn were all the school students and teachers had assembled. Athena was standing off to the side looking mortified.

"That spell worked, didn't it?" said Rosemary.

"I'm so sorry, she said. I didn't mean to..."

"Let's find somewhere to sit down," said Neve. "It seems Athena has some explaining to do."

"She certainly does," said Rosemary.

Athena broke into tears before she'd even sat down. They were in a little alcove on a bench outside the staff room, an undamaged part of the school. Rosebushes in full bloom surrounded the bench, perfuming the air, but Athena barely noticed them.

"I'm sorry," she said. "It's all my fault."

"It's okay," Neve said in a calm voice. "Just tell us. Tell us what you think happened."

"I didn't realize," said Athena. "I... at first, I was just experiment-ing. At night... I'd go down to the forest. I thought of it as a kind of practice."

"What were you practicing," Neve asked, nudging Rosemary, clearly to keep her quiet.

"Just practicing cutting a door through to the fae realm," said Athena.

Rosemary gasped.

"It felt so good," Athena explained. "I... I really miss being there."

"Where did you get the idea?" Neve asked.

Athena shrugged. "I don't know," she said. "I saw Finnigan do it to let us through. When I came back everything felt so grey. Actually I might have thought of it after the dinner we had with our cousins. Elamina wanted to talk about the fae realm, at least. Mum never did. It got me thinking that I might be able to cut through... just a little bit. Being there was *amazing*. It felt like home and maybe... it's kind of addictive. I don't know. I couldn't stop thinking about it and I felt really good. But I was so tired and drained when there wasn't enough fae realm energy around and... I had no idea I was letting anything through until..."

"Until what?" Rosemary said.

"Until I showed Elise when I was at her house. I didn't cut all the way through, ever, just a tiny bit. Just enough for some of the energy to come back to me. Elise understood why I'd do it. She missed the far realm too. But... she saw something fly out. And she said it was some kind of fae and a spiritual form. Maybe a fire sprite."

Rosemary and Neve looked at each other.

"I'm so sorry," said Athena. "I didn't mean to cause any trouble at all. I wasn't trying to create a fire of anything. You believe me, don't you?"

"It's actually really hard to believe you're right now," said Rosemary, her voice heavy with disappointment.

Neve sat down in the seat next to Athena with a great sigh.

"I'm sorry, Neve," said Athena. "I really didn't mean to."

"It's not that," said Neve. "In fact, I think the problem is even bigger."

"What do you mean?" Rosemary asked. "Athena just explained it to us."

"Well, we found the source... of the person who let the fire sprites in to the earth realm," said Neve. "That's who the spell led us to."

"But?" said Rosemary. "There definitely sounds like there's a but here."

"If Athena was only letting them in by accident, then there's somebody else we're looking for."

"What do you mean?" Athena asked.

"Based on the research that I've done fire sprites are relatively friendly. In fact, I've interviewed a couple just to get more information. They were hard to track down as there aren't many around and the ones that live here, well they are much more stable and well-adjusted than their wild counterparts, but even they wouldn't just go around lighting magical fires and summoning the Cavalia."

"See you are good at your job," said Rosemary. "You have way more of an idea of what's going on than I do."

Neve sighed. "Anyway, from everything that I've learned, I'm absolutely certain that there is something deliberate going on here. These fires are serious. It couldn't possibly have all happened by accident."

"I swear it wasn't on purpose," said Athena. "As soon as I found out what I was doing I stopped."

"I'm not accusing you," said Neve. "Besides, I don't see what your motive could possibly be. Someone else must be behind this. I'm not sure if they knew what you were doing. They're definitely using it to their advantage."

"That's giving me the creeps," said Rosemary. "Do you think it could be somebody close to us?"

Neve looked around suspiciously, confirming Rosemary's fears.

"Why are you so sure it's deliberately?" Rosemary asked.

"Those kinds of fires wouldn't happen by accident," said Neve. "Like I said, fire sprites tend to be quiet peaceful unless they're specifically summoned charged with doing something else. We may have found the source who's letting them in," she looked at Athena. "But we haven't found the source of the biggest problem."

"It couldn't have just been a coincidence?" Rosemary asked as Athena dried her eyes.

"What we're dealing with is really old magic," said Neve. "Someone has been weaving it together, expertly, in a way that allows the fire sprites to connect with the divine plane."

"The what?" Athena asked.

"The divine plane, where the gods are."

"There's another plane, all together?" Rosemary asked. "I'm going to need a multi-dimensional map for this."

"Anyway," said Neve. "The only reason I'm more concerned now, is that it seems like you've played some kind of role in someone else's plan without even knowing it.

"I didn't mean to," said Athena.

Rosemary let out a long, slow breath. "It's okay."

"You're not angry?" Athena asked.

"I am angry," said Rosemary. "But I'm starting to realize something."

"What?" Athena asked.

"You didn't want to tell me any of the stuff about missing the fae realm because you were worried about me being over protective, right?"

"Right," said Athena.

"And if you hadn't been worried about that, you would have talked to me more about this stuff."

"Exactly," said Athena. "So it's really your fault."

Rosemary narrowed her eyes. "I wouldn't go that far."

"Also, if I'd been able to hang out with Elise more often she probably would have told me what I was doing wrong, much earlier."

"Don't rub salt in wound," said Rosemary. "You're still in trouble."

"I'll be grounded forever, right?"

"No," said Rosemary. "I'm starting to see that grounding you is part of the problem. We're going to both have to work on being more open and trusting, okay?"

Athena sighed. "Okay, Mum. I'll be more open with you if you stop being so freaking controlling."

Rosemary made an exasperated noise. "Fine. Now we just have to figure out who the creepy spies are who've been manipulating us and taking advantage of the fact that you missed the fae realm so much."

On the way back to Thorn Manor, Athena and Rosemary sat next to each other in the back of Neve's car while Tamsyn sat in the passenger seat.

Athena's school had sent all the students home, due to the fire, and she'd insisted she was far too embarrassed and overwhelmed stay anyway.

On the drive, they collectively mulled over the suspects.

"Do you think it could be Dad?" Athena asked.

"Well he's certainly got the fae realm experience," said Rosemary, feeling her blood run cold. "But why would he want to do something like that?"

"He's quite mischievous, you know," said Athena.

"True," Rosemary groaned. "I never should have trusted him again... or gone to all their effort to help him."

"Mum, it was just a possibility. I doubt it's him."

"Well if it is, he's got another thing coming."

"There are actually lots of possible suspects," said Neve, as she turned into the driveway of Thorn Manor. "A lot of people have even been around the house, lately."

"Obviously Marjie and Nesta," said Athena. "But I doubt either of them would have any motive to summon deranged fire beasts."

"Then there's Sherry," Rosemary added. "She has record of being deceptive in the past."

"That's true," said Neve. "But I wouldn't have thought she'd want anything chaotic to happen after what she's been through"

"We've had quite a few visitors," said Athena. "And it could even be somebody who hasn't been to the house at all... someone with other ways of spying on us. Or maybe it really is just be a coincidence. Someone was doing this magic and happened to make use of all the extra fire energy around."

"It's a pretty big coincidence," said Neve. "This is complex magic. They're not fooling around. I suspect they needed the fire sprites in order for it to work, a bit like Marla and Agatha Twigg suspect. Not many people have the power to open up doors between the realms the way you do, because or your fae and witch heritage, and most people don't know about that you, either."

"That's true" said Athena, but I'm not the only witchy fae person around

"Not Finnegan!" said Rosemary. "You haven't heard or seen him again since you left the fae realm?"

"No, of course not," said Athena, crossly.

"What if he's behind it?" Rosemary continues. "He might have been letting through a lot more fire sprites than you."

"That's certainly a possibility,' said Neve. "There are a few people with fae heritage around."

"Like Una," said Rosemary. "But I have no idea what kind of motive she would have."

"That's the problem," said Neve.

"The Bloodstone Society could have spies everywhere. Athena thought that blonde woman looked familiar – the one in the mask who attacked us, but who is she?"

"That's true," said Athena looking her mother in the eye. "How many blonde women do we know?"

"There's Ashwyn," said Rosemary. "And Elamina, of course, but I'm sure I'd recognise my own cousin, even masked, and I'd be able to smell her sickly perfume a mile away. Besides, she wouldn't be caught dead in an outfit like that."

"What about the new girl at Marjie's shop? Lamorna?" Neve suggested. "We don't know anything about her."

"It's silly, really," said Athena. "We're grasping at straws. The woman was probably wearing a wig."

Neve sighed. "You're right. Oh, by the way. I checked the records at the spa the day you were there. Apparently there was a women checked in who looked a lot like Despina, registered under the name Merriweather Wurster."

"I knew it!" said Rosemary. "I bet it was her."

Neve frowned. "The problem is we just don't know enough. If we'd been able to find the person responsible today then we would hopefully have a little time before Beltane tomorrow night."

"I would offer to try again," said Tamsyn. "But it'll take a few days for my magic to recharge after such a big exertion."

"Never mind that," said Neve. "Whoever is doing this had found very clever ways to hide their tracks. Another seeing spell might just lead us to Athena again or someone else who's unwittingly helping them and there's not enough time. All these other fires are just dress-rehearsals. If my deductions are correct, then whoever is doing this is going to want to celebrate Beltane, whether the rest of the town is there or not."

"So we'll be able to find them," said Rosemary.

"Exactly," said Neve. "Tomorrow night is our best bet."

CHAPTER

THIRTY-SIX

"You saw it, didn't you?" Rosemary asked Neve as they sat around and the living room later on that day, after returning to Thorn Manor.

"Yes. That beast was terrifying," said Neve. "What did he say he was? A minotaur?"

"That's right. Sid said she's heard rumours for fire beasts like that. Rosemary leaned back in her armchair, grateful that she wasn't the only one to see it. She was also pleased to be freshly showered and feeling much better. However, the atmosphere was tarnished with anxiety.

"What was it like?" Athena asked. "I couldn't see anything from where we were standing."

Rosemary tried to explain the terrifying flaming minotaur.

"Your mum was incredible," said Neve. "She somehow summoned water out of thin air... or made it. I've never seen anything like that."

Rosemary shrugged. "I didn't know what I was doing. I really wish that I did."

"But you killed it, did you?" Athena asked.

"Not exactly," said Rosemary. "I just kind of pushed it back through. The fire was sort of like a portal."

"That makes sense," said Athena. "The fire sprites energy must be being used to open up a portal to the Divine Realm to let Belamus through. Beasts will come through along with the ancient god of light. That's what the Cavalia is supposed to be... according to Granny's books anyway. It's all becoming clearer."

"God of light that sounds kind of nice," said Nesta.

"I don't think there's anything nice about it, unfortunately," said Athena. "The Old Gods aren't like Brigid or any of the other ones that we normally hear about. They come from a different time and aren't likely to value human life all that much, or so I've read. Although I admit, there's not all that much written about them."

"Do you think the gods are trying to come in and take over?"

"Or maybe somebody is else is trying to bring them through so that *they* can take over," said Rosemary.

"Quite possibly, something along those lines," said Neve.

"Compared to how epic the Cavalia sounds, the flaming huge beast I fought today was probably nothing," said Rosemary.

"I bet it's Sid," said Nesta, bitterly. "She's suspicious. Plus, aren't firefighters all secret pyromaniacs?"

Rosemary looked between Neve and Nesta. "This is one conversation I'm not going to get involved in, but I'm pretty sure the blonde woman who attacked Thorn Manor wasn't Sid – not even in a wig.

Nesta sighed. "It's probably a good thing that Beltane was cancelled."

"Neve didn't seem to think so at the town meeting," said Rosemary.

"Why not?" Athena asked.

"Without the Beltane celebration, I'm worried it will only get worse," said Neve. "Whoever is doing this is bound to hold a ritual, anyway, to draw on the energy of the season, and no one will be there to stop them."

"You're probably right about that," Dain chimed in. He'd been sitting quietly as if lost in thought for some time. "They're increasing in intensity and frequency. It's got to build up to something. But we could use that to our advantage. Beltane could be a chance to confront whoever's doing this, and put a stop to it, maybe even to push some of the sprites back through the portal."

"So you're saying we should have the ritual anyway?" Athena asked.

"If we don't take control of it, someone else will," said Neve. "That will be the benefit of leading the ritual ourselves. At the moment, whoever is behind all this has scared everyone off, successfully."

Rosemary felt a prickle of suspicion as Neve continued to talk. The mayor had cancelled Beltane. Maybe he wanted them out of the town centre for a reason.

"If we don't go down there and take charge, then they'll have the whole run of the place," Neve said. "They'll be in total control, which is what they're wanting. And we can't risk that. But then again, it's not fair for me to put you at risk either."

"We want to help," said Rosemary.

Neve looked around the room. "I've tried to call in more enforcement from the magical authorities, but I'm afraid they're not taking this very seriously. They think the real Beltane ceremony is in Edenborough. I'm afraid they're stationing most of their enforcements up there, even though many of the fires have been around Myrtlewood."

"But not all of them?" Rosemary asked.

"No. In fact, there have been some in Burkenswood, and a few dotted all over the country. The authorities are trying to keep them quiet in case whoever is doing this is just wanting attention. My superiors were hoping they'd just stop on their own."

Rosemary and Neve shared an unimpressed look.

"I had no idea there've been so many," said Athena. "I'm so sorry for whatever role I've played."

"We'll let you make it up to us later," said Neve, with a smile.

"You're on dishes duty for a very long time," Rosemary added.

"I suppose I deserve that," said Athena. "Luckily, we have a very cooperative house that likes helping out."

Rosemary squinted at her daughter. "Don't try and get out of this, someone needs to teach you that there are consequences for your actions and your deceptions and not telling your mother about them..."

"Yeah, tell me about it," said Athena. "I'm never gonna live this one down, am I? Is there any way I can help?"

"I'd prefer to keep you well out of it," said Neve. But I'm afraid we're going to need all the help we can get to hold the ritual, and hopefully stop whatever is trying to come through."

"Do you think it will be in the town circle?" Rosemary asked.

"I assume so," said Neve. "That's where all the rituals are, it's a kind of nexus of power for the town, right in the middle of those ley lines. That's an obvious choice."

"Maybe it's too obvious," said Athena. "Maybe they'll try and hold it somewhere else. Like in the forest somewhere."

"That's quite possible," said Neve. "Though that could be to our advantage as well. The town circle holds so much energy that we could use it to channel a lot of the Beltane energy and divert any other attempts that somebody tried elsewhere to summon the Cavalia."

"Sounds dangerous," said Rosemary. "Maybe we're playing right into their hands. I hope you've got a plan."

Neve gave a stiff nod.

"Tell me where to sign up," said Dain.

Rosemary looked at him feeling slightly suspicious. They'd allowed him to sit in on the conversation since the children were all occupied eating pudding. Rosemary had wanted to see his reaction to all this. He'd taken it very calmly, so far, perhaps a little too calmly. Though, what he'd have to gain from all this chaos, Rosemary had no idea.

"You want to be part of this?" Rosemary asked.

"Of course I do," Dain said. "I'm not just a glorified babysitter, you know."

There was an edge of anger to his tone. He got up and stomped out of the room.

Rosemary followed him. "Dain, what's going on? Tell me the truth," she asked.

"I don't think you want to know," said Dain.

Rosemary felt a lead weight in her gut. "Do you have something to do with all this? The fires? If you do then tell me right now."

Dain laughed. "Don't be ridiculous," he said, "I'm not a fan of fire sprites at the best of times, let alone the old gods."

"What do you know about them?" Rosemary asked.

"Enough to know that I don't want anything to do with them, that's all," said Dain. "They're dangerous and archaic, not something you want to mess around with."

"So why are you in this mood, then?" Rosemary asked.

"Because you keep side-lining me," Dain said. "No matter what I do, I can't seem to make up for the past and I know it'll take time but... give me a chance."

"I've given you a lot of chances," said Rosemary.

Dain sighed, pressing his hands over his face. "Look, it's hard for me, seeing you with all these suitors, hearing about you kissing some vampire in the middle of town."

"Nonsense. I don't have any suitors, for the last time! And the only reason that town incident happened was because of the stupid fire."

"No, it isn't," said Dain. "I know you, Rosemary. I know you wouldn't be caught dead kissing anyone that you weren't already attracted to, magical pull or not. You're powerful, more than even you know. And it's not just your magic."

Rosemary recalled seeing herself through Dain's eyes. The warmth of the love he had for her.

"Why won't you open up to me?" he asked.

"This is not about you," said Rosemary. "We've been through, way too much, Athena and I..."

"And part of that was my fault," said Dain. "I accept that. I just wish you'd give me another chance, now that I'm free of my addiction. I wish I could show you how much I care."

Memories of his past tenderness, swam through most Rosemary's mind. She closed her eyes. Dain stepped towards her and grasped her shoulders. Rosemary opened her eyes and looked into his.

She shook her head.

"We're meant to be together," he said. "And it hurts to think of you with anyone else."

She stepped away from him. "No, we're not, Dain. There's nothing destined about us. We were just two kids that found each other in the wrong place at the wrong time, had a terrible turbulent relationship, and managed to get a wonderful daughter out of it. That's all."

"It can't be all," said Dain. "You're everything to me. You and Athena."

"And that's part of the problem," said Rosemary. "It's not healthy, I can't be everything to anyone. You need to have your own life."

"I know I do," said Dain. "I've been thinking about that. I want to start a business. And I probably need to move out of here."

Rosemary sighed, wondering what she'd do with all the children without Dain's help.

"See, exactly," said Dain. "You're worried about how you'll cope with the kids. You treat me like a babysitter. You just want me here to help out around the house. You don't want *me* here."

"Thank you for all your help," Rosemary said. "I know the fae don't like to be thanked, but seriously, thanks for all the things you've been doing to help with the kids. I'm not sure what we would've done without you, probably shunted them off into substandard foster homes by now. It's taking a lot longer than I thought to find them homes."

"It hurts that you only need me because of them," Dain said.

"And because of Athena," said Rosemary.

"She doesn't need me." He looked down at the ground, his voice cracking as he said it.

"She does. She needs her father around... as long as you're going to be a good influence." Rosemary nudged him with her elbow. He took hold of her hand, gently and looked her in the eyes.

"Just tell me, Rosemary. Honestly, I need to know the truth. Tell me you don't have feelings for me."

Rosemary looked into Dain's eyes feeling a wave of vulnerability. She couldn't say it, because it wasn't true.

A cheeky grin spread over his face. "I knew it! You do! You do have feelings for me."

She elbowed him again, hard this time.

"I can't help the way I feel about anyone," she said. "We have a past. And I admit, we have chemistry. But..."

"Yeah, I know you're not having any relationships. That's fine," said Dain, maintaining his grin. "I just need to know that there's still hope. Take all the time you need Rosemary. You're not getting rid of me anytime soon. Not unless you really seriously want me out of your life. And if that ever happens, you're going to have to tell me. Be straight with me. I've never loved anyone like I love you. I don't know if I could."

With that, he walked away, leaving Rosemary feeling dizzy, confused and heartbroken all at the same time.

Yes, she had feelings for Dain. She always had, despite the fact that she'd tried to suppress them quite a lot of the time. And if she was completely honest with herself, she also had feelings for Burk, and possibly for Liam as well.

"Feelings," Rosemary muttered. "Who needs them? Way too complicated."

"Are you talking to yourself again, Mum?" Athena asked, coming out of the living room. "What was up with Dad? Why did he storm out?"

"I think he's just sick of being treated as the babysitter, like you thought," Rosemary replied. Clearly she wasn't going to tell her teen anything about the conversation she'd just had. Rosemary had enough to be teased about already.

"Oh yeah?" said Athena. "So if he quits his job as a babysitter, what are we going to do with the kids?"

"I have no idea," said Rosemary. "Hopefully, the authorities can find them some good foster homes as quickly as possible."

"They need to be magical foster homes," said Athena. "The kids aren't really practicing magic yet but they sure are otherworldly, and strange things will happen around them from time to time, things that mundane people will struggle to understand."

"That's why it's taking so long to find them homes, I think," said Rosemary. "But you're right. We need to come up with some other kind of solution, because even the most placid children in the world are a handful."

"Thank you for what you said before," said Athena. "I know you were just trying to control yourself. Because there were all those other people listening in. I know that you're still mad at me."

"It was the truth," said Rosemary. "I've never had to worry about protecting you so much before because you never went to parties or got into trouble like other teenagers. And now that things have changed since we've been in Myrtlewood, I've gone totally overboard, treating you like a toddler when you're almost an adult, as you keep saying. If I treated you that way from the beginning, then you wouldn't have gone to the fae realm, without telling me. Well you might have, but things could have been different. And you would have told me how you were feeling about that place. We could have figured it out together instead of you sneaking out at night, and cutting holes in the veil."

Athena nodded. "I guess if you didn't pry into my life so much," she added, "Then I wouldn't feel like I needed so much privacy or to protect myself from you."

"I guess it's time for me to let go a little bit," said Rosemary. "You're so strong. You can protect yourself. You know your own mind. I'm incredibly proud of you. I'm still angry, but also incredibly proud."

"Thanks Mum," said Athena, giving Rosemary a playful push.

"What was that for?"

"Just trying to break the tension. I'm a teenager I can't handle these serious earnest conversations, remember?" she giggled. "So since you're going to trust me to live my own life, you're going to let me come to this Beltane ritual, right?"

"My initial reaction is not on your life," said Rosemary, looking her daughter in the eye. "It's bound to be dangerous, possibly more dangerous than anything we've faced yet, including the Bloodstone society, although I wouldn't be surprised if they are the ones behind this. But I have a feeling that if I try to hold you back, and keep you at home with the kids, not only will we be in more trouble, because we won't have you there with your powerful magic. But you'll also find some way to sneak out anyway. And then we won't be well-orchestrated. And we'll be in even more danger. So, this is me, living up to what I've said. Walking the talk or whatever."

"No one says that anymore, Mum,"

"I'm not trying to be cool," said Rosemary. "It's just a figure of speech."

"I'm glad you're not trying to be cool because I don't think it would ever work," said Athena. "But also. Thank you."

"I'm trusting you to make up your own mind," said Rosemary. "I still don't think you should come. But if you are going to, then let's work as a team."

"I think you already know that I'm definitely coming," said Athena. "And I'm bringing my friends too."

CHAPTER
THIRTY-SEVEN

"I know you're up to something," said Marjie, the next morning. She'd arrived at Thorn Manor a few moments before, carrying a big box of Sally Lunn buns including some dairy free ones for Dain. "Don't even think about not including me."

They sat around the table, drinking tea and eating the fresh baked goods.

"It's going to be dangerous," said Rosemary. She filled Marjie in on the details. "Actually, it'd be great if you could stay here with the kids."

"I'm not just some babysitter, Rosemary Thorn," said Marjie. "Not when there's danger that I could help to fight. I'd ask Herb to help with the kids but you know he's not the best, with his bad leg. He won't be able to run after them. How about Una and Ashwyn?"

Rosemary glanced at Neve across the table, wondering if the sisters could be trusted.

"What was that look about?" Marjie asked. "Don't tell me you're suspicious of those two. They're both absolutely lovely and highly trustworthy."

"How can you be sure?" Rosemary asked, a whir of different suspicious thoughts flicking through her mind. "Una's father was fae, and maybe she could have some kind of motive to do with their realm."

"That does sound like a stretch when you say it like that, Mum," said Athena. "Una is so nice."

"Nice people can do terrible things, remember that sweet little girl who turned out to be an ancient vampire and came after us?"

"She was *not* nice," said Athena. "Genevieve was pure evil. I could tell from the very beginning."

"Don't be silly," said Rosemary. "You were just jealous."

Athena pierced her with an evil look.

"I know!" said Neve, clearly trying to break the tension. "How about we invite them over and ask them some questions. We can ask if they'll babysit. And that will also give us a chance to make sure that they're comfortable with the kids before we leave them with the children."

"I don't know about that," said Rosemary. "Can't you just stay?" she asked Nesta.

"I'm afraid not," Nesta said. "When Neve's working I'm only able to go out for short intervals at the moment, when my neighbour pops over to look after Neve's aunt. I can't very well leave her and Mae alone for hours at a time in the evening."

"Well, they could all come here," said Rosemary.

"My aunt's refusing to leave the house at the moment," said Neve." She says there's too much evil afoot."

"That's probably true," said Athena. "She was right about me after all."

"What you did wasn't evil, love," said Rosemary. "Just misguided."

"Thanks for the vote of confidence," said Athena. "That's what it will read on my tombstone. 'Not evil, just misguided.'"

"You're not going to have a tombstone," said Rosemary, frowning. "At least not while I'm around."

"That is not exactly inspiring confidence," said Athena.

"Are you sure you don't want to stay, Dain?" Rosemary asked, hopefully.

"Absolutely not," said Dain. "There's no way I'm going to miss out on the chance to see you fighting." He laughed.

Rosemary glared at him.

"But more seriously," Dain continued. "I need to be there to help protect you two."

Rosemary sighed. "Oh, fine. We'll call Una and Ashwyn and see if they're able to come over and look after the children. But—I want Neve to interview them before we allow them anywhere near the kids. Use your detective interview powers Neve."

Neve gave her a questioning look. "You want me to interrogate them? Have you got a swinging lightbulb in a bleak concrete room?"

Athena laughed. "Look, we can just ask them some questions. If they're acting weird, we'll tell them not to worry about it, and then we'll follow them around until they do something evil. And otherwise, we'll have a babysitter."

"It still doesn't seem like the wisest idea," said Rosemary.

"It might not, but we're running out of options," said Athena, holding up an old leather-bound book. "We need to get organised. This book makes it sound like we'll have to appease the gods in some way."

"That doesn't sound good," said Rosemary. "In fact it sounds rather 'adult' especially when you think about the effect that the fire seems to have on people. I'd really prefer if you didn't come," she said to Athena. "Can't you babysit?"

"No, Mum. We've been over this. You need my magic."

"How do you appease the gods, then?" Rosemary asked.

An idea popped into her head relating to magical protection.

She could use a shield spell and adapt it to cover the Myrtlewood residents to protect them from the fire. It would be complicated, but it might just pay off.

"Well, we can try milk and honey," said Athena. "That's the kind of thing that Brigid likes."

"Okay, add that to the shopping list," said Rosemary. "What else do we need?"

"Yellow topaz, carnelian red agate, ruby, garnet," said Athena. "Basically all the red, yellow and orange stones."

"We should make some more battle charms," said Marjie. "That's how I'm going to help."

"Okay, sounds great," said Rosemary. "Plus, I'll make sure you're all fed. I've got a batch of beef pies, baking in the shop. In fact, I better go and get them. I'll meet you in town later on."

Most of the day was spent in preparation for the ritual. Rosemary was relieved that there were no more fires and nobody had tried to attack her for a change, but there was lots of work to do in the meantime to prepare for the evening.

"We'll arrive in town, just after nightfall," said Neve who was in charge of strategy. "That way. We'll have less chance of the mayor finding out and kicking us out of the town circle before we can set up."

"Alright," said Rosemary.

She checked her phone to find another missed call from Liam. Her heart sank. She had promised she would help him soon. But she had other more pressing issues. Surely, he could just do whatever he normally did if it was too close to the full moon. He'd been caught out couple of months before, but he'd assured her that wasn't normally the case and he had some kind of cage setup that he usually used when he went all wolfie. She pushed thoughts of Liam out of her mind. She had plenty of other things to think about.

There was a knock at the door.

Rosemary opened it to find Burk standing there, his skin looking pasty. He was holding an umbrella.

"I didn't know you could go outside in daylight," said Rosemary. It was only slightly awkward seeing him for the first time since their little incident in the middle of town.

"It's cloudy day," said Burk. "Plus, I'm wearing incredibly high SPF sunscreen and the umbrella's for shade."

"I figured," said Rosemary. "What do you want?"

"Can I come in?" Burk asked. "It's a bit risky being out here."

"Sure," she stepped aside and let him in through the front door. "How can I help you?" There was slight rigidity in her voice considering everything else that was going on. She hardly needed the disruption.

"I know you're doing something for Beltane to try stop fires," said Burk.

"Did Marjie tell you?" Rosemary asked. "There's no such thing as a secret in this town, is there?"

"I might have just figured it out myself," said Burk. "I heard about the fire at the school. The mayor thinks that cancelling Beltane is going to help settle things down. But he's wrong, isn't he?"

"That's what I think," said Neve's stepping towards them. "Look, you're not going to be able to stop us. We know it's risky, but we've got to do something."

"I'm not trying to stop you," said Burk. "I'm trying to help."

"Oh, good," said Rosemary. "Now... you can help by staying out of the way and stepping in if necessary."

"Is that all?" Burk asked, sounding a little disappointed.

"Look, do you actually want to help?" Rosemary asked. "Are you just getting your action kicks?"

Burk gave her a slightly offended look.

"I know you're a vampire. You've been around a long time, life gets boring. Maybe you're here for a little entertainment."

"I'm just offering to help," Burk said, defensively. "Is something wrong? Did I do something to offend you?"

Rosemary shook herself. "No, sorry. I'm just a bit stressed. Sure you can help. I just I don't have the bandwidth to figure out how at the moment."

"Never mind, leave that to me," said Neve. "Come this way, Mister Vam... I mean Mister Capricorn man."

Rosemary laughed at Neve's deliberate use of the code word for vampires that she and Athena had come up with.

Burk raised his eyebrows, questioningly, but didn't ask any questions.

As Burk followed Neve through the house, Dain came out of the living room, raising himself up to his full height and squaring his shoulders in some kind of display of Alfa maleness.

Rosemary giggled.

"What's *he* doing here?" Dain said.

"Helping," said Rosemary, cheerfully. "Which is what you're supposed to be doing, remember? And it would be in your best interests to listen to Neve, instead of bothering me. I've got enough to think about with the spell."

"What's the spell? I might be able to help," said Dain.

"Since when do *you* do spells?" Rosemary narrowed her eyes.

"I have fae magic," said Dain, defensively.

"Yes, but fae magic is not the same as witch magic," said Rosemary.

"Just run along and see what Neve's strategy is, and we'll ask you to pitch into the magic if necessary."

"Okay, fine," Dain huffed and walked away.

"All right, then," said Rosemary, walking into the kitchen where her daughter was dutifully doing her chores. "As soon as you're finished that. I need you to help me with a few things."

"Okay, Mum, but I meant what I said. I asked around, and my friends are going to help us."

"Do their parents know?" Rosemary asked. "Actually, it's probably better if you don't tell me. We need the numbers. This might be dangerous, but it's going to be a heck of a lot worse if we don't pull it off."

"I'm glad you think so," Athena said, crossing her arms in satisfaction.

There was another knock at the door. Rosemary sighed, dramatically. "Not more disruptions!"

Athena opened the door to find Una and Ashwyn. "Thanks for coming," she said.

Rosemary felt more guarded than her daughter's cheerful smile seemed to indicate.

"Come through here," Athena showed them into the dining room as the living room was currently occupied by the strategy department, meaning Neve, accompanied by Burk and Dain.

Rosemary had plenty of prep work to do and she would have much rather had been watching the rooster-like behavior of the two men and laughing at them than having to have this awkward conversation.

"Maybe I'll go and get Neve," she said.

Athena shot her mother a warning glance.

"What?" Rosemary asked in her mind.

"I'm going to go and make tea," said Athena, slightly too loudly. "Why don't you sit down and be polite, Mum?"

Rosemary reluctantly sat down at the table.

"You look stressed," said Una. "What's going on?"

"It's complicated," said Rosemary.

Neve came in a moment later. "Oh, you're here!"

"What's this about?" Una asked. "I thought it was supposed to be babysitting."

"Yes, err..." Rosemary wanted to leave the room but Athena had made it too awkward. "We just have a few screening questions first," she said.

Neve gave her an odd look.

"Why can't I do anything right at the moment?" Rosemary asked.

"Look," said Neve. "Something strange is going on around town and we want to make sure that you're not part of it, so we do want to ask you a few questions. If that's all right."

"Of course," said Ashwyn, smiling in a friendly way.

"Is this to do with the fires?" Una asked, concerned. They both sounded so genuine and earnest. With each question they were asked Rosemary ceded a little bit more mental ground to the realization that they must be innocent in all this.

Athena brought in the tea and Rosemary followed her out.

"What was all that about?" Rosemary asked.

"You were trying to avoid an awkward situation," Athena said with an accusatory tone.

"So what?" asked Rosemary.

"Mum, you're the suspicious one here. If you're really worried about those two, you needed to be there to hear them out. Otherwise you weren't going to stop being suspicious of them, and it would defeat the whole purpose."

"Oh fine," said Rosemary. "You have a point."

"And?" said Athena bracing her hands, questioningly.

"And they seemed perfectly innocent to me," Rosemary conceded. "I'll trust them to look after the kids."

"That's perfect," said Athena. "Now come and help me with this spell."

"I thought I was in charge of the magic," Rosemary said, crossing her arms.

"Mum, don't pout. It's ridiculous," said Athena laughing. "You're just getting wound up. Why don't you go have a bath and relax. You're no good to any of us if you're frazzled. You need to recharge your batteries."

"There's no time for baths," said Rosemary.

"Yes, there is. We've still got several hours and everything is in hand. I'll make you a cup of Marjie's special tea and your job is to relax."

"Why is relaxing the hardest thing to do sometimes?" Rosemary complained. But after a lot more magical preparation, she took Athena's advice and stalked upstairs to have a bath. After all, baths were important.

The relaxation actually did help her to clear her mind somewhat. She remembered several things that would be helpful for the ritual. She also remember to put on the heirloom emerald necklace to help her focus. She had avoided wearing it recently because she wanted to hone her powers without the crutch of the magical talisman, but tonight, she wasn't going to take any chances.

CHAPTER

THIRTY-EIGHT

Rosemary emerged in her fluffy bathrobe after what had turned out to be a rather long and relaxing soak in the tub. A glorious sunset lit up the sky outside her bedroom window.

"Athena!" she called out. "Look."

Athena came through from her own room and they watched the fiery sky.

"I should be getting dressed," said Rosemary. "But just look at that."

"Red sky at night, shepherd's delight, isn't it?"

"I hope it's not a warning," said Rosemary. "Although we hardly need a warning for danger when we know we're going straight into the thick of it."

"We'll be alright, though," said Athena. "We always are. We've gone through lots of dangerous situations before, at least since we moved here."

"I told you this town was trouble," said Rosemary.

"It might be that," said Athena. "But is there anywhere you'd rather live?"

"No, of course not," said Rosemary. "Plus, I figure now we've got access to the Thorn family magic, danger is going to follow us wherever we go."

"That's right," said Athena. "And this town needs us. It's good to be needed."

Rosemary thought back to what Dain had said earlier about how they didn't need him. They'd done all right in his absence. That was true, but she could see that there was pain behind his words. He needed to be needed.

Everyone needs to belong and be part of something that isn't just themselves. And this little quirky and oddly dangerous town is where we belong.

"You're right. We'll get through this," she said to Athena. "But either way, you're not going to get out of doing the dishes."

"I wouldn't dream of it," said Athena with a smile. "Now, get dressed, or we're going to be late."

CHAPTER
THIRTY-NINE

As soon as darkness had fallen, they left Thorn Manor, driving in procession to the town centre.

Athena felt a nervous flutter in her chest as they drove through the quiet streets. "There would normally be a lot more people around on the night of a seasonal festival," she muttered from the back of the car as Rosemary drove with Dain in the passenger seat.

He'd insisted on coming with them. Burk had taken his own car and so had Neve.

"It does seem awfully quiet for a Saturday night, in general," said Rosemary. "But I guess the shops do close early around here."

Athena felt even more nervous as she realised how eerie the deserted town seemed.

They pulled up next to Marjie's tea shop. She was waiting outside, holding a rolling pin.

"What's that for?" Rosemary asked.

"It's a weapon," said Marjie. "I've got a broom too."

"Maybe try a sword or something," Athena suggested.

"Where are your weapons, then?" Marjie asked.

Rosemary held up her hands and twiddled her fingers around. "This is all I need."

"Dear, dear," said Marjie. "Look, the pies are ready."

She nipped inside the shop and returned with a tray containing paper bags of delicious smelling beef pies.

"Feel free to pop in if you need anything to drink," said Marjie. "I'll leave the door unlocked while we're here."

Athena took a pie and bit into it. Despite the fact that her brain was occupied with a million different worries, she couldn't help sighing at the delicious, rich gravy and crumbly pastry.

"Marjie, you're a legend," she said with her mouth half full.

"Close your mouth when you're talking," said Rosemary. "I mean, don't speak with your mouth...eat with your mouth full, don't speak with your mouth open up. Oh! You know what I mean!"

"Athena!" a voice called out.

She turned to see Elise approaching with Felix in his fox form just behind her, followed by a rather large bear. Sam brought up the rear.

"You came!" said Athena.

"Of course," said Elise.

Athena smiled and gave Elise and Sam hugs. "Thanks for coming," she said. "We're in way over our heads. We have no idea what we're doing."

"We wouldn't miss it," said Sam.

"I'm a little surprised, actually," Athena admitted. "I wondered if...after yesterday at school, nobody would ever want to talk to me again."

"I figured what must have happened," said Elise. "I hope you don't mind, I explained it to the others."

"That's fine," said Athena.

"But we were sure you hadn't done anything on purpose," said

Sam. "And then when you texted today...Well, of course we had to help."

"You're our friend and that's what's important," said Elise. "Regardless of what you accidentally let into the earth realm."

"Thank you," said Athena. She was still getting used to having real friends.

"Umm..." She ogled the slightly terrifying bear who she knew was probably Deron. "What are we going to do with a couple of stray animals?"

"They're much stronger in their shifter forms," said Elise. "You'll see."

"Ahh," said Marjie. "There you all are!"

"You knew we were coming?" Elise asked.

Athena looked around awkwardly, hoping Marjie wasn't about to send her friends packing.

"Of course you'd come. I prepared some special charms just for you. If any creatures appear, throw them and duck." Marjie held out a brown paper bag to both the humanoid children.

Felix looked up expectantly.

"You're only allowed one if you're in human form," said Marjie sternly. "Foxes can't throw."

Felix looked down at the ground, making a whining noise, and sculked off.

Athena laughed nervously. She knew the evening ahead was going to be dangerous and hoped she didn't regret inviting her friends. Even with the additional people they were still going to be a bit light in terms of holding a proper town ritual, let alone fighting off potential hordes of flaming beasts.

Mum's protection spells better work!

"Right. So what's the plan?" Elise asked.

Neve frowned and turned towards Rosemary. "Are you sure it's a good idea to allow children to be here?"

"We're almost adults," said Elise. "And Mum's even here."

"She is?" Rosemary asked.

They turned to see Fleur locking up her car, holding a big tray of something sparkly.

"I told her all about it," said Elise. "She insisted on coming to help."

"And so have I!" said a familiar voice. Ferg has appeared from a side street. He was wearing a brown cloak.

"What are you doing here?" Rosemary asked.

"I've come to officiate, of course," said Ferg.

"I thought you'd be following the rules," said Marjie.

Ferg looked stern. "Unfortunately, this was a difficult situation for me. I'm usually a stickler for the rules as you know, but I can't abide a town festival being cancelled, especially not on such short notice. It was outrageous.

"Great," said Rosemary. "The more the merrier!"

They began setting up the ritual, placing the red crystals at strategic points in the town circle.

Athena noticed that her father and Burk seemed to be studiously avoiding each other. She found it hilarious, the pickle her mother was getting herself into with these various men who were obviously interested in her and Rosemary's flat-out refusal to be involved with any one of them. Though she did feel a little bit sorry for both men. For Burk, who had done nothing but be the perfect gentleman, and who Rosemary was treating with slight coldness, and also for her father, who might have been totally useless at times. He wasn't so bad, and it wasn't just because he'd had a hard life that Athena was close to forgiving him. There was also everything he'd done to try and make up for it lately.

Everyone deserves a chance to redeem themselves, she thought. *If people can forgive me for letting the fire sprites into the earth realm, then maybe I can work on forgiving dad.*

They began laying out crystals and herbs to prepare for the ritual. Marjie set up the Beltane fire. Meanwhile, Ferg walked to the centre of the circle and set a little brown drawstring pouch gently on the ground.

"What's that?" Rosemary asked, her hands poised with a bundle of protective herbs she was laying around the perimeter.

Ferg didn't reply. He took three paces back and muttered a charm under his breath.

The brown pouch twitched slightly and then out popped a candy-striped pole, ten feet high and strung with ribbons.

"The maypole, of course," Ferg said.

Athena clapped and her friends cheered.

Rosemary narrowed her eyes at Ferg. "You could have warned me. I was getting worried."

Ferg turned towards Rosemary. "Nothing to worry about." He saluted and then walked off towards Marjie and her fire, leaving Rosemary shaking her head.

CHAPTER
FORTY

Rosemary glanced around for one final check to ensure the herbs and crystals were all in place for the protective spells she'd prepped for.

Everything was laid out in preparation for the ritual and they'd arranged themselves in a loose circle on the grass, leaving enough space in the middle for something dangerous to enter.

I hope this works!

Ferg stepped slightly further into the centre and began to officiate the Beltane ritual. He was so comfortable, as if this were a normal festival and not a last minute attempt to stop arsonist cults.

"At this time of year, we give thanks to the start of summer," he said. "And the many blessings of richness and fertility it bestows upon us."

Rosemary had a prickling at the back of her neck as if she was being watched.

She looked around to see more people from the town had appeared, including Nesta who must have found someone else to look after the child and old woman at their house. Sherry was there, and so was the mayor's husband, Zade, along with Agatha Twigg and Covvey. Ashwyn appeared too. Either she'd come to help once the children were settled in for the night, or perhaps something more sinister was afoot.

It seemed that a lot of people had kind of summoned themselves to the ritual, and Rosemary was slightly suspicious of all of them.

She eyed them one-by-one, wondering if any or all the uninvited guests were involved in the fires.

Mum, stop glaring at people. It's awkward. Athena's voice sounded in Rosemary's head.

But how did they know to come here? Are they all Bloodstones?!

Athena gave her a meaningful look from where she stood across the circle. *Didn't you stop to think that this ceremony has been practiced here for centuries? People weren't going to stop just because some mayor called it off.*

Rosemary made a point to smile instead of anything that could be misconstrued as glaring. *Maybe you have a point, but they shouldn't be here. They probably have no idea they're putting themselves in grave danger.*

Athena didn't respond. Maybe she had stopped listening in to Rosemary's thoughts.

As Ferg continued to talk, Rosemary wanted to warn them all off. It wasn't safe. But she knew it was too late. Even if the townsfolk tried to leave now there was no guarantee they'd escape what was to come, and besides, there was a certain strength in numbers.

Instead, she connected mentally with the earth beneath her. She could sense the crystals and flowers she'd placed strategically around the circle. She linked her magic through them now – both the old Thorn family magic that coursed through her veins, and her own unique brand of magic.

She felt the crystals respond to her as her magic pulsed through them, beginning to weave the spell around them all, protecting the circle from harm, wrapping delicate white protective light around them.

Ferg raised his hands and announced that the circle be cast.

Marjie walked around the perimeter, waving a little wooden wand with a crystal stuck to the end of it, adding her own magic to that which Rosemary had already woven, strengthening their protections further.

A third source of magic joined in the mix. Rosemary glanced at Athena, who nodded. She smiled back. Her daughter's magic was powerful on both sides. The fae magic from Dain's side had a distinctly aromatic quality that Rosemary hadn't noticed before. It reminded her of elderflower cordial.

"The circle is cast. We are between the worlds. Beyond the bounds of time," Marjie said. "Where light and dark meet as one. Together we are safe. Together we are strong."

She resumed her place in the circle.

It was time for the directions and elements to be called.

Athena turned to the east, and everyone followed suit. She summoned element of air, with intellect and clarity.

Then turned to the south and Rosemary summoned the element of fire, passion and drive.

Marjie summoned the element of water, emotion and empathy, and then finally, Neve summoned the element of earth, matter, prosperity, and the physical world, grounding and determination. Rosemary smiled as she felt the energy click into place. Neve had been hesitant to take part as she wasn't particularly magical, but that kind of grounded practicality was just what they needed for the earth element.

After the quarters and the elements were summoned, Athena called out to the maiden goddess, Brigid.

Oh great maiden, Brigid, we honour you tonight.

Then Rosemary did the same for the crone goddess, Cerridwen.

Cerridwen, we call you forth to our circle, oh grandmother, guardian of the old ways and of inspiration, goddess of transformation and rebirth. We honour you.

They had figured if an older god was trying to break through, it wouldn't hurt to have some of the more modern, and hopefully more spry, god relatives present, or at least in their favour.

They lit the small fires they'd prepared inside the circle, then began to circle around it, as was the traditional practice at Beltane.

It seemed a rather solemn affair compared to what Rosemary would have expected from a usual festival. After all, they were supposed to be celebrating fertility and the beginnings of summer.

As the ceremony continued, the atmosphere lightened to one of merriment. Ferg began patting a drum to a jaunty beat. Fleur pulled out panpipes and played a little tune.

The participants came forward, taking handfuls of flower petals from the baskets that Marjie had brought, to scatter around the circle. Some took ribbons from the maypole and skipped around it, weaving the colourful strands over and under each other as they went.

Sherry, Zade, Agatha, and Ashwyn began dancing around the circle and were joined by others, as they made their way towards the small Beltane fire.

Traditionally, those who wanted children or to bring something to fruition in their life, would jump over the fire, thinking of what they wanted. And Rosemary figured, since nothing else in a dramatic nature had occurred, she might as well jump over it thinking of her dream chocolate shop. Though she was pleased to see that Athena didn't jump over it at all.

Rosemary certainly wasn't ready to be a grandmother yet.

She carried on around the circle, turning back to watch as Nesta jumped over the tiny fire, tripping a little as she did so, landing with a laugh as Neve caught her. Rosemary smiled at her friends. They really did make a lovely couple.

The joy and laughter of the celebration was interrupted by a shriek and then a banging sound.

Rosemary turned to see the dreaded and familiar hooded figures approaching.

"I knew it!" she cried out to Athena. "It's the Bloodstone Society. They are the ones behind all this."

The woman in the middle peeled back the hood of her cloak. Her pale blonde hair gleamed in the low light of the lanterns around the town centre.

Rosemary breathed a sigh of relief that her paranoid suspicions about her various blonde friends were unwarranted. She glared at the woman. "Still masked, I see. What's the matter? Not brave enough to show your face?"

The woman threw back her head with a gravelly laugh. She removed her gleaming butterfly mask to reveal a beautiful pale and familiar face.

"Lamorna!" Marjie shrieked. "I cannot believe this! I trusted you to work in my shop and all the while you were plotting against us."

"And spying, no doubt," said Athena.

Lamorna smiled in glee. "It was so easy to put on a simpering act and win your trust," she said, pouting.

"Shut it, blondie," said Rosemary. "It's time for you and your Bloodstone cronies to get out of my town!"

"I don't think so," said Lamorna. "In fact, we quite like it here."

"Move out of the way," Rosemary cried, motioning to people to run around to the other side of the circle. She sent a blast of bright purple energy out towards the newcomers.

It seemed to hit an invisible barrier on the inside of the magical dome that encased the ritual. Rosemary hadn't realised that when they'd cast the circle they'd created an actual energy membrane or forcefield, an unfortunate own-goal.

The energy ball made its way through with some encouragement but it was too slow. The Bloodstone members just stepped to the side.

Lamorna laughed. "You told me she was silly, but I didn't realise she was this silly."

"That's just my Gemini ascendant," Rosemary muttered.

Athena gave her a sympathetic look.

"Anyway, who are you talking to? Who told you I'm silly?"

Lamorna turned to the figure next to her whose cloak slipped back enough for Rosemary to recognise Despina with her perfect shiny bob of hair and her pastel pink collar.

"Not now!" said Rosemary. "The last thing I need is to get a rash."

"She's not an estate agent anymore," said Athena from the east of the circle. "I told you your so-called allergy was psychosomatic."

"Once an estate agent always an estate agent."

"What are you talking about?" Lamorna asked. She was clearly the leader.

Rosemary grimaced. "Well, at least it looks like we're protected in here. Plus, we've got way more power than the three of you. Why don't you just go on home?"

Lamorna threw back her head with another gravelly laugh. "We have reinforcements coming."

"Of course you do," said Rosemary. "Why wouldn't you have planned ahead when you've orchestrated all this?"

Lamorna looked at her in shock. "What do you mean? We thought you and your silly witch friends were behind the fires."

"Why on earth would we do that?" Rosemary glared at Lamorna. "It's not like we're in a dodgy power-mad secret society or anything!"

"Don't act all innocent," Despina said. "Why else would you be here when the ritual was supposedly cancelled?"

"Wait a minute," said Athena. "If you're not here for the Cavalia, what are you doing here, then?"

"We're here to stop you," said Lamorna. "Messing with the old gods is a step too far. The Bloodstone Society is coming back, and believe me when I say that *we* are going to be the major magical power in these parts. No old gods are getting in our way."

Rosemary looked around the group in confusion. "So you're here to stamp out the competition?"

"That's right," said Despina. "Whatever cult of Belamus you're trying to start here – it's not going to happen!"

"I'm not bloody starting any cults!" Rosemary cried.

Despina rolled her eyes. "Then who?"

There was a sudden crackle from the tiny fire in the circle, and the little cauldron burst into life as an enormous fire lit the centre of where they stood.

Rosemary reached for her magical light barrier, sending more energy through it, around the circle, in the hopes that people wouldn't be affected by the magical fire.

"It's too late," said Despina. "He's here."

"Let's go!" Lamorna cried.

There was a great crackling sound followed by booming laughter.

A series of beasts burst through the flames.

Rosemary looked back at the Bloodstone members to see their eyes bulging.

"I think we'll just leave you to it," Despina said and they backed away into the shadows.

Rosemary thought about going after the Bloodstones, but she had bigger fish to fry. Her problems had just grown astronomically larger. She eyed the flaming beasts in horror. Some were at least eight feet tall. Others had wings. "This is going to get messy."

"Let us out of the protection," said Marjie, hammering against the invisible barrier that Rosemary had put up, which seemed to have grown and warped to encase all the ritual participants individually. "We need to fight. We're prepared." She held up a bright yellow bundle from her patchwork carry bag.

Covvey growled and flexed his muscles. "Let us fight, lass."

Rosemary tensed. "It's not safe."

"We came prepared to fight," said Fleur.

Rosemary looked around to see Ferg holding a staff and Ashwyn with bottles of potions. Everyone had some kind of weapon or magical tool. Even those who Rosemary had assumed had just wandered into town for the ritual.

"But how did everyone know to bring weapons?" Rosemary asked.

"After Elise told me what was going on I called up some allies around the town," said Fleur. "We couldn't let you face this alone."

It was all kind of moving, but Rosemary didn't have time to be sentimental.

"Alright, then," she said. "I'll drop the barrier, but if things get out of control I want everyone to run away."

"We're not stupid," said Sam. "We're here to fight, not to be annihilated."

Rosemary allowed her magic to shrink back, so that it was no longer a barrier, but she kept a small coating in place, covering the participants, to protect them against any inappropriate effects of the fire.

A huge minotaur lumbered forward. He raised a gleaming golden bow, aiming a flaming arrow towards Rosemary, and let fly.

She raised her arm and blocked it with a magic shield, just as Marjie hurled a yellow parcel at the beast. It exploded into dozens of enchanted butterflies that swarmed around its head and chased, tripping it to the ground.

"That was unexpected," said Athena.

Covvey shifted into an enormous wolf and growled just as Felix in fox form lunged at one of the fiery nymphs.

Rosemary shrieked. "Don't get burnt!"

"Don't worry," said Elise. "His fox form is impervious to fire."

"Including magical fire?" Rosemary asked.

"We'll soon find out," said Athena.

Rosemary strengthened the protective magical barrier over herself and extended the same favour out to the townsfolk around her, hoping that it would keep them from danger of either the violent or seductive kind. She could sense Athena's magic working with hers, fortifying their protections.

Rosemary looked towards her daughter, just as Athena cried, "Mum!"

She turned to see a fiery centaur running towards her.

"Don't worry, I've got this," Athena said and blasted it out of the way with a big sizzling ball of lightning.

"That was impressive." Rosemary beamed. "You've been practicing!"

The fight continued. The giant wolf that was Covvey barrelled down multiple beasts at a time before taking a break and shifting back to human form to help Agatha as she wielded an enormous double-headed staff that shot blasts of water in multiple directions.

"What's that?" Rosemary called out.

"One of my little inventions," said Agatha. "I call it the Aquifyer."

"Handy!" said Rosemary. She noticed Fleur and Elise nearby as they sparred with some fire nymphs not far away, moving with a kind of fluidity that Rosemary wouldn't have thought possible. It almost looked like a dance as they ducked and kicked and punched the nymphs that darted around out of their reach and then circled back, baring their teeth and claws as they hissed at their opponents.

Elise and her mother joined hands. Bright rainbows burst from between them, circling the fire sprites, delicate flaming creatures that they were, and wrapping around them, binding them and sending them sprawling into the ground.

Zade wielded an impressive-looking glowing sword. He stood back-to-back with Ferg who got to work using his staff like a spear. He battled a large hairy fire creature bearing a flaming pitchfork. Ferg was nimbler than Rosemary had expected. The creature lunged for him with the sword and Ferg ducked, rolled on the ground, and then sent his staff straight towards the chin of the creature.

Burk stood off to the side with an intense expression on his face. No doubt he was holding back because of the damage the fire would do to his vampire form. Dain, on the other hand, was right amongst it, punching nymphs, sprites, and beasties alike. He was a ball of chaos, grabbing them and spinning them around, flinging them into each other.

Rosemary raised her hands, pressing her fingers together. She wove a much stronger fire-protection spell in mid-air and sent it floating towards Burk. His expression transformed into one of glee as it coated him like liquid. He nodded in her direction and then barrelled into the fire, no longer afraid of the flames.

Ashwyn threw a potion towards the centre, nearly striking the largest beast who had been standing there, roaring for a while. The beast stepped out of the way and continued roaring. The potion hit the ground, crackled and hissed, sending bright silver sparks into the air in a cloud of steam. The earth beneath it melted.

She sure knows how to brew up something nasty. Remind me to never get on her bad side.

The battle was in full swing. The smell of smoke and charred earth hung thick in the air, but above that was a sweeter scent note, it was heady, almost soapy, but Rosemary didn't have time to think about it. Between sending out blasts of magic and hurling flaming beasts to the ground as they attacked, Rosemary watched the chaos unfold all around. The bear and fox and various magical people all attacked or were attacked by the fiery creatures.

Sid and her firefighting team had been called in by Neve. They lined up around the outside of the town square. They had hoses and all the hydrants on full blast, dousing the flames that tried to escape the outskirts of the circle, but they hadn't gained much ground.

Rosemary tried to connect with the element of water, but it evaded her. It turned out that in the heat of battle, she needed to fight fire with fire.

The Myrtlewood townsfolk had managed to hold back the swarm of flaming beasties well, but the tide seemed to be turning, as more and more creatures emerged from the flames. Some flew through with fiery wings. Others formed a stampede.

Rosemary threw up the barrier spell she'd practiced, but it was all she could do hold them back.

Suddenly, there was an air wrenching crack and an enormous chariot burst through, hovering in mid-air. It glistened and gleamed in gold. Atop it sat an enormous man, who gleamed golden himself with huge horns stretching up into the sky.

"The Cavalia begins!" he cried. "I have been summoned."

"Belamus!" The fire creatures all began to chant and bow before him.

"Heed my power and delight!"

"Delight?" Rosemary called back. "What kind of delight is this?"

"It is a celebration of all that is bright in the world!" the old god bellowed. The sheer size of him made Rosemary feel tiny.

The old god's voice rumbled through them; Rosemary felt it shaking her bones. "Thank you for summoning me, human creatures, frail as you are. I heeded your call."

"It wasn't us," said Athena, but Belamus took no notice.

"Now I'm ready to receive my sacrifice."

"Sacrifice?" Rosemary asked. She looked around at the other townsfolk who were all looking as equally terrified as she felt. "We didn't hear anything about a sacrifice."

Belamus roared. "You must sacrifice a beast to me. A beast of the earth to appease and delight me." He looked around. "But here, you have only young little beasties." He gestured towards Deron and Felix. "Is this meant to be a befitting sacrifice?"

"No!" Athena shouted. "They're not sacrifices!"

Just then, a howl sounded off in the distance.

Rosemary looked around, but she couldn't see anything.

"Are you saying you summoned me here without a sacrifice?" Belamus growled.

"The thing is," said Rosemary, her heart racing almost as fast as her mind as she struggled to come up with a solution to their catastrophic predicament, "we didn't exactly want you here at all. It's all a big misunderstanding and I hope you don't mind just turning around and going home. Sorry for the inconvenience."

The god glowered at her. "You frail and worthless humans! How dare you insult my power like this!"

There was another howl and Rosemary turned to see a huge wolf-like creature stalking towards the circle.

Oh no! It's Liam!

She hadn't returned his calls and now it was too late. Somehow, he'd not managed to keep himself shackled up and had come to join the party.

Marjie and some of the others were glaring at the huge wolf-man as if he were part of the evil, and for all Rosemary knew, maybe he was. He certainly wasn't up to any good.

"Aha!" said Belamus. "A great beast! A great beast befitting to be sacrificed for me! That will do. Kill him!"

"No!" Rosemary shouted as Liam, or at least the werewolf that Rosemary assumed was Liam, lunged towards the circle.

Rosemary raised her arms to try to stop him, but hesitated. If she blasted him with her magic, his secret might well be revealed in front of half the town. Before she had time to weigh up the risks, Burk flew across and attacked, blocking the werewolf's path, and so did Dain.

"A great battle in my honour!" Belamus bellowed again and laughed.

"Werewolf, vampire, and fae," Rosemary muttered. "It seems remiss not to make a bad joke about a bar." She wasn't bothering to censor herself as she wondered how much water she could draw from the four hydrants around the town.

"Not now!" said Athena. "We've got plenty of time for your awful sense of humour later on. We've got to stop them!"

"I'm sure they'll be fine," said Rosemary.

"No, not them." Athena gestured back towards the flaming beasts, who were slowly advancing towards Rosemary's would-be suitors.

"What about your essay?" Rosemary asked.

"This is no time to be asking about schoolwork, Mum!"

"No. Just think. Is there anyone we could call on...anything that could stop Belamus?"

"Depending on which source you believe, once the beast is sacrificed," said Athena, "the door will be flung wide open, and thousands of fiery creatures will come through and ravage the human realm, bringing a renewed era of Belamus!"

"You didn't think to tell me there was a sacrifice?!" Rosemary asked. "Oh, never mind. That part's not very helpful. Anything else? If only there was somebody who could stand up to him."

"Now that gives me an idea," said Athena, ducking out of the way of a flaming arrow. "Remember how we called on the gods as part of our ritual. What if I actually tried to summon Brigid?"

"Brigid? Why Brigid? Do you think she's any match for this dude?"

"I don't know," said Athena, blasting a nymph with her magic. "But she is the patron goddess of this town. Maybe she'll be listening. Granny's books say that reciting Brigid's ancestry will bring protection."

"Worth a try," said Rosemary as she hurled a flaming beast aside. "Only...Do we know what it is?"

Athena pulled out her phone. "Hold them off for a second."

Rosemary blasted white light out towards all the fiery creatures nearby, knocking them back. " I won't be able to hold this up for very long."

"Here goes!" said Athena, and she began to recite.

This is the genealogy of the holy maiden, Brigid.
Radiant flame of gold,
Daughter of Dugall the Brown,
Son of Aodh, son of Art, son of Conn,
Son of Crearer, Son of Cis, son of Carmac, son of Carruin,
Every day and every night
That I say the genealogy of Brigid,
I shall not be killed, I shall not be harried,
I shall not be put in a cell, I shall not be wounded,
Neither shall Spirit leave me in forgetfulness.
No fire, no sun, no moon shall burn me,
No lake, no water, nor sea shall drown me,
No arrow of fairy nor dart of fay shall wound me
And I under the protection of the great goddess
And my gentle foster-mother is my beloved Brigid.

Athena raised her arms in the air and said, "Fair Brigid, patron goddess of Myrtlewood, our people need you. Please come forth. I summon you, I beseech you!"

"That was a bit dramatic," said Rosemary. "Remind me to sign you up for drama lessons."

"Shush!" said Athena. "I'm trying to focus."

The air around them seemed to still and then a big gust of wind blew through, bringing a flurry of flower petals with it. The maypole ribbons began to spin as it swept around the circle. With it came the warm floral scents of spring.

An enormous white light burst into the town square.

Rosemary shielded her eyes and peered through the glare. An enormous being stood there, towering over them, six stories high.

"Goddess Brigid," said Athena.

The goddess looked down at them curiously and then turned her attention across the circle, fixing her gaze on the old god.

"Ah..." said Athena. "As you might notice..."

Belamus stood there with a somewhat sheepish grin now plastered across his face.

"Grandad!" said Brigid. "What are you doing here? This is *my* town."

"I'm...I'm here for the Cavalia," said Belamus. "These people summoned me. They...need my help. They want to bring things back to the old way."

His words stirred something inside Rosemary's memory. She couldn't quite put her finger on what.

"No, you absolutely will not do that," said Brigid. "The old ways are over, granddad. You're coming with me." She snapped her fingers, and the entire fiery scene in front of them vanished, along with the beasts, leaving no trace behind, not even scorch marks.

"Fair people of Myrtlewood," said Brigid. "My apologies for the disruptions. I'm afraid I must go now, to attend to some family matters."

"Thank you!" Rosemary and Athena both called out after her as she vanished slowly, leaving a floating trail of spring blossoms hovering magically in the air in her wake.

"Well, that was unexpected," said Rosemary. "I'm glad your Brigid thing worked."

"Yeah. Thank goodness I'm becoming a bit of a swot. Getting geeky about my assignments."

They surveyed the carnage, including a large scorch mark in the middle of the town square, much bigger than the one from the previous fire from a few days before. At least a few people seemed to be limping or mildly injured. Everyone was accounted for.

"Everything's going to be alright," said Rosemary, somewhat surprising herself with this realisation. "We did it."

"I did it, you mean," said Athena. "You just stumbled and floundered, then I led us to victory."

"You're still on dishes duty," said Rosemary. "For a very long time."

Athena sighed. "Oh, well. It'll be good practice for my automancy magic, I suppose."

Rosemary elbowed her playfully. "Seriously though. Thank you," she said. "I'm pretty sure we wouldn't have gotten out of this mess without you, at least without any serious injuries."

"No problem," said Athena. "When I make a mess, I like to be the one to summon a goddess to clean it up."

"That's how I raised you," said Rosemary proudly.

People milled around asking each other how they were for a few minutes, and then began cleaning up.

"You're all welcome back at my place," Rosemary announced.

"I'll bring the cake," said Marjie.

"I'll bring the wine," Sherry added.

"All right, it's settled," said Athena. "I'll take these bags to the car."

The scent of lily of the valley wafted over the town square and Rosemary turned to see someone standing in the entrance to one of the side streets.

"I'll meet you there," she said. "I've just got to take care of something."

She bolted after the shrouded figure, chasing them down the street next to Burk's law office.

"Stop where you are," Rosemary called. "Or this is not going to be pretty."

The person stopped and then turned back and lowered the scarf from around her head.

"I knew it!" said Rosemary. "Well, I didn't at first, but I did suspect you were up to something when you invited us to dinner, and then I got caught up with thinking it was the Bloodstone Society..."

"Must you ramble?" Elamina asked.

Rosemary noticed that despite her haughty tone, her cousin looked somewhat dishevelled. Her white blonde hair, normally perfectly in place, looked mussed, as if she'd been through some quite frantic endeavours, herself.

"Did the Bloodstones have no idea what was going on?" Rosemary asked. "Or was a that lie? Are they secretly working for you?"

Elamina threw back with a haughty cackle. "Those plebs? I wouldn't dream of working with anyone of their station."

"So even when you've been apprehended, you still insist on being an arrogant nutball?"

Elamina glared at her. "What gave me away? You all seemed perfectly occupied. You didn't even notice that I was watching from a distance."

"For a start, there's the stench of that god awful flower," said

Rosemary. "That's a dead giveaway. Plus, when you invited us over for dinner at your house, you did talk about wanting things to go back to the old ways, which was kind of what that big horned guy said. I didn't remember until just before."

"You speak about the gods with such disrespect," said Elamina.

"Who's being disrespectful now?" Rosemary asked. "It's pretty rich accusing me, considering you set the town on fire and almost blew up the whole place. I've heard about blue-blooded conservatives romanticising the past, but this is ridiculous. And probably a whole lot more carnage would have happened if we hadn't stopped that guy."

"*That guy*," said Elamina, "is an ancient and respected being. He's incredibly powerful!"

"I don't really see the appeal," said Rosemary. "He's a little bit large and hairy for my liking."

Elamina scoffed. "If you only knew."

"Look," said Rosemary. "I don't mean to kink-shame you, but what on earth did you think you were playing at?"

"I'll have you know that I've managed to do what my father had been aiming to for decades."

Rosemary raised her eyebrows. "I don't want to know about your daddy issues! How did you even do it?"

Elamina glared at her. "There were various manoeuvres necessary, if you must know. For a start, I managed to get hold of some wild fire sprites through some of my contacts. They were the missing link, you see. With the power of my magic, and drawing close to Beltane, I managed to light the first fire."

"The one at the old Twigg farm," said Rosemary. "But that wasn't enough for you?"

Elamina laughed bitterly. "Not by a long shot. To have a chance of instigating the Cavalia I needed more sprites, but the only way I could think of was through the fae realm. It was fate really, that my own little cousin held the key."

"That's why you wanted to spend time with Athena wasn't it? You knew she had the power to cut through the veil. You know *what* she is...But you don't know *who* she is. She's not a play thing. You manipulated Athena. How?!"

"I might have planted some seeds," said Elamina. "I might have tried to hint to her, very subtly so that you wouldn't pick it up, that she had the power to get back to the place she missed so much. The place that you would be trying to keep her away from."

"I don't buy it," said Rosemary. "You're not *that* compelling. And Athena isn't gullible."

"If you really must know it was a simple suggestion, over dinner, followed by some carefully crafted chants to lure her outside and make her think it was a good idea to open the veil. Then my own ancient magic had the power to summon them through. After that first time I simply attached an invisible charm to her and she did the rest. It was brilliant, if I do say so myself."

Rage rose like bile in Rosemary's torso and she hurled a ball of red lightning at her cousin. Elamina deflected, but it sent her reeling into the side of the wall.

"How dare you enchant my daughter!"

Rosemary expected retaliation, but Elamina merely shrugged. There was something odd about her; she seemed almost deflated.

"I didn't hurt her," Elamina said quietly.

"That entire thing was totally inappropriate and dangerous. Not to mention all the fires that we've had recently which sent people into all sorts of strange behaviours."

"Inconvenient, but necessary," said Elamina. "The magic on the other side of my family goes back many thousands of years. It comes from the cult of Belamus. To truly harness it and master it, we needed his return. All my life I was told tales of the great power of Belamus. My father mourned the loss of the old gods to history. I was merely fulfilling my legacy."

"And did you get what you wanted?" Rosemary asked, unimpressed.

"The old ways..." Elamina began, but her voice trailed away.

"Well, that's just lovely," said Rosemary. "But this was all about power. What were you *really* seeking here, cousin? Did you want some kind of apocalypse?"

"The power is rightfully ours. The Bracewell family..."

Rosemary laughed. "How foolish to think you could harness the powers of an old god."

Elamina looked bitter, and Rosemary could tell she had regrets.

"I guess it's a bit late for a be-careful-what-you-wish-for moment," said Rosemary.

Elamina glared at her. "If you hadn't meddled—"

"What? You'd have fire and brimstone raining down on us? Is that honestly what you wanted?"

Elamina crossed her arms. "Mama and Papa may have been mistaken as to the risks. It is difficult to understand ancient history as not much was recorded and many things that were are not entirely accurate."

"I suppose that's as close as I'm going to get to you lot admitting you were wrong," said Rosemary. "At least you admit to all of it. That's very convenient because I have a detective friend who's right over there...I wonder what the magical authorities will think."

"I don't think so," said Elamina. "You owe me one."

"I only owe you some potion ingredients," said Rosemary. "It's not a get out of magical jail free card."

"Now, that's where you're wrong," said Elamina. "You owe a lot more than that. Imagine my surprise when my sweet, innocent, yet somewhat idiotic cousin came to me asking for spell ingredients, only to ask for something totally banned and illegal. Of course I helped out with what I could, but werewolf blood? That's something else entirely. If I was to possess such a thing, the authorities would come knocking on my door. Indeed, the witching authorities do not show mercy to people possessing and using dangerous illicit substances like that. Let alone the fact that it now appears that you *know* a certain werewolf...one who turned up here tonight, no doubt. I don't suppose you'd like to end up imprisoned in Bermuda for the next decade or two?"

Rosemary was speechless. Though Elamina had not specifically issued a threat, she'd certainly laid it all out. If Rosemary went to the authorities now, Elamina would be sure to tell them about the werewolf blood, which would not only put Liam in danger when they tracked him down, it would also land her with a whole lot of charges for harbouring a werewolf and using illicit magical substances or some such things.

"How can you—"

Elamina smirked. "Now, I know you're going to tell me how much you care about your daughter. And I know you do. I also know you're not about to risk everything you care about and set yourself up to be locked up in a prison cell, where you can't care for her."

"You absolute garbage face," said Rosemary. "How dare you?"

"How dare I what?" said Elamina. "I have not threatened, dear cousin. I'll let you do that yourself. I have more important things to do with my time."

"So that's it then?" said Rosemary. "You create total chaos, unleashing an old god and a whole lot of fiery beasties, and then you toddle off to your castle."

Elamina looked bitter. "I didn't really get what I wanted to out of the whole thing."

"Oh great," said Rosemary. "So you're bitter that Belamus was sent back?"

"It is a shame he disappeared so fast, before Derse and I had a chance to harness his energy for our own gain. But there's no point in wasting anymore time, cousin. I'm afraid I can't stay much longer. Things to do, people to see. You know the drill."

Rosemary sighed. She hated being caught in a checkmate situation like this. She couldn't put Liam at risk and she couldn't go to jail. She needed to be there to protect Athena.

"I won't go to the authorities," Rosemary conceded. "You win on that front, there's too much at stake."

Elamina smiled – not the fake smile she'd put on over dinner, but her genuine smile which was a lot colder and more frightening.

"See now, cousin. You are a bit slow but you do catch up, eventually."

"Maybe I won't go to the authorities," said Rosemary. "But I can still kick your arse and you're not going to tell anyone about it."

Rosemary held up her hands, summoning a giant purple ball of energy, crackling with lightning and fire.

Elamina screamed and dashed out of the way before disappearing into the night.

Rosemary laughed at herself, trying ease the bitterness she felt at being trumped like that. "At least it solves the mystery," she muttered. "Though I don't know if I can actually explain any of that to anyone else."

"You don't have to, Mum," said Athena, stepping from around the corner. "I heard all of that." She looked around to check that nobody else was listening. "It's Liam, isn't it? He was the werewolf."

"Athena, I..."

"I know. I won't tell anyone," said Athena. "It seems that werewolves are rather stigmatised in magical society. It seems a bit prejudiced if you ask me."

"I thought so," said Rosemary. "Anyway, what did you think about our dear cousin?"

"She's a nasty piece of work, isn't she?" Athena linked arms with her mother as they walked to the car.

"I'm glad you realise that," said Rosemary. "I'm sure Elamina thought I'd hide it from you so that I didn't share Liam's secret. She's still going to try and use you for something. I can tell by the way she talks about you as if you're some kind of treasured prize."

"That's one thing you don't have to worry about," said Athena. "Hell's going freeze over before I let that happen."

"Don't say that," said Rosemary. "I'm sure this town has a seasonal festival for exactly such a thing."

Athena laughed. "Okay, then." She put her arm around her mother. "Let's go home. We can talk about all of this and what it means another time."

"That sounds like a good idea," said Rosemary. "I'm in the mood for hot chocolate and a bit of good conversation, followed by a lot of very quiet time."

CHAPTER

FORTY-ONE

R osemary stirred the enormous bubbling pot of hot chocolate on the stove, inhaling the heavenly scent.

Most of those who had been at the impromptu ritual had decided to come over to decompress after the dramatic events of the evening.

Marjie lined up mugs, ready for hot chocolate for Rosemary, while Athena showed her friends around the house, since only Elise had seen the inside of it before. Ashwyn admired Granny's crystals and chatted to Sherry while Fleur and others followed Dain into the living room. Of course, Liam was nowhere in sight, and Rosemary hoped he was okay. Dain had informed her that Burk had escorted him away from the town square and was keeping him somewhere safe. Rosemary wondered if this would mean letting the vampire in on his secret, but that wasn't her issue to worry about.

Rosemary added an extra pinch of cinnamon and a dash of vanilla into the brew of hot chocolate.

"Mmm, smells delicious," said Ferg. He sat at the kitchen table as if he were someone incredibly important, staff still clasped in hand, while the foundling children stood around him, looking awestruck.

Rosemary had returned to find them all tucked up asleep in their beds, and Una sitting in an armchair with a book looking slightly tired herself, but satisfied. The children's slumber had not withstood the sounds created by so many people arriving. They had gotten up, confused and excited, and proceeded to run around the house. They were all going to be tired in the morning, but Rosemary didn't mind. Hopefully that would mean a proper sleep in.

With over a dozen visitors, Rosemary was pleased to see that the living room had grown to be bigger than usual. She and Marjie carried in trays of mugs filled with steaming hot chocolate.

Rosemary and Marjie entered the living room to find that the mayor had arrived at Thorn Manor.

"That's funny," Rosemary whispered to Marjie. "I thought he'd be too embarrassed to show his face after cancelling the ritual and everything."

"Oh, Don never misses a party. He must have snuck in," said Marjie. "I didn't notice him arrive."

Mr June insisted on doing a round of speeches, in which he thanked the townsfolk for all their hard work and somehow made it seem as if all of the good ideas were his own.

"How does he manage to take credit for everything when he wasn't even there?" Athena asked. "While he's supposed to be thanking us all?"

"Must be a gift," said Rosemary quietly, smiling at her daughter.

"Never mind," said Ashwyn, who was sitting next to Rosemary. "This hot chocolate is so divine that it makes up for any pompousness."

"Believe it or not, it's his way of apologising," said Marjie. "I know it sounds silly, but he's got a bit of a complex, and he's trying to include himself in things to show how much he approves."

Rosemary shrugged. "Oh well, it shows I have a lot to learn when it comes to our most esteemed town official."

Una giggled. "I'm so relieved it worked out. Ashwyn did some scrying after you left and saw what kind of danger everyone was going to be in. It really could have gone either way. So she decided to join in."

"It was probably good that she did come down," said Rosemary. "It was kind of touch and go there for a while. A lot of chaotic influences, including our local neighbourhood secret society and a couple of enormous gods."

"Sounds like quite the adventure," said Una.

"What about you?" Rosemary asked. "How did everything go?"

"It was lovely," said Una. "The kids are wonderful, so charming. I always wanted to have a big family. I love children, I just can't have any of my own."

"Well, they're free to a good home," said Rosemary.

"Seriously though," said Una. "What is going to happen to them? Surely they can't stay here indefinitely."

Rosemary pressed her lips into a thin line. "That is a problem. Now that Neve and Nesta are back at their house all the time, and Dain wants to have a life of his own...I don't know how we're going to manage. Neve's tried to find them foster homes, but they are clearly magical and need special supervision."

"They certainly are," said Una. "That's partly why I find them so delightful. They remind me of something. Maybe it's to do with my fae lineage, I'm not sure, but I find being around them so soothing."

"They are particularly placid aren't they, for young children," said Rosemary. "Still, they need to run around a lot and they need to eat and so on."

"I managed to get them to make their own sandwiches for supper," said Una.

"That's an impressive start," said Rosemary. "You'll have them doing chores in no time."

Una watched the three children across the room. They were now all sitting dotingly around the mayor who continued to speak. He'd moved on to telling grand stories about the town and its relationship with gods and Beltane over the centuries, some of which would have been helpful to know before the evening's fiasco.

Rosemary watched Una's face light up at the sight of the children, before turning back.

"You wouldn't..." Una started. "I mean, I'm hardly qualified, but Ashwyn and I could look after them, at least for a while. I've always wondered about being a foster parent."

"Really?" Rosemary asked. "It's a big job. They're quite placid for children, but still, any kind of parenting is a lot of work."

"We have a big old house, not quite this big," said Una. "And if we can figure out some kind of childcare arrangements for during the day while we're in the shop..."

"Marjie has been talking about enrolling them in the local kindergarten," said Rosemary. "We just didn't know how long they were going to stick around Myrtlewood for, or whether they'd have to go further afield to find suitable foster homes."

"They really have nowhere else to go?" Ashwyn asked.

Rosemary shook her head. "Neve's tracked down some of the historical records she thinks relate to their families, but the problem is they're all from so far in the past that we have no idea whether their very distant, great, great nephews and so on, would want anything at all to do with them. We certainly can't force them off into people's lives like that. We really need to find foster carers who are ready, willing, and able...really prepared to have children around."

"They shouldn't leave Myrtlewood," said Ashwyn. "Surely not after all the change they've already gone through."

"That's probably right," said Rosemary. "Are you really serious, you'd consider adopting them, or fostering them temporarily at least?"

"Of course," said Una. "I was talking to Ashwyn about it, wasn't I? After we met them at your house a little while ago, I knew they needed a more permanent home, but I didn't want to be too pushy or anything. It's quite a big deal to come into somebody's house and say I want to foster the children you found in the fae realm."

"I'm almost certain nobody's ever done that before, actually," said Rosemary. "It's quite a unique predicament. But I'm thrilled that you're even considering it. Right now we've got so few options."

"Really?" said Una. "That's wonderful, isn't it, Ashwyn? We might be able to foster the children!"

Ashwyn grinned at her sister. "What are we getting ourselves into?"

Rosemary smiled and rubbed her hands together with glee.

Everything seemed to be falling into place. However, there was that small matter of Athena's school...the school that had almost completely burnt down in a magical fire.

Perhaps she'd be home-schooling Athena for a while, which didn't sound like the sort of endeavour either of them were prepared to embark on, especially when Rosemary was supposed to be trying to set up her own business.

After the hot chocolates, the townsfolk went home, leaving Athena, Rosemary, and a blissfully quiet house, after Una had offered to put the children to bed and sleep in the adjoining room.

Rosemary was glad she and Ashwyn hadn't got cold feet about the potential foster situation. Dain had called it a night, yawning and excusing himself, saying he'd had quite enough excitement for one millennia.

Athena was dutifully doing the dishes, although Rosemary did notice she was staring quite intently at the sink, perhaps trying to use her automancy magic to get the job done a lot faster.

"I wish I could show you," said Athena. "You should have seen that dynamo go...and the look on Beryl's face. It was priceless!"

"Speaking of school," said Rosemary. "It's such a shame about the fire. You know it's funny, with all those children gone the house is going to feel quite empty. Think we'd have room for a few dozen more kids?"

"What are you talking about?"

"Just my very random thoughts. I've seen your school. There's only a handful of pupils in each class. Surely there's not more than fifty on the entire campus, despite how big and sprawling those old buildings are."

"Probably something like that." Athena's voice had a sharp edge to it. "Why are you talking about this now?"

"Maybe Thorn Manor can temporarily be Rosemary Thorn's Educational Establishment for Challenging Magical Students."

"Is that the official title?" Athena asked with a laugh. Rosemary laughed too. It was clearly a joke.

"That would be terribly embarrassing," said Athena. "I've got to keep you as far away from my classmates as possible. Although, imagine the look on Beryl's face if she found out she had to go to school at my house!"

A cracking and rumbling shook the house.

"What was that?" Rosemary clenched her fists as the rumbling continued. Then they noticed a shimmer of gold running around the room.

"Oh no," said Rosemary and Athena simultaneously.

"It's the house!" said Rosemary as they followed the sound to the west wing of the house. She pulled open the door to find the cobwebs being cleared from before their eyes, as the dusty abandoned looking wing was swept clean, and the wood began to gleam. New rooms formed around the corridor.

"Oh no!" said Athena. "I think the house was paying a little bit too much attention to your joke, Mum."

"Maybe it wasn't a joke." Rosemary crossed her arms.

"It's making classrooms!" Athena cried. "It's kind of amazing, but also, there's no way I'm going to school at home."

"It would just be a temporary arrangement," said Rosemary. "After all, your education is very important."

EPILOGUE

Lightning crashed through the sky, followed closely by rolling thunder.

The cloaked figures assembled in the old ruin of a castle, high up in the tower, overlooking the stormy ocean. Wind whipped through the busted stone walls.

A bald man with a pointed nose spoke first. "Why did you call us here, Despina? The weather is atrocious!"

Despina said nothing, as if she wouldn't dignify his protestations with a response. She merely pulled her pastel pink cloak tighter around her shoulders to protect her from the cold.

All eyes turned as a woman entered via the old spiral staircase. She wore a deep blue cloak and her white blonde hair tumbled out from the hood making her easily recognisable among her fellow society members. "We have more important things to think about than weather, Geoffrey," said Lamorna, her pale skin glistening in the moonlight.

Her mouth twitched at the corners as they all stared at her. They could tell she wasn't quite human, but none of them knew her secret. Not yet.

A loud wave crashed outside and Lamorna smiled.

"Hem, hem," said Despina. "Now that all the cell leaders of the Bloodstone Society are present and accounted for...and quiet." She eyed Geoffrey as she spoke. "We have some news."

There was a pause so full of anticipation, Despina wanted to prick it with a pin, but she drew it out, waiting for Lamorna.

"Those Myrtlewood pests with their fire sprites have given us a brilliant idea," Lamorna said. "Of course, you'll be aware of the rather fortuitous celestial alignments coming up this Solstice. Neptune will be in harmonious aspect to the full moon eclipse in Capricorn."

"Will you stop babbling about the stars already?" Geoffrey grumbled. "It's freezing!"

"Very well," said Despina. "You might be more interested in this!"

She pulled a black cloth from the small table in front of her.

Gasps echoed through the room as they all took in the sight of the small carved wooden box.

Geoffrey scoffed. "You really mean us to believe *she's* in there? After all this time..."

Despina frowned and glared at him. "Three months is hardly a long time where other dimensions are concerned. You're just trying to make a play for leadership. But guess what? It's not going to work, werewolf. You're too weak!"

The man growled and looked up at the half-moon, visible through the gaping holes in the ceiling. He bared his teeth and lunged for the box.

"Stop!" Despina cried, but Lamorna opened her mouth and a strange sound escaped.

Geoffrey froze, spellbound. They all watched, transfixed, as Lamorna opened a tiny silver vial, humming as she did so.

Glimmering liquid rose up from the small vessel as if coaxed by her voice. It sped towards Geoffrey, covering his face.

He screamed as the metallic liquid hissed, burning through his skin and clothing. He stumbled around the room and leapt from the open side, screaming as he fell.

The remaining attendees looked out to see that he was dead.

"Now then," said Despina, dusting her hands together. "Are there any others who feel like challenging us?"

Order Myrtlewood Mysteries book four!

A NOTE FROM THE AUTHOR

THANK you so much for reading this book! I so much fun writing it. I love Myrtlewood with all it's quirky characters and cozy magical atmosphere.

If you have a moment, please leave a review or even just a star rating. This helps new readers to know what kind of book they're getting themselves into, and hopefully builds some trust that it's worth reading!

You can also join my reader list or follow me on social media. Links are on the next page.

ABOUT THE AUTHOR

Iris Beaglehole

Iris Beaglehole is many peculiar things, a writer, researcher, analyst, druid, witch, parent, and would-be astrologer. She loves tea, cats, herbs, and writing quirky characters.

facebook.com/IrisBeaglehole
twitter.com/IrisBeaglehole
instagram.com/irisbeaglehole